PRAISE for *Witchful Thinking*

"Mallory's writing is fun, and her protagonist is empathizing this book an edge. ing the pace until the and questions answered entertaining series."

—...

"Mallory's strong-willed, sharp-tongued, and extremely fallible heroine; an unusual take on necromancy; and a surprising ending make this an enjoyable read."

—*Publishers Weekly*

"I was immediately sucked into the story from the very first page. . . . A perfect novel to start with if you haven't read the rest of the series because the author gets you caught up to date on what has happened so far."

—*Night Owl Romance*

"Light, fun, and interesting as well as drama filled and suspenseful . . . The ending of this fabulous book will leave you wanting more and I am so excited I found a new author to look out for! Go grab this series today and be prepared to laugh your butt off."

—*Romantic Fiction*

"H. P. Mallory is amazingly gifted. . . . All of her characters, both primary and secondary, are memorable, and the story is humorous and engaging. It held my attention from page one."

—*Romance Junkies*

"This book in three words: Thrilling, Witty, Amazing! Now that I gave you 3 words to describe this book, let me give you a few more. This book is an emotional roller coaster ride that will take you through twists, turns, action, romance, danger and mystery. Just when I thought I had it all figured out, H. P. Mallory hits us with an ending that we never saw coming! . . . UNPUTDOWNABLE."

—*Paromantasy*

By H. P. Mallory

THE JOLIE WILKINS SERIES
Fire Burn and Cauldron Bubble
Toil and Trouble
Be Witched (novella)
Witchful Thinking
The Witch Is Back
Something Witchy This Way Comes

THE DULCIE O'NEIL SERIES
To Kill a Warlock
A Tale of Two Goblins
Great Hexpectations
Wuthering Frights

Something Witchy This Way Comes

A JOLIE WILKINS NOVEL

H.P. MALLORY

BANTAM
NEW YORK

Something Witchy This Way Comes is a work of fiction. Names, characters, places, and incidents are the products of the author's imagination or are used fictitiously. Any resemblance to actual events, locales, or persons, living or dead, is entirely coincidental.

A Bantam Books Mass Market Original

Copyright © 2012 by H. P. Mallory
Excerpt from *Witchful Thinking* copyright © 2012 by H. P. Mallory
Excerpt from *The Witch Is Back* copyright © 2012 by H. P. Mallory

Published in the United States by Bantam Books, an imprint of The Random House Publishing Group, a division of Random House, Inc., New York.

BANTAM BOOKS and the rooster colophon are registered trademarks of Random House, Inc.

ISBN 978-0-345-53158-2
EBook ISBN 978-0-345-53159-9

Cover design: Anne Keenan Higgins
Cover illustration: Eileen Carey

Printed in the United States of America

www.bantamdell.com

9 8 7 6 5 4 3 2 1

Bantam Books mass market edition: October 2012

Thank you to the following people:

My husband for all your support.

My mother for all your help.

*My editor, Shauna Summers,
who always makes my books so much stronger.*

My agent, Kimberly Whalen.

My son, Finn, just for being.

*And to all my readers—
thank you from the bottom of my heart.*

Something
Witchy
This Way
Comes

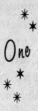

One

I blinked.

I blinked a few more times, and even then my vision was still cloudy, like I was just waking up with a massive hangover in a room bright with sunlight. I covered my eyes with my hand, trying to ward away the garish attack of light, hoping that my sense of hearing might help me figure out where I was. But my heart was beating so fast, it sounded like waves crashing into my ears.

I dropped my hand from my eyes and forced myself to focus, to concentrate on the scenery around me so I could get some sense of where I was and what had happened. Once I was able to make out the rocks that interrupted the otherwise deep blue ocean before me, I realized it wasn't my heart that was echoing through my ears at all, but the actual waves. I glanced down at my shoes and took in the sand, feeling the sea breeze as it whipped around my ankles and caused me to shiver involuntarily.

"Jolie."

I felt like I was moving in slow motion as I turned to face Rand. His dark brown eyes showed his concern for me as he smiled, and his dimples made him appear almost boyish. His deep chocolate hair was tousled, as if he'd just awakened from a restless night. He was breathtakingly beautiful, as always. At the sight of him, something warm began to grow within me and I recognized the feeling—relief melded with love.

If Rand was here, I was safe.

But the question remained: Where exactly was I?

I swallowed hard, trying to bridge the gap that was growing in my mind. I'd been home in . . . Los Angeles only moments ago and now I was . . . now I was . . .

I glanced around again, at the beach and then behind me. I took in the craggy hillside that led up to pastures of heather, dotted with enormous pine trees and a three-story white mansion, the plaque of which proclaimed itself to be KINLOCH KIRK. Somehow, the title resonated with me and carried me to a place in my mind that I hadn't visited in a while.

Kinloch Kirk is the home of the Queen of the Underworld, I told myself. *It's my home.*

"We're back in Scotland," I whispered to Rand as I faced him again, the dawning realization forcing the clouds from my mind. He said nothing, just nodded and reached for me, engulfing me in his strong arms. I leaned my head against his chest and inhaled his spicy, masculine scent, relishing the feel of his embrace.

"You failed."

It was a woman's voice—austere and calculating—and I knew it well. I turned to face the prophetess,

Mercedes Berg, who stared past us, her mouth angry. The prophetess was the highest of all the witches and also the Queen's chief ambassador, *my* chief ambassador. But what struck me was how upset she was that her plan hadn't succeeded. Actually, it had been a complete fiasco.

And that was when it all came back to me, like someone had just pumped memory juice directly into my brain.

Mercedes had broken the rules of time by sending the vampire Sinjin Sinclair two years back in time to meet me before I ever became Queen . . . hell, before I was even aware that I was a witch. And Sinjin's purpose? To get to know me before Rand did, thereby ensuring that I would never fall in love with Rand, which is what truly happened. Sinjin had wanted me to fall in love with him instead, and as much as I now hated to admit it, he'd succeeded.

But luckily for me, Rand hadn't given up. A gifted warlock, he had recruited the help of Mathilda, a fairy. They'd traveled back in time to beat Sinjin at his own game. Why Mercedes had orchestrated the whole thing, I still didn't know. And why had Sinjin agreed to it? Well, I also didn't know for sure, but I did have my suspicions. He undoubtedly wanted the promise of power that went along with being the paramour of the Queen of the Underworld.

"I attempted."

At the sound of Sinjin's voice, I felt something within me constrict. I had to fight the feeling, though, because I'd promised myself I would get over him.

I refused to look at him. The power of his betrayal still felt like a knife in my back. Instead, I faced Mercedes and felt anger riding up my throat. She appeared so nonchalant, almost indifferent, as if sending Sinjin back in time and royally screwing up my life was no big deal. She acted like it was no more serious than if she'd just stepped on an unfortunate beetle.

"And apparently you failed," Mercedes said, facing Sinjin with an expression that was none too friendly. I didn't miss the fact that Sinjin had no comeback. But I still refused to look at him.

"Why did you do it?" Rand demanded of Mercedes. He took a step toward her, his shoulders tight. She turned away from him without answering. "Why the bloody hell did you do it?" he repeated, and his voice was rough, his English accent more pronounced and heated with his anger. I was suddenly afraid of a possible confrontation between the two of them.

"You must not doubt the prophetess," Mathilda suddenly piped up from behind me. I turned to face her, in surprise, not having realized she was present. The oldest and wisest of the fae, Mathilda was slight, barely four feet tall. Her long, silvery hair flowed around her body. When I looked at her, I sometimes couldn't tell how old she was. She'd told me a long time ago that each person's perception of her was different—they see her however they choose to see her—apparently my confused mind was unable to distinguish her age.

But back to the time-travel thing . . . Right before Mercedes sent Sinjin back in time, I was looking for my cat, who had escaped from the house. Instead of finding her, I stumbled across Mercedes as she was performing a time-traveling charm on Sinjin. It was on the beach, just below the bluffs of Kinloch Kirk.

Knowing it wouldn't be long before everything I knew was whisked away from me, I used my telepathic connection to warn Rand—who was miles away at the time—about Mercedes' intentions. Then, boom! When I woke up, it was two years in the past, in Los Angeles. I was completely unaware of the fact that I was officially Queen of the Underworld. Truth be told, I hadn't even met Rand or Sinjin because they had yet to venture into my life.

To make a long story short, Rand, Sinjin, and Mathilda were able to return to the present. (I hadn't traveled back in time to begin with, so I didn't have to make the trek back.) I was surprised that everyone had returned to the same place—right here on the beach where Mercedes had first sent Sinjin on his merry way into the past. I wasn't sure why, but I had guessed that upon returning, each person would reappear wherever he or she had departed. Well, clearly that wasn't the case. 'Course, I also couldn't say I understood the hows and whys about time travel, so maybe I shouldn't have been surprised.

"Damn not doubting her," Rand raged.

"I had but one goal," Mercedes answered in her same level tone, fixing her gaze on Rand and then on me.

"What was it?" I asked, my voice sounding hollow and drained, which wasn't surprising considering everything going on around me.

"I made the decision to ensure the safety of our Queen and sovereign," Mercedes finished, raising a brow at Rand as if to say, *How can you argue with that?*

"Her safety against what?" Rand asked as he wrapped his arms around me, pulling me close. It seemed as if just the very thought of a threat to my safety bothered him.

Mercedes didn't alter her straight-lipped expression. Instead, she stared at him vacantly for about two seconds. "The Lurkers," she finished succinctly. "Sending the Queen back in time would give us another two years to train her in an environment free of Lurkers." I was about to respond when she held up her hand. "I never told you, Jolie, but I could sense something was coming, something dangerous."

"So you decided to send Sinjin back in time to avoid it?" I asked.

She nodded. "It was the only way I could protect you, to give us more time to plan our retaliation."

"Fat lot of good it did," I muttered. The Lurkers, a breed of half-human/half-vampire creatures who had a vendetta against all Underworld residents, had done as good a job of attacking me in the past as they had in the future—well, now my present. Shit, this time-travel stuff was going to get confusing fast.

"What do you mean?" Mercedes pressed.

"She means that the Lurkers found her even though you upset the balance of time. So your reasoning was completely flawed," Rand finished, his eyes burning.

"The Lurkers found you?" Mercedes asked slowly, spearing me with her eyes.

I nodded, reliving my fear as I remembered my brush with the Lurkers and how they had poisoned my dreams. "Yes."

"How?"

"They sent me a dream," I answered, remembering

the images—a battlefield littered with bodies, an image of a throne unattended. It was a dreamscape that appeared to me twice in my sleep. The first time, I awoke with the realization that the Lurkers were not only half-vampires, but also possessors of magic. The second time I had the dream, I was back in Los Angeles, two years ago, and the images resulted in an attack on my psyche. "My magic wasn't strong enough to fight the images and I became very sick."

"She could have died," Rand finished for me, his lips tighter than before. I could feel his hands fisting around me, and I glanced up at him and smiled, loving the fact that he was so protective.

It's going to be okay, Rand, I thought the words, knowing he could hear them. Even though I didn't believe my own words, it felt good to say them. I wanted to trust that this was all going to work out just fine and that the Lurkers weren't such a huge threat after all. Wishful thinking.

Instantly, I felt pride and love welling up within me, a feeling that threw me for a second because they weren't emotions that belonged to me. No, they were Rand's feelings making themselves known to me. That was when it dawned on me—Rand and I were still bonded, which meant we were soul mates, for lack of a better description.

I wasn't sure why I was surprised. I mean, we had bonded after he, Sinjin, and Mathilda traveled back in time. I guess I hadn't thought the bond would survive when Rand traveled forward in time, but apparently it had. And I had to admit I was elated. I've always known Rand was the only man for me. I love him like no other, and now I knew our bond had cemented us permanently. With it, we could hear each other's thoughts and feel each other's emotions. Bonding is like the ultimate union achieved between two witches, and it's forever. The only end to a bond is death.

Mercedes and Sinjin manipulated you, Jolie, and that is not okay with me, he responded, shaking his head as he thought the words. But I couldn't say I sincerely agreed with him. Things were not as black and white for me as they were for him. And knowing that Mathilda trusted Mercedes so wholeheartedly spoke volumes, because I trusted Mathilda.

"We will discuss the dream later," Mercedes said resolutely as she faced me. I noticed she was careful not to glance at Rand, who probably looked furious.

"So that was your plan?" I asked her, trying to decide if I believed it. "To send Sinjin back in time to avoid the threat of the Lurkers?" She just nodded. "Then what about saving yourself?"

Mercedes was the prophetess, yes, but not all Underworld creatures believed in her existence—mainly because no one had ever seen her because she'd imprisoned herself in the year 1878. Why? She'd received a vision that if she didn't relive the year 1878 repeatedly, she'd be killed by the Lurkers. Luckily for her, she was able to harness my power to bring me back to 1878, and we returned to the present together. Thus, in sending Sinjin back and changing the course of history, she would also have changed the course of her own history, possibly sacrificing herself . . .

"I gave the vampire express instructions on how to train you until your powers were strong enough to send for me yourself," Mercedes answered.

"So you had it all planned out," I said, swallowing down the lump in my throat as the pieces began to fall into place. Did I actually buy her explanation? Any way I looked at it, I couldn't think of another reason why she would have bothered with such a grandiose plan. And I had to admit that I did believe Mathilda when she said every action by Mercedes was intended to protect the kingdom, and likewise, to protect me. So, in a way, I guess I had to believe her.

Yes, I was still angry about the whole thing, but when I thought about it in this new light . . . well, it offered an angle I hadn't yet considered. And it also meant something else—that Sinjin had been telling me the truth. He'd insisted that he'd done Mercedes' bidding because he wanted to protect me. Prior to the whole time-travel thing, Sinjin had been a guardian to me, the Queen. He'd insisted that he was and always would remain my loyal protector.

Even though I didn't want to, I turned to face him.

Sinjin Sinclair is in a word . . . stunning. He's about six-foot-four and lean, with broad shoulders and long legs. His hair is the color of midnight—so dark that it sometimes appears almost blue, his eyes a much lighter blue—like the color of alpine water. He is the quintessential rogue, a real Casanova, and he's six centuries old.

I felt something inside me rise up. It was a sort of numbness that quickly gave way to anger and pain, then feelings of betrayal. I refused to give in to them, though, and instead took a deep breath, already facing him. "Is that true?" I asked him.

"Of course," he answered simply. "It was to protect you." His eyes bored into me as if he could see into the depths of my soul. I felt myself swallow hard. "As I told you earlier."

"Jolie, don't believe a word from his mouth," Rand interrupted. "He's done nothing but lie to you, and he will continue to lie to you," he spat, staring at Sinjin.

"Poppet, I have only ever spoken the truth," Sinjin continued, not even sparing a glance at Rand. It was the same as always between them—Rand wore his emotions on his sleeve, and where Sinjin was concerned, those emotions were usually anger, protectiveness, and jealousy. Sinjin, on the other hand, while he probably did experience the same emotions, was always even-keeled and level-headed. I attributed it to the six hundred years he'd had to master his art.

"You conniving—" Rand started.

Sinjin merely cocked a brow in his direction and turned to face me again, wearing a smirk. "I have always been and will always be dedicated to the protection and longevity of my Queen."

Okay, so I was willing to suspend my disbelief for the moment and lend a little credence to Mercedes' and Sinjin's story, but there was one part of the whole thing that still didn't sit well with me. Well, aside from the fact that they both attempted to change the course of my life without my permission. I faced Mercedes and took a deep breath. "Was it your intention for me to develop feelings for Sinjin?"

I suddenly felt deeply depressed, then recognized that I was experiencing Rand's reaction to my words. I glanced at him quickly and smiled, letting him know exactly how much he meant to me. Even though Sinjin had in a way tricked me into falling in love with him, it wasn't something that would ever be long-term. No, I would beat this. I knew I would because I loved Rand and always had, and ours was the type of love that was forged by fate, set by the fires of destiny.

"That was not my intention," Mercedes said as she eyed Sinjin suspiciously. "But apparently it was a by-product?"

A by-product.

If only my feelings for Sinjin could be dissected and archived as nothing more than a "by-product." I said nothing, though, since I recognized the situation for what it was. Mercedes just didn't understand the language of emotions—she was one of those people who lived only for the facts; there were moments when I envied her for that.

"I do not believe any of this," Rand spat out at last. "And I have never trusted you," he finished, glaring at Mercedes. "What you did was in no way defensible. You changed Jolie's life when it was not your right."

And Rand was correct. One hundred percent. Whatever their reasoning, I couldn't deny that the wool had been pulled right over my eyes, that I'd had no say whatsoever.

And then something interesting happened. Mercedes' eyes narrowed as she faced Rand, and I could see heat building in her face, staining the apples of her cheeks to a handsome shade of cherry. Mercedes is very pretty—she has long dark hair and the most gorgeous green eyes you've ever seen. At the moment, though, those eyes looked like they were about to resurrect World War II.

"Perhaps there was one other reason I sent the vampire back in time, warlock," she said between gritted teeth. I couldn't remember the last time I'd seen her so upset.

"And what was that?" Rand persisted, seemingly unconcerned that she was so angry, which hinted at his courage. The prophetess could have made a peanut butter and warlock sandwich out of him in two seconds flat.

"It was a test," she finished squarely.

"A test?" he repeated, and I felt my heart rate increase. Tests are never good, particularly when you haven't studied.

"What do you mean?" I demanded.

She glanced at me and frowned. "You have admitted yourself that your feelings for Rand have caused you pain. As far as I was concerned, your feelings for him were getting in the way of your duty to your kingdom and your people."

I swallowed even harder. This was going to end badly. I could see it already. "That was not your place—" I started.

"It was and is my place," Mercedes interrupted, her eyes ablaze. "I am responsible for your safety and your happiness. And as far as I could tell, Rand has caused you nothing but agony."

"But—" I started, but she wouldn't be silenced.

"Do you recall the time when you begged me to send you back to 1878 because, in your own words, you 'hated your life'?"

Damn, I did, and now those words were coming back to haunt me. But it's not like I'd really meant them. I mean, at the time, Rand was being his usual obstinate self and I was having a pity party for myself, remembering 1878, when he and I had loved each other openly. But it wasn't like I really wanted Mercedes to send me back . . . or was it?

You asked her to send you back to 1878? Rand's words echoed through me, but I couldn't face him. His voice sounded too hollow, surprised in its sadness.

Yes, but I didn't . . . I didn't mean it, I responded, feeling guilty. Looking back on it, I was happy that Mercedes hadn't sent me back. Somehow I hoped all those thoughts translated over to Rand.

"I wished to spare you the heartache inflicted upon you by this man," Mercedes finished. She crossed her arms against her chest as if daring any of us to argue with her. I couldn't really find it in myself to be that angry with her because I did believe her. And somehow it's hard to be super irate with someone when they can't see the full picture, since they probably had good intentions. As it was, I actually felt sorry for her.

"That's just life, Mercedes," I said, shaking my head. "You can't control people's destinies. You aren't God."

She swallowed hard. "I was only doing what I thought right."

"Well it wasn't right," Rand insisted. "And Jolie is much more forgiving than I'm willing to be." He gritted his teeth. "Because of you, I nearly lost her."

"But you didn't," Mercedes snapped. "I had to ensure your worthiness to court my Queen," she continued. "This was a test of your loyalty and affection for her and of whether you were the ideal recipient for her love."

I watched Rand swallow hard as his arms tightened around me, his anger suddenly consuming me.

"Then you knew I would go after her? That I would time-travel just as Sinjin did?" he asked.

Mercedes glared at him for a few seconds before responding. "I did not know, but I suspected, or rather, hoped you would."

"And?"

She cocked a brow and frowned. "Obviously, you passed the test. That is proven not only by the fact that you are standing here, but also that you are bond mates again."

There really wasn't anything Mercedes didn't know. I'd reached that conclusion a long time ago. She had an uncanny ability to detect things, our bonding status being a prime example. I mean, it wasn't like bond mates had to wear matching shirts. It was just one of those things Mercedes inexplicably knew.

"You are bonded?" Sinjin asked, turning to me. His expression was tight, his fangs indenting his lower lip. He didn't look happy. Instead, he seemed surprised, yes, but more than that—hurt.

"Yes," Rand responded before I could. "You lost, Sinjin," he said, his eyes angry as he took a few steps closer to the vampire. "Even though you did everything in your power to ensure that I would lose Jolie, you failed."

Sinjin said nothing, and I faced forward again. I didn't want to see pain in his eyes. I just couldn't believe it—couldn't believe he'd ever cared for me.

You know he cared for you, a small voice piped up from within me. *Don't try to kid yourself, Jolie.*

Sinjin tricked me, I responded. *I don't care what*

Mercedes says or what excuses Sinjin makes—he isn't being honest. Yes, he wanted to protect me but he also hungers for power, and I've always known that. Everyone knows that.

"At any rate," Rand continued. "Punishment must be doled out to those who transgressed against the Queen. I will not allow this to be swept under the proverbial rug."

I gulped as I considered it. It wasn't like Mercedes could be punished. Or could she? She was like this supreme being—way more powerful than any of us—so how could we hope to punish her? I wasn't sure. Which left one person. I couldn't help it—I glanced back at Sinjin, only to find his eyes trained on me.

"I await my punishment with bells on," he said as he disappeared into the cold night air.

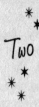

Two

I just couldn't stay at Kinloch Kirk that night. I wasn't sure why. Maybe it had something to do with Sinjin, who was also staying there, back in his room in the basement. It was like things were just the same as they'd always been, only now Sinjin was being held in confinement with a guard posted outside his door. Or maybe it was just that I needed a little alone time and my house was teeming with people, busy doing this and that. Either way, I had this irrepressible desire to hide away at Pelham Manor, Rand's home in Alnwick, England. Luckily for me, it was just a hop, skip, and a jump away (otherwise known as a thirty-minute trek straight down the A1 from Kinloch Kirk).

Rand didn't seem averse to the idea of spending the night at his place either, so we agreed to regroup in thirty minutes, giving me ample time to pack. Yes, as a witch, I could have just magicked myself a clean outfit, toothbrush, and hair tie for the night, but I felt drained and didn't want to waste my energy. Sometimes it was just easier to act human.

I plopped my backpack on my bed, zipped it open

and piled my pink-and-black pjs inside as I watched my cat, Plum, loop herself between my feet.

"You're on your own tonight," I said, and smiled as she purred up at me. Reaching down, I picked her up and snuggled her against my cheek, loving the feel of her soft fur. She started spreading her paws against my neck, like she was kneading bread, and I giggled against her, suddenly overwhelmed with a feeling of gratitude. Why? Because I loved my life, as complicated as it was. And everything I'd worked so hard for had almost been torn away from me. In fact, if it hadn't been for Rand, I wouldn't be here now. I'd be in a parallel life, with no knowledge of what I was missing.

And that was when it struck me. Even if Mercedes and Sinjin believed they were acting in my best interests, even if they were convinced that they were saving me from a death at the hands of the Lurkers, they had gone about it in entirely the wrong way. And for that they deserved to be reprimanded. Because in the end all anyone has is control over his or her own destiny, the ability to make his or her own decisions. And that innate right had been snatched from me.

I walked over to the window, feeling suddenly claustrophobic. I had this sudden and blinding desire to lose myself in the beauty of the clouds as they eclipsed the moon. Even though I hadn't done any time-traveling myself—well not since I'd traveled to and from 1878 months ago—I still felt exhausted. It was as if the strata of memories I now had from two separate realities were constantly in conflict with one another, and it was hard to remember what was true. It was pretty damn confusing when you had two sets

of memories about the same events. It was taxing—
no, exhausting, to say the least.

And what was even more exhausting was trying to
catalog my feelings toward Sinjin. I still cared about
him, a lot. And, yes, I was still hurt over what happened between us. Did I love him still? I wasn't sure.
Ever since I'd bonded with Rand, the feelings I har-
bored toward Sinjin had been somehow numbed. I
mean, they were still there—it wasn't as if they'd
disappeared—but there was a general detachment
that just felt strange to me. Strange because it was as
if my feelings and emotions had been papered over
rather than fully dealt with.

I just wished, more than ever before, that things
between Sinjin and me could be the way they were
before he changed the course of history. The sad truth
of the whole stupid thing was that I missed his friendship. I missed his witty banter and the fact that I
could always rely on him for a laugh. But more than
that, I'd felt I could always rely on Sinjin . . . period.
He had been my protector and guardian, yes, but he'd
also been so much more than that. He'd been my
friend, and the loss of his friendship was impossible
for me to accept. Especially because I couldn't feel the
ache and void of losing him.

But what about his ulterior motives, Jolie? A voice
inside me piped up. *You're remembering the good
times and none of the bad.*

I always knew Sinjin was selfish and power hungry,
but I had accepted those shortcomings, figuring they
were just part of the enigma known as Sinjin—part of
what made him who he was. His imperfections had
almost been endearing, charming in their limitations.

But after this whole time-traveling mess had reared its ugly head, it was suddenly clear that his imperfections weren't quite so harmless . . .

Maybe he was telling the truth when he said his sole purpose was to protect me, I argued with myself.

You know there's more to it than that. Sinjin is admittedly selfish, so really, what would he gain by purely doing it to protect you? Nothing. No, he wanted you to fall in love with him so he could control you, and in doing so, control the crown.

Maybe, but maybe not. That just sounds so cut-and-dried, and you know Sinjin is anything but easy to figure out. No, he's the most frustratingly complex person you've ever met—well, aside from Rand.

Don't give him the benefit of the doubt. You've always given him the benefit of the doubt, and look where that's gotten you.

Well, I'm also not about to believe that he cares only about himself. Not when he's proven his goodness on multiple occasions.

There you go, trying to give him human attributes again. He's not human, dummy!

I know that! I insisted, irritated with myself for the name calling. *But what if there weren't more to the time-travel bit? What if Sinjin's reasons were purely selfless? What if Sinjin really loves me?*

Seriously? Wow, you're dumber than I thought!

"Jolie?" Rand's voice came from the doorway. I turned to face him and smiled with embarrassment, realizing I hadn't finished packing before I'd started arguing with myself. And then something horrifying occurred to me.

"Could you hear any of that?" I asked, hoping—no

praying—that the answer was no. I knew Rand wouldn't take any of it well—his stance on Sinjin was pretty obvious.

"Any of what?"

I took a deep breath. "My argument with myself?"

Rand chuckled and shook his head, his eyes warm as he smiled down at me. "No. Rest assured that you can keep your lunacy to yourself."

I laughed, and then just gazed at him for a few seconds, still not quite able to believe he was fully mine. Through the course of our relationship, we'd endured so many ups and downs, so much back-and-forth, that it almost didn't seem real.

"Are you still arguing with yourself?" Rand asked with an amused grin as he crossed his arms against his expansive chest and leaned against the wall.

I shook my head and felt my cheeks color. "No."

"Well then?" he asked, gesturing toward my half-packed backpack.

"Okay, I'll just be a minute, promise," I said with a smile. Rand approached me and took the cat from my arms, pausing to give her a pat on the head. Then he set her down and we both watched her scamper out of the room.

"Jolie," he said, and I brought my attention to his handsome face. "You realize we can't avoid this situation forever?"

I exhaled. "Yeah, I know, but I don't think it will be a big deal for one night."

He nodded, and I walked into the adjoining bathroom to fill my toiletry case. Emerging, I dropped the case into my backpack and zipped it up. I felt Rand behind me as he reached his arms around me, pulling me into him. He was so warm, an electrical pulse shot through me at his touch. It reminded me of the first time we met—how he touched me and I instantly knew he was some kind of ethereal being.

"I know you've been through a lot," he whispered into my ear, and squeezed me reassuringly. "Are you okay?"

I thought about it. Was I? I wasn't sure. I mean, I was happy that we were all back in the proper time, and that I had all of my memories back. So that was a plus. But as far as the future went? That part wasn't all roses and chocolates. "I'm honestly worried about the Lurker threat," I said, and turned to face him, running my hands down his shirtfront. "If what Mercedes said was true, then we might be on the cusp of something huge."

Rand nodded and sighed, tracing the outline of my cheek with his index finger. "If the Lurkers attack us, they attack us."

I frowned, thinking it wasn't quite that simple. 'Course, maybe it was. I mean, there was only so much we could do to thwart the danger, only so much we could do to prepare. And the scary part was, everything we'd been doing still wasn't enough. "Maybe it would have been better for all of us to seek asylum in the past?" I asked, swallowing down the fear that was suddenly choking me.

Rand shook his head. "It would be merely prolonging the inevitable, and as you witnessed yourself, the Lurker threat was just as real two years ago as it is now."

I nodded. The Lurkers seemed to have the power to

reach me no matter where I was in the spectrum of time. "Then what can we do?"

He cocked his head to the side and frowned. "What we've been doing, I suppose. Continuing reconnaissance missions and hoping to uncover any information about them that we can get."

It didn't seem like much. But therein was the problem—we just didn't know what we were up against with the Lurkers. It wasn't anywhere near as cut-and-dried as the war with Bella had been. Then, we'd known exactly how many were fighting with her, and more exactly, what they were capable of. We didn't even really know what the Lurkers were— half-vampire, half-witch, or both. And speaking of Bella . . . "Is Bella still in confinement here?"

Rand nodded. "Everything is as it was when Sinjin was sent back, Jolie."

Which meant that Bella was still my prisoner. And since she had refused to take a loyalty oath to become one of my subjects, she was still as much of a threat as she had always been. Well, at least she no longer had an army to command. But she still wasn't exactly a ray of sunshine.

"We can worry about all of this tomorrow, Jolie," Rand said with a small laugh, then smiled down at me. "Tonight, you need to focus on you and nothing else."

I nodded and accepted his hand, throwing my overnight bag over my arm, only to have him pull it free, hoisting it over his shoulder. Then he escorted me from my bedroom and down the stairs. When we reached the vestibule, I recognized his black Range Rover just beyond the front doors.

"Your chariot awaits, my lady," he said with a smile, holding open the front door for me. Glancing at the SUV, I was suddenly overcome with memories—memories of when I first moved to England with Rand, and how he'd trained me to become the witch I was today. It just seemed that every part of me, every facet of what made me who I was, had something to do with this man. It was nice to know that I'd have him by my side as I faced the biggest threat to myself and my kingdom.

He opened the door for me and I threw myself into the plush black leather of the Rover. I buckled up and leaned back in the seat, enjoying the classical music piped from the speakers. In many ways Rand had never outgrown his nineteenth-century roots. It was evident from his manners to the antiquated way he sometimes spoke to his musical tastes.

"What is this?" I asked, motioning to the CD player.

He listened for a moment or two, as if trying to decipher the melody, then nodded. " 'Carnival of the Animals' by Saint-Saëns."

I just shook my head in wonder and laughed. "Do you have a catalog of music in your head or what?"

He glanced at me and shrugged. "I'm a classical music enthusiast."

I just nodded and allowed myself to enjoy the music, trying to drown out the nervous humming of my thoughts.

"I can feel your anxiety, Jolie," Rand said as we pulled onto the A1107, headed for the A1. It was so dark outside, I couldn't see anything other than the moon, but even that was periodically shielded by the clouds. "What's bothering you?"

I took a deep breath, knowing that this would be a touchy subject. "What if what Mercedes and Sinjin said was true?" Rand immediately started shaking his head, but I wasn't going to back down just yet. "What if they *were* just trying to protect me?"

He glanced over at me and scowled. "Jolie, I nearly lost you."

I took a deep breath and nodded. "I know but—"

"But nothing. They completely stripped you of your freedom of choice. How can that not bother you?" His voice was becoming heated, as if this conversation were quickly on its way to Argumentville.

"It does bother me," I responded, taking a deep breath. "Of course it bothers me, but I just wonder if it's worth punishing them, and come to think of it, I don't even really understand what punishing them means . . ."

He glanced at me and arched a brow.

"I mean, I don't know if punishment is going to be a major thing or just a slap on their wrists. And not only that, but our focus should be on the Lurkers and how to stop them. Should we really waste time reprimanding Sinjin and Mercedes?" He took a deep breath but didn't say anything, so I continued. "You heard Mathilda. Mercedes only acts to protect me and the kingdom."

Rand was silent for another few seconds, appearing to zone out on the headlights as they lit up the dark road ahead of us. "Perhaps I can apply more lenience to Mercedes . . . but Sinjin does not deserve it."

I knew Sinjin would be the sticking point. "I . . .

I think I believe him, Rand. I think he was protecting me."

Rand's jaw was tight. "No."

"Try to divorce yourself from the situation, Rand. Try to look at it objectively."

He said nothing as we merged onto the A1. Then he turned and faced me, looking irritated. 'Course, I didn't need to look at him to know that—I could feel it churning in my gut. "Jolie, you have the tendency to think people are better than they are. I don't know how many more times I can warn you against Sinjin. You saw what he did when given free rein. If things had gone his way, he would have forced you and me apart. He used you, wanted to control you, and if I hadn't been able to time-travel myself, he would have succeeded."

I swallowed and nodded, thinking it was difficult to make a good case for him. Sinjin really had manipulated the situation and me. There was no point in trying to find the good in him, because maybe Rand was right, it might not exist. But somehow I couldn't shake the feeling that there was more to it. Somehow, in my heart of stupid hearts, I was sure that Sinjin did care for me . . . that his actions were motivated by emotions far different from selfishness and ambition.

He glanced over at me quickly. "He must be punished for his transgressions, Jolie. What he did cannot be glossed over." He was silent for a few seconds. "I believe he should be banished as an example that those who transgress against the Queen will not get away with it."

"Banished?" I said, even though I realized I was beginning to sound like Rand's echo. "The Lurkers are growing more powerful. Who knows what could happen to him if he's banished?"

"That isn't your problem or mine." Rand's hold on the steering wheel tightened. "He has been alive for centuries. He is a master at surviving. I've no doubt that he'll figure it out."

There was no point in discussing this any further. Rand was obstinate and I couldn't imagine his point of view changing. And I supposed he had good reason, considering Sinjin had attempted to steal me away from him.

When we pulled up to Pelham Manor, I was all too eager to get out of the car, even though the English night was frigid, as I expected. I glanced up at the old stone edifice and felt my heart sing. I felt at home—more so than I'd ever felt at Kinloch Kirk. I'd spent so much time here and had learned so much. Yes, it was home.

Rand unlocked the front door and opened it for me, smiling down at me warmly as he took my bag and locked the door behind us. As soon as we walked over the threshold, the lights came on, a fire roared from the fireplace, and music filtered into the room. This piece I knew well—Ravel's "Bolero." It was the same as it always was—almost like Pelham Manor welcoming us home.

"I missed this place a lot," I said with a sigh as I wrapped my arms around myself.

Rand reached for my hand and started up the stairs with me in tow. When we reached his bedroom, he lifted me up bride-style and carried me over the threshold.

"What's this?" I asked with a laugh.

"We're bonded now," he answered with a large grin. "So this is our wedding night."

I laughed and allowed him to place me on the bed while I looked around the room. He lit a fire in the enormous fireplace with no more than a glance, the orange flames flickering against the rich mahogany wood paneling that matched his oversized furniture. The hunter green of the bed linens and curtains gave the whole place a deeply masculine feel. I watched Rand kick off his shoes, and moments later he offered me a glass of champagne, which he conjured from thin air.

"To you, Jolie," he said, holding his fluted glass high.

"No, to us," I corrected him, and smiled up at him as we both took a sip. I glanced at the bubbling liquid in the glass and laughed. "Not bad. You could give Cook's a run for their money."

He chuckled, even though he probably wasn't familiar with the cheap champagne. But then his smile fell and he regarded me seriously. "I'm happier than I've ever been, Jolie. Knowing that you have been the only woman for me—both in the past and the present—is a gift."

He was referring to the first time that we'd bonded, back in 1878. When I returned to the present, my absence nearly killed Rand. Thank God, Mathilda had nursed him back to health, and in the process wiped his memory clean of me. He'd continued on with his life, all the while imagining that his bond mate was dead. He'd only recently figured out that I had been his bond mate all along. The weird part was that our bond hadn't survived my return to the present time from 1878, but our new bond—formed when we had sex after Rand time-traveled to rescue me—had survived Rand's return to the present day.

"It seems the whole bonding thing only works when one of us travels to the past," I said with a smile.

He was quiet for a few seconds and then grinned in return. "Perhaps only time travel can reverse a broken bond." Then he shrugged as if he wasn't sure what the rules were. Neither of us were.

I nodded and handed him my glass, which he placed on the side table, setting his just beside it. "Rand, I love you and I've always loved you," I said. After my confession, I looped my arms around his neck and got up on my knees to kiss him.

He met my lips immediately, fire burning in his kiss. A similar burning had started deep within my belly and was now almost painful. Rand pulled off his V-necked navy sweater, taking his undershirt off with it. When my eyes beheld his bare chest, complete with its rambling valleys and hills of muscle, I could only lick my lips in preparation for what was to come. My eyes fastened on the trail of light brown hair that started at his navel and disappeared beneath his waistband.

He lowered himself on top of me, probing his tongue into my mouth, and I eagerly accepted it, meeting it with my own. I moaned underneath him, wrapping my arms and legs around him, wanting nothing more than to feel as close to him as I possibly could. Then something occurred to me. This was the first time we would have sex as a bonded pair. I wasn't sure what that meant or how it might make things different, but I was definitely up for finding out.

His hands migrated down my sides, bunching my shirt up past my waist as he nimbly pulled it over my head. He reached around and unclasped my bra, pulling it down my arms slowly, as if he wanted nothing more than to drive me insane with his patient teasing.

"Your pants," I whispered, and was pleased when he immediately unbuttoned his fly and pulled his jeans down the swells of his thighs rather than teasing me. His erection strained behind the cotton of his boxer shorts.

"And yours," he whispered, not waiting for me to respond. Instead, he unzipped my jeans and pulled them down my thighs, his eyes settling on the white lace panties that peeked out between the junction of my legs. His fingers traced my upper leg back and forth until he reached the soft lace. At the feel of his fingers over my panties, I arched up, gasping my pleasure.

"Rand," I whispered. "I need you."

He made a throaty sound and raised up, bringing his face to my neck as he kissed his way down, plying each of my breasts with his large hands. I felt his tongue on my left breast and closed my eyes, arching my back. He sucked and teethed at my nipple while I moaned beneath him, allowing the fire of passion to ignite within me. He gripped my panties, his finger lightly brushing up against the nub between my legs, and I thought I'd shoot right off the bed. He laughed gently and pulled my panties down my legs until I was entirely naked.

"I love you, Jolie," he whispered as he gazed down at me.

He spread my legs wide, settling himself between them as the head of his erection perched at my opening. My breath caught as he drove himself into me. Gasping at the feel of it, I wrapped my legs around him and he pushed harder into me.

"I love you," I managed between moans. Rand didn't respond, but he leaned down and kissed me again. Our tongues mated as he pushed himself harder and deeper into me. All of a sudden it was like he'd unleashed a river inside of me, because I could feel what he was feeling as he thrust into me and pulled out again. "I can—" I started.

He laughed and nodded. "Yes, I can feel you too."

I was quiet as I focused on the feelings—finding it difficult to distinguish between his emotions and mine. One moment I could feel him pushing within me, and the next I could feel soft, slick, tight wetness, which had to be me experiencing myself through Rand's eyes.

"This is amazing," I said as I opened my eyes and watched him. "I can feel myself through you."

"I've never—" he started and closed his eyes as he pushed inside me again. Once he'd apparently regained control of himself, he opened them again and gazed down at me. "I've never felt anything like this."

I could feel myself growing wetter, hotter. I was going to come soon, I knew it. "I'm nearly there, Rand."

He said nothing but nodded, encouraging me as he clenched his teeth, revealing that he too had to be close.

I arched up against him, throwing my head back,

and gasped as bliss rained through me. At the same moment, he grabbed hold of my waist and forced himself in and out of me, moaning deeply. I could feel his intense release only seconds later. He collapsed against my chest, panting.

"Holy crap," I said with a smile. "I don't smoke but, damn, I sure feel like I could use a cigarette right about now."

Three

The next morning, Rand and I returned to Kinloch Kirk, knowing there was much to do and not much time to do it in. There was the whole problem of determining the right punishment for Sinjin and Mercedes. Then the threat of the Lurkers, and add to that the problem known as "What in the hell am I going to do about Bella?" (who was still my captive), and my life was a mess and a half.

But before I started thinking about any of those unfortunate topics, I was going to talk to my best friend, Christa. She and I had been through a lot. We'd grown up in Spokane, Washington, together, had known each other nearly all our lives. Christa had moved with me from Spokane to Los Angeles, acting as my assistant when I owned my own tarot card–reading store. Once Rand ventured into my life and I moved to England, Christa stuck right alongside me. She was like my shadow and always had been. Well, until recently.

Of late, Christa had gotten engaged to her were-wolf boyfriend, John, and moved out of Rand's home, Pelham Manor. She was still serving as Rand's assistant, but she'd chosen to live with John. After the whole time-traveling deal, I felt the intense need to reconnect with her. Of course, as far as she was concerned, it had never happened (seeing as how she wasn't in the loop). So technically the last time we'd connected was only a few days ago. But still, I missed her.

When we talked on the phone, it was like no time had gone by at all. She was super excited about her wedding and anxious to share all the details of when, where, why, and how. And I was excited for her, although there was also a side of me that was so overwhelmed with my royal duties that it was difficult to concentrate on something as trivial as centerpiece colors or whether her dress should be long or short. But I tried. Really, I did.

"My Queen?" It was Mercedes knocking on my door. I glanced up from my bed and motioned for her to enter. As she walked into the room, I said goodbye to Christa, making plans to meet her for dinner one night that week. Clicking off the phone, I stood up and turned to face the prophetess.

"What's up?"

"Your representatives have come, as you requested. They are assembled in the library."

I nodded and gave her a quick smile, signifying that she could leave. She closed the door behind her as I thought about the evening that faced me—and most particularly, figuring out whether to punish Sinjin and Mercedes. I was still torn regarding the whole subject because I couldn't imagine Mercedes would stand for it; and if she didn't, how fair could it be to punish Sinjin? Well, that was the beauty of having a panel of representatives—I didn't have to make the decision myself. God knows I was too personally invested to be impartial.

I took a deep breath, and figuring I couldn't delay the inevitable any longer, strode to the door. I made my way down the hallway, feeling like I might pass out because my heart was beating so quickly. At moments like this, I detested being the ruler of the Underworld.

I paused outside the library door and without further ado pushed it open. As soon as I entered the room, everyone stood up and bowed. Everyone included Rand; Mathilda; the King of the Fae, Odran; Trent (a werewolf and my ex-boyfriend—also the representative of the werewolves; Varick—to my knowledge, the oldest vampire, and Sinjin's boss (that is, before I emancipated Sinjin, allowing him to be his own Master Vampire); and, of course, Mercedes.

"You may be seated," I said impatiently, finding all this fussy courtliness irritating. I mean, it wasn't like we were living in King Henry VIII's court—we were in the twenty-first century, for God's sake. It wasn't necessary for everyone to kowtow to me.

I watched as everyone in the room took their seats—most of them were sitting around the fireplace, which offered a radiant fire. Rand remained standing, as he always did. It seemed he did his best negotiating on foot. But in actuality, he just needed the floor so he could pace back and forth and run his hands through his hair in the usual exasperated Rand form.

"Where is Sinjin?" I asked, realizing he was the only one unaccounted for.

"We didn't think it proper for him to be here," Rand answered.

"Because we're deciding his punishment?" I finished, and Rand merely nodded his assent. He dropped his eyes to the ground as he exhaled. I felt something rebel within me.

Mercedes' attendance, I guess, answered the question of her own unlikely punishment. Since Sinjin hadn't been invited and Mercedes had orchestrated the whole meeting, chances were, her head wasn't on the chopping block. And, no, that didn't seem just to me at all.

"Let's begin discussing the vampire," Mercedes started.

"So why aren't you being tried as well?" I asked her with a shrug. "I mean, it was your decision to send Sinjin back, wasn't it?"

Mercedes' jaw was tight. "I am the prophetess. I cannot be punished."

I felt something in me burst and anger flooded me. "Aren't you one of my subjects?"

"I am your advisor," Mercedes corrected as she glanced around the room in obvious trepidation, clearly uncomfortable that we had an audience.

"Isn't an advisor still considered a subject?" I demanded.

Mercedes cocked an irritated brow and merely nodded. "Perhaps if you had allowed the conversation its natural progression, you would have found that I do not believe the vampire should be punished. Both he and I were acting in your best interests."

"That is debatable—" Rand started, but I silenced him with a wave of my hand.

"Then Sinjin's sentence, or lack thereof, will be decided by everyone in this room? And he doesn't even have the benefit of being present? That hardly seems right," I said, adding, "and it hardly seems just."

"As we are the ambassadors to the Queen, it is fer oos all to decide the vampire's sentence," Odran responded, nodding his head as a stray tendril of golden hair crossed his handsome face.

Odran is very striking—he has the overall look of a lion—broad, high cheekbones, wide lips, square jaw, and large, beautiful hazel eyes. He's also built like a wall and has the muscle mass of a WWF wrestler.

I cleared my throat, somehow uncomfortable with the fact that Sinjin's future would be decided without him even being present. "Is he still downstairs?" I asked, and Mercedes nodded. "Then someone get him so he can give his side of things."

Mercedes shook her head. "He has requested not to be in attendance."

"What?" I demanded. "He needs to represent himself!"

"He said, and I quote," Mercedes started, "that he 'did not care to partake in our festivities,' and I was to inform him of our decision."

I swallowed hard, but figured we could move on since Sinjin had willed it so.

Mercedes took a few steps forward. "Can we proceed, please?" she asked, eyeing me impatiently.

Frowning, I just nodded and watched as she walked to the center of the room, everyone's eyes on her. She cleared her throat and looked at each person in turn before she finally opened her mouth. "I am of the persuasion that the vampire should be forgiven."

"Of course you would say that," Rand said, shaking his head. "You two were working together."

Mercedes turned her fiery green eyes on him, and I had to imagine that a lesser man would have caved under the pressure of her gaze. But Rand wasn't a lesser man.

"My motivation for sending the vampire back in time was different than the vampire's," she finished simply.

"What does that mean?" I prodded.

"It means," Varick suddenly piped up from his chair beside the fire, "that from the moment Sinclair had his freedom handed to him," and he glanced at me with a frown because I'd been the one to grant Sinjin his freedom, "he has acted however he pleases. Had he remained under my control, I would never have agreed to this." He paused for a second or two and then glared at me again. "Without his independence, this would never have happened."

I shook my head and tried to control the anger that snaked through me. I was the Queen and therefore had to lead by example. Losing my temper and blowing up at the bloodsucking jerkoff wasn't the best choice right now.

Mercedes eyed him indifferently. She probably figured he was full of it, just as I did. Varick was selfish and his every decision was intended to ensure his own future comfort. Had he still been in control of Sinjin, I'm sure he would have been all for Sinjin's role in Mercedes' plan, since he'd stand to gain if his subordinate became more powerful. Yeah, he was full of it, and then some.

"Sinjin said he acted to protect me," I replied in a soft voice.

Rand frowned at me and shook his head but didn't say anything.

"He said the same to me," Mercedes admitted, but then narrowed her eyes as she apparently weighed the sentiment. "Although I do believe he also had an agenda."

"An agenda?" I repeated.

"And yet you defend him?" Rand asked Mercedes.

"I believe his reasons overall were good," she said quickly, "regardless of his personal goals and ambitions."

"He wanted to force Jolie to love him," Rand said in an angry tone, shaking his head in apparent disbelief. "And his reasons were anything but chivalrous. Sinjin wanted nothing more than to control Jolie, thereby controlling the crown. As far as I'm concerned, both are treasonable offenses."

Mercedes pursed her lips and glanced at me quickly before facing Rand again. "Regardless of the vampire's intentions, he forced her into nothing. It's impossible to force someone to love you."

Rand frowned at that because he had to know her words were true, just as much as I knew it. Sinjin had certainly led me to water, but I'd been the one to take the first sip.

"What it comes down to," Trent suddenly piped up from the couch, where he sat beside Odran, "is that Sinjin decided to plan your life without clueing you in." He added with a frown at me, "And for that, he should pay the price, I think."

Trent isn't a bad guy to look at—he's shorter than

Rand and has a stocky build—like he played college football. He has wide-set brown eyes, high cheek-bones, a full mouth, and a generous nose. He was an attractive-looking guy and definitely had enough women in his life who would echo that sentiment. But I didn't find him attractive in the least, not anymore.

Rand nodded—probably the first time he'd ever agreed with anything the werewolf said. The two don't exactly see eye to eye, given their tumultuous past. It went back to when Trent and I were dating and Rand had gotten . . . jealous.

"Sinjin should be banished," Rand said with final-ity. "He cares about no one but himself, and this was an absolute act of narcissism."

The word "banished" caught in my throat, and try though I might, I couldn't swallow it.

"Banishment is a heavy price to pay," Mercedes said, sighing as she glanced at me. "And I do not agree."

"I agree with the warlock," Trent said.

"Aye, I do too," Odran said, nodding as he stretched his long legs out before him, the sides of his kilt be-ginning to separate. I glanced away because I was all too aware that he never wore a damn thing under-neath it.

"As do I," Varick said, eyeing me down either side of his long, snipelike nose. Varick is nearly as tall as Odran, but whereas Odran exudes health and vivac-ity with his broad shoulders and bulky frame, Varick is so thin, he looks emaciated—like he hasn't had anything to eat in ages, which I guess is pretty close to the truth. He's got bright orange hair and the whitest, most anemic skin you've ever seen.

I took a deep breath, forcing myself not to buck at Varick's words. It couldn't be any clearer that he had a personal vendetta against Sinjin. He had hated him ever since I'd granted Sinjin his emancipation. "I don't agree to his banishment," I said in as regal a tone as I could muster. Odran shook his head in apparent surprise, while Trent glanced at me and frowned. I made a point of not looking at Rand, since I knew what his reaction would be.

"At the very least, his title as Protector of the Queen should be stripped," Trent said, still facing me.

I exhaled for a count of three, not at all happy with where this was going. Maybe I was just being too easy on Sinjin—maybe I should have been as angry as everyone else appeared to be—but I couldn't deny that there was something in me that believed in him. Maybe it was just wishful thinking and I was still attributing Sinjin with qualities he didn't possess, but I couldn't help my feelings. I just . . . didn't, couldn't, believe that he deserved to be banished.

"Aye," Odran agreed. "He cannoot be troosted."

Mercedes sighed and glanced at me. "Perhaps stripping the vampire of his title is punishment enough?"

I had to agree and started to nod when something occurred to me. "Who will act as my guardian in his stead?" Varick raised his eyebrows and gave me a significant look. I adamantly shook my head, wanting nothing to do with him. If he were my protector, I'd need to worry about who would protect me from him. Varick was the type who would turn on you in an instant. "No," I said to his unspoken suggestion.

"Then I shall inquire with Klaasje concerning who would be an apt replacement," he said in a droll tone.

Klaasje was an old "friend" of Sinjin's who also shared his role as my protector. Although I'd been somewhat jealous of their close friendship, now I had to admit that I liked Klaasje and that she was very good at her job. I trusted her fully to find Sinjin's replacement.

"Okay, that is fair," I said, relieved that Sinjin hadn't fared too badly in the punishment department.

" 'Tis noot enough," Odran said, shaking his head as he smashed his fist into the side of the couch. "That is noot enough ta teach 'im his lesson."

"He should be banished," Rand repeated, his jaw tight as he ran his hands through his hair. He glanced at me and his expression was imploring.

"No," I said firmly. "I will not banish him."

"Perhaps we cannot rely upon the Queen's counsel," Varick said as he studied me in a detached way—like he was dissecting a bug. "Perhaps she is still in love with Sinclair?"

I hated the sound of the words because I couldn't deny the truth in them. I still cared for Sinjin deeply. "That has nothing to do with—" I started, but was interrupted by Rand.

"Jolie is not in love with Sinjin," he said. His voice sounded hoarse as I felt a wave of anger and resentment pour through me—Rand's feelings.

It's okay, Rand, I said in my head. *You know you're the only one for me.*

He glanced at me and smiled, almost embarrassed, nodding quickly as he did so.

Trent suddenly chuckled and shook his head. "Looks like a triangle if ever I saw one."

"You shut up," I said, and glared at him before I faced everyone in the room again. "And my personal life is not up for discussion. It's none of your business! Any of you!"

"Actually—" Varick started, but I turned my scowl on him and he wisely chose to back down.

"What is up for discussion is Sinjin's punishment, and all that should be considered are the facts. That's it." I took a deep breath. "And I am willing to admit that he definitely should be reprimanded, but I believe exile is too extreme. I'm comfortable with stripping him of his title of Protector of the Queen, but I refuse to allow anything more than that."

"I do not believe he should be banished either," Mathilda said softly, shaking her head as the silvery tresses of her hair bounced around her, seemingly weightless.

"Then 'tis ah draw," Odran announced. "The womenfolk in disagreement with oos."

"Maybe," Trent started, cocking his head as if carefully considering his words, "maybe this is another case of women being the weaker sex. Maybe you three are just too lenient to see this situation clearly," he finished as Mathilda, Mercedes, and I all glared at him at the same time.

"Do you want to say that again, Trent?" I asked. "Either Mercedes or Mathilda could turn you into dog stew in five seconds flat."

"As could you, child," Mathilda added.

Rand chuckled while Mathilda and Mercedes continued staring at the stupid were. I had no clue why I'd ever dated him. It was just one of those things I preferred to sweep under the rug and forget. "I'm firm in my decision," I said, and felt my jaw tighten.

Jolie, Rand interrupted in my mind. *You need to divorce yourself from your feelings for Sinjin and look at this rationally.*

I looked up at him and frowned, feeling heat beginning to brew inside of me. *I am looking at this rationally. Banishment is way too heavy a price for him to pay . . . and . . . and I refuse to agree to it.*

Then perhaps this must be a case in which you defer to the vote of your panel. His voice was silent for a second or two. *Perhaps your personal feelings are getting in the way?*

I shook my head as I felt acid begin to build in my stomach. *This has nothing to do with my feelings!* I railed back.

Then what does it have to do with?

Maybe you need to ask yourself the same question!

Seemingly taken aback, he glared at me. *I do not begin to guess what you mean by that.*

Rand, you need to separate yourself from your own jealousy regarding Sinjin and ask yourself if this truly is the right decision.

I watched him swallow as he took a deep breath. He said nothing, though, so I continued. *I simply won't agree to banishing Sinjin, no matter what anyone says. And I'm the Queen—my word is final.*

I choked on that last sentence. His eyes were narrowed on me, his lips pressed into a tight white line. *Ah, then you are now playing the part of a dictator?*

No, I thought immediately, then shook my head, realizing how bad it had sounded. *No, of course I'm not a dictator. You're . . . you're blowing this way out of proportion, Rand.*

Pray tell me, then, what is the difference between what you just said and the way a dictator would act? You refuse to allow for a democratic vote among your panel of representatives?

Rand—I started but he shook his head.

Jolie, I will leave this decision to you. Yes, I fully admit to my jealousy, but in this instance I have done my best to divorce myself from it. I believe Sinjin should absolutely suffer for the fact that he attempted to thwart his monarch for his own selfish reasons. And for what it is worth, I wouldn't mind if you chose to forgo my vote if you believe me too biased.

I realized then that if I truly wanted to lead as the Queen I had envisioned myself to be, one who valued democracy and justice, I couldn't override a majority of the people in that room. No, I had to rule justly and fairly, and that meant I would have to be open to a majority vote . . . as much as it pained me. "Although I am opposed to Sinjin's banishment, I will allow his fate to be decided by this room," I said, feeling my heart riding up into my throat. I then glanced at Rand. "By everyone in this room." I nearly felt myself choke on the words, knowing I was casti-gating Sinjin even as I uttered them. "But before you make your decision, I would advise you to consider all facts in this case and realize that banishment is no light subject."

"You could very well be sending him to his death,"

Mercedes added as she glanced at each person in the room.

"His death?" Varick scoffed.

Mercedes considered him without amusement. "The Lurker threat is ever present," she said simply.

At the mention of the Lurkers, I felt my stomach sink.

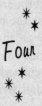

Four

An hour later I found myself alone in the library, my head aching as I realized what I had to do. We had debated for another two hours before reaching a decision about Sinjin. In the end it was agreed that he should be banished.

I was mostly exhausted, but I did see Rand's point. What it boiled down to was that even if I did believe that Sinjin meant to act in my best interests, he shouldn't have tried to ruin my relationship with Rand—that was the true evil. That was the sticking point. Sinjin had wanted me to fall in love with him for his own selfish reasons, and that was why I had to punish him with a heavy hand—why he needed to be banished.

Knowing that what I had to do was going to be unpleasant, I took a deep breath and started for the door. I took the stairs two at a time, and when I emerged in the basement hallway, I could feel my heart beating wildly, thumping throughout my entire body.

I spotted the vampire guards outside Sinjin's door immediately. Sinjin could have destroyed either of the younger vampires in a heartbeat, had he the desire. But he had obviously chosen to play by the rules, not causing any upset in my kingdom. For that, I felt strangely drawn to him—and appreciative.

The vampires bowed when they recognized me, and I smiled my greetings in a hurried and absentminded way. "I need to see the vampire," I said.

"We have been instructed not to allow you near him, my Queen," one of the guards said.

"Rand does not have the authority to dictate whom I see," I said sternly, realizing who the perpetrator was as soon as the guard spoke. Rand hadn't wanted me to deliver Sinjin's verdict to him in person, pointing out that according to Underworld custom, there would be a ceremony during which Sinjin was stripped of his position and officially banished. If anything, the fact that he would be so publicly humiliated made me want to see him alone all the more. I had to somehow explain everything to him.

The guard just nodded and stepped aside. I approached the heavy wooden door, but from the feeling of energy reverberating off it and stinging my cheeks, I realized it was charmed. I closed my eyes and held my palms up, facing the door, and imagined the magic fading away, breaking the spell. Why Rand had bespelled it was beyond me, because it wasn't like witchcraft worked against vampires. Just extra precautions, I assumed.

I knocked, and didn't hear a response from the other side. But moments later the door cracked open, revealing the breathtaking vampire on the other side. Of course, he knew it was me—he'd probably known from the moment I stepped into the hallway. I'm sure he could smell me, and his incredible hearing would also have allowed him to eavesdrop on my conversation with the guards.

"My Queen," he said with a grin as he bowed low.

I didn't like the sound of "Queen" on his tongue. No, truth be told, I preferred it when Sinjin referred to me as "poppet" or "love," his pet names for me. I closed the door behind me and took a deep breath, clasping my hands in front of me as I thought about the best way to start.

I found it difficult to even look at him. He was staring at me so unabashedly and appeared so . . . stunning. Yes, my feelings toward Sinjin Sinclair were lessening day by day, but I couldn't deny that he meant something to me and always would. That was when I realized I'd always been in love with this man. Maybe not to the extent I was now, but there had always been a part of me that loved him—really, it was impossible not to love him.

But I knew that thoughts like those would do me absolutely no good, so I shut them down and focused on the task at hand. "You really outdid yourself this time," I said, frowning at him.

"Perhaps and perhaps not," the debonair vampire replied, continuing to stare at me in a way that made my heart rate increase.

"You have been stripped of your title as my protector," I blurted, suddenly wanting nothing more than to say what I had to say and retire to the solitude of my bedroom.

Sinjin didn't respond for a second or two, but then nodded as if he weren't surprised. "Please inform Klaasje that Saxon should take my place. He is the only vampire I would trust with your safety, aside from Klaasje herself, of course."

I couldn't help but remember the moments when Sinjin had been there for me. When I delivered my first speech as Queen and was so nervous I thought I might wet myself, Sinjin had given me the strength to carry on. Just glancing back at him and seeing those hard ice-blue eyes and his gentle nod had given me the courage to continue.

"That's not all," I managed, feeling as if I were choking on the words.

"Yes?" Sinjin said in a small voice. I glanced up from my fidgeting hands and found his gaze focused on me.

"You've been banished," I said quietly.

Sinjin's eyes narrowed, but almost immediately his expression was once again stoic. He just stood there, watching me. I tried to meet his gaze but found it increasingly difficult to do so. Feeling like I might pass out, I took a seat on his bed and rubbed my temples, sensing an ache beginning to build behind my eyes.

"This is a decision that will threaten your safety," he said solemnly.

I glanced up at him in surprise. "My safety?"

He nodded. "The Lurker threat is ongoing, and I am the second strongest vampire in your kingdom." The strongest was Varick.

"It isn't a verdict I can rescind," I said softly, focusing on the fibers of my headache so that I could unravel them with magic and do away with the pain.

"You are the Queen, and your word is final."

I shook my head. "I may be the Queen, but where you're concerned, I can't be impartial. Therefore, I must rely on my panel of advisors. Your case was voted on and I can't and won't reverse that order." I took a deep breath. "You've been banished," I said again.

"You do not support this decision," he said softly.

I glanced up at him, surprised. Sometimes he was just so damned intuitive. "Why do you say that? I'm the Queen; obviously, I support it."

But he shook his head, a small smile beautifying his lips. He was handsome—just as he always had been. "No, you do not." And then he was silent for a second or two. "I can tell by your delivery."

"My delivery?" I repeated.

He nodded and appeared amused. "Yes, you said 'you've been banished' as if it were outside your control. Had it been solely your decision, you would have said, 'I am banishing you.'"

Sinjin had been around too long for me to try and pull any fast ones on him. It was futile to argue with him when he was right—I'd just dig myself into a deeper hole. "Well, that isn't to say I'm not angry and upset with you," I managed, wanting him to understand that while I might not support his exile, I was still angry and hurt by his actions.

He nodded. "I only ever acted to protect you, my love."

I swallowed hard at the mention of "love." But I ignored it. "You are much more enigmatic than that, Sinjin," I said, and shook my head with a small laugh, as if to tell him I wasn't dumb enough to swallow his words hook, line, and sinker. "I know you well enough to know that there's never just one motive for you."

He smiled, no doubt liking my comment. He seemed to enjoy being unpredictable and complex. "Perhaps."

I took a deep breath, feeling light-headed and dizzy—like I hadn't eaten anything in days and had just run a marathon. "There will be a . . . a ceremony," I started, wanting to warn him. This was the part I liked least, but according to Rand and Mercedes, it was Underworld protocol.

Sinjin merely nodded. "Yes, of course." Then he eyed me and shook his head with a small smile. "Do not imagine I am anxious about the silly thing."

I glanced up at him, surprised. I had figured it would bother him. I mean, it would have bothered me. It did bother me, and I wasn't even the one being banished. "You're not?"

He chuckled. "It means nothing to me . . . just pomp and circumstance."

I nodded and then remembered the rest of his verdict, wanting to prepare him. If I was in his shoes, I wouldn't want any surprises. "After the ceremony ends, you will need to pack your things and vacate Kinloch Kirk within the hour."

"That will be quite simple—I have no need of anything from this room," he said, and glanced around with apparent languor before his eyes settled on me again and he smiled. "Save for one."

Not wanting to touch that statement with a tenfoot pole, I changed the subject. "You, uh, you aren't allowed back here ever again, Sinjin." I felt something inside me break as the words fell off my tongue.

"I understand the terms of my banishment," he said.

I nodded and stood up, feeling like I was going to implode. I started for the door, but realizing that this was the last time I would ever see him alone, I turned back to face him. I just wanted to imprint his male beauty in my memory, wanted to be able to recall his gently curving smile, the intelligence in his striking gaze, the splendor that was Sinjin Sinclair. Then I looked away.

"When someone dies," Sinjin started, and I glanced up at him in surprise, "they say the friends and family of the deceased are able to recall his features, his mannerisms, and his voice for one year. Beyond a year, the memories become more and more obscure."

"Why are you telling me this?" I asked, afraid of the answer.

"Remember me well," he said, a small laugh accompanying the macabre sentiment.

"I'm hardly sending you to your death," I said, even though I doubted the truth in my own words. Who knew what awaited him out there?

Sinjin won't die! I promised myself. *Sinjin can't die!* I mean, he'd been alive for six hundred years, so he could easily survive for another six hundred . . . right?

"Very true," he said simply and shrugged.

"I'm . . . I'm sorry, Sinjin."

"One thing I would like to make quite clear," he added, wanting to have the last word. And I suddenly hoped he would belittle me, tell me he never cared a damn about me and, yes, had been acting out of self-ishness all along. It would have made my decision that much easier.

"Yes?"

He took a few steps toward me, and I nearly suffocated on his clean scent. I tried not to inhale. "I care more for you than I have cared for anyone . . . ever."

I closed my eyes against the tears threatening to break through and shook my head. "No, Sinjin," I started, then opened them, a sudden anger burning me from the inside out. "It's too late for this. Grant me enough respect not to play with my emotions anymore."

He reached out and grasped my shoulder. I reeled back at his icy touch, but it wasn't the cold that warded me away—it was the way my heart fluttered when he touched me.

"You can banish me to the ends of the world, poppet, but you will never banish my feelings for you. You cannot deny me my own emotions."

"Sinjin—" I started, but he shook his head, indicating that he wasn't finished.

"And for that matter, your bloody panel can strip me of my position, banish me from Kinloch, but I will always remain dedicated to your protection, damn what anyone else says or thinks."

I refused to look at him. "Sinjin, you can't . . . your job here is done."

He grasped my chin and tilted it, forcing my gaze upward, forcing me to take in his beautiful blue eyes. "As long as the Lurker threat continues, you are in danger." He took a breath. "You are as aware of that as I am, poppet."

"Klaasje and Saxon—" I started, trying to reassure myself that the Lurkers weren't as much of a threat to my safety as Sinjin imagined they were.

He shook his head. "You know you are safest with me."

"Sinjin . . ." I said his name and felt the rest of the sentence fall right off my tongue. I wasn't even sure what I'd been about to say. He stayed silent, just smiling at me. But his smile spoke volumes—it said that this was by no means the end, that he wasn't finished with me.

"I will see you at the ceremony," I finally managed when it seemed like he was done with talking. I stepped away from him, but he just stepped closer to me again. "Take care of yourself, Sinjin," I said as I started to turn around and palmed the doorknob.

His cold breath fanning across the back of my neck caused my own breath to catch in my throat.

"I know I never said the words you wanted to hear," he whispered.

I closed my eyes and shook my head, refusing to allow him to bring this up now. "Sinjin, it's way too little and way too late."

Before I could take another breath, he whirled me around so I was facing him, his hands on my upper arms. I started to pull away but he was resolute, his eyes boring into mine. "I care for you more than I care for myself."

I shook my head. "No, Sinjin, I don't want to hear this." And that was the truth. I didn't want to hear it because I knew it could do no good. I was in love with Rand, just as I always had been, and while there was once a time when I'd imagined carving out a life with Sinjin, that time was long gone.

"You will hear it, dammit!" he railed back, and his urgency surprised me as much as the heightened tone of his voice.

"I came here to say goodbye," I started, feeling myself begin to spiral out of control. This wasn't what I'd been expecting—this wasn't what I'd come here for—and now I needed to escape.

"Damn saying goodbye to me, poppet," he spat back and shook his head, an odd smile curving the ends of his lips. "You came here because you couldn't keep away from me," he insisted. "You came here because you still feel the same way for me that I feel for you."

"Stop it!" I seethed at him, feeling tears welling in my eyes.

"You love me, Jolie, just as much as you always did, and I . . ."

I narrowed my eyes, suddenly hanging on his words. And although I knew this conversation was absolutely pointless, somehow I couldn't let go of the fact that he had been about to say something . . . something I had so longed to hear . . . well, that is before Rand and Mathilda returned my memories to me. "You what?" I demanded, surprised by my need to hear him utter the words.

But Sinjin had already dropped his gaze to the floor, as if any boldness he'd previously experienced had withered and died.

"You what?" I demanded again.

But he dropped my arms and stepped away, shaking his head as he did so. The tears that had been threatening me only seconds earlier abruptly receded, replaced by anger. Why I was angry, I didn't really know.

"It's just as well," I said in a soft but disappointed voice. I pulled away and opened the door, disappearing into the sanctuary of the dark hallway.

* * *

The ceremony was held a mere two hours later. My panel and I were in attendance in the Green Room of Kinloch Kirk, so named because the entire room, with its amphitheater-style seating, was painted a sage green. It was the same room where only a few months earlier Sinjin had helped me defeat my nerves before I gave my first speech as Queen.

But of course I firmly pushed all kind thoughts about Sinjin to the deepest recesses of my mind, knowing they would only spawn useless feelings of guilt. As I glanced around the room, I was quiet, depressed. I watched Odran and Trent make small talk as they sat in the first row, four rows of unoccupied seats behind them. Meanwhile, in a corner, Mercedes struggled with her "projection charm" to ensure it was working. She raised her hands a few times, closed her eyes and uttered a few words as lights flamed up from between her hands like a fireworks show. The projection charm was basically like a magical video camera. The ceremony that was about to start would be broadcast to the entire Underworld community. The witches and fae would need to go into a visionary trance and Mercedes' charm would act like a film reel against the backdrop of their minds. Those less magically inclined, like the vampires and werewolves, could tune in on their television sets. They just had to turn on the channel that offered the most static, and Mercedes' magic would do the rest, broadcasting itself like a television show. Or at least that's how Mercedes had described it in her announcement.

The fact that Sinjin's disgrace was going to be aired like the Rose Parade made me sick to my stomach. In some ways the Underworld reminded me of medieval times—some of our customs were just as outdated.

"I know this must be difficult for you," Rand said as he took the seat beside mine.

I glanced up at him, half expecting him to be jovial since he was about to witness the banishment of someone he had always disliked . . . intensely. But instead his expression was grim and I could feel his gloomy mood.

"It isn't easy," I said with a frown.

He nodded. "Well, for whatever it's worth, I think you did the right thing."

"This wasn't my idea," I reminded him, second-guessing it even now. The thought of what was about to happen to Sinjin was making me feel physically ill.

"I wasn't referring to Sinjin's punishment. I was referring to the fact that you allowed your panel to vote, and you carried out their decision." He smiled down at me and appeared to be proud. "You are every inch the Queen you wanted to be."

I nodded, trying to find comfort in his words. But I couldn't. I mean, yes, I was proud of myself for choosing to support a democratic vote, but at the same time I was uneasy because I didn't support the verdict. I just had to wonder what was worse—ruling with an iron fist and feeling justified in my decisions, or . . . this?

I watched my fingers drum against my knee, and then glanced around the room nervously, wondering when the guards would escort Sinjin in and, more so, when this whole ordeal would be over. My attention turned to Klaasje, who was sitting beside Varick. The older vampire was prattling on about something, but I could tell she wasn't listening. She was pale and her normally bright, wide eyes were even wider, scared. She hated every second of this as much as I did—hated the fact that her friend was about to be banished and then God only knew what would happen to him.

"It's still not a decision that leaves me with the warm fuzzies," I said, and sighed.

Rand nodded but was spared further comment when the double doors opened and two burly werewolf guards walked inside, Sinjin between them. I wasn't sure what I was expecting, considering that Sinjin was for all intents and purposes a prisoner, but he certainly wasn't dressed like one. Now, in his midnight-colored suit, he looked like he was heading to a black-tie event. There wasn't a chain or a handcuff to be seen. He strolled inside casually, pausing when he reached the center of the room. The guards took their positions on either side of the doors and stood there, wearing solemn frowns.

"The party can begin," Sinjin said with a smile as he scanned the room, his smile broadening when his attention settled on me. I felt my stomach drop.

"Sinjin Sinclair," Mercedes started as she approached him. She was dressed in a long flowing purple velvet cape with a hood over her head. She looked like she was trying to impersonate a monk.

Sinjin had been right when he'd described this as nothing more than pomp and circumstance. It seemed especially heavy on the pomp.

"Mercedes Berg, the prophetess," Sinjin said with that devil's smile, a smile that said he wasn't taking any of this seriously, that it was all just a big game to him—like, well, most things in his life.

"You might do well to wipe that grin off your mouth, as you have been denied the privilege of protecting your Queen from this day forward," Varick called out from his seat on the opposite side of the room.

Sinjin glanced at him and smirked. "Ah, my dear comrade Varick, why should I not smile when I am so enjoying myself?"

Mercedes cleared her throat. "I do not want to make this task long or arduous," she said firmly.

"We have that in common," Sinjin responded, dropping the smile as he faced her again.

"Then I will not delay," she finished, and turned toward me. "My Queen, before you stands your former chief protector, do you approve of his removal from this office?"

I swallowed hard. "Yes."

She faced Sinjin again. "As our Queen has vested within me the power to free you from your responsibilities as her chief protector, you are hereby stripped of that office."

Sinjin glanced at me but said nothing, merely nodded in an almost humble sort of way. Then he bowed in a practiced form and turned to face Mercedes again, expectant. Mercedes simply sat down in the seat beside me as Odran stood up and lumbered toward Sinjin.

"As ah representative ah the Queen's panel, I declare that Sinjin Sinclair, Master Vampire, is ta be stripped ah 'is title ah Master Vampire and banished froom the Queen's kingdoom . . . forever."

Sinjin nodded again and said nothing apparently,

just listening to Odran's words. Once the King of the Fae lumbered back to his seat, Sinjin must have recognized the floor was his own. He cocked a brow and narrowed his gaze on me, until it seemed as though no one else in the room even existed.

"I recognize and abide by my Queen's will," he began. "I have only ever wanted to protect her, to ensure her longevity and happiness."

Rand grumbled something. I ignored him.

"My Queen, these are uncertain times in which we are living," Sinjin continued, as if Rand's reaction were of no consequence to him. "And it would serve you well to rethink my banishment."

"The decision is made," Rand said furtively. "Endure your punishment like a gentleman, Sinclair."

Sinjin faced him then and his eyes narrowed. "The Queen will require all the protection available to her. Banishing me could be cutting off her nose to spite her face."

Rand stood up and shook his head. "Don't think you're going to worm your way out of this one, Sinjin. You've been decreed a public enemy, and as such, you will be banished."

Sinjin said nothing more to Rand, but he turned back toward me. "Poppet, if ever you should need me, you have only to ask and I will come running."

Of course, I replayed the conversation with Sinjin repeatedly in my head—I mean, how could I not? Questions poured through my brain and it was all I could do to focus on one at a time. Was what Sinjin said true? Was banishing him cutting off my nose to spite my face? I glanced outside the window at the darkness of the Scottish sky, thankful that I was in the solitude of my bedroom. I needed some alone time in order to contemplate the enigma that was Sinjin. As Queen, it seemed I never had any time to myself, so these few moments were precious.

Sitting at my bedside vanity, I stared at myself as if my blue eyes might hold an answer—as if they could tell me whether Sinjin truly cared about me. But of course, my vacuous expression was reflected back at me. I couldn't help but notice that my eyes were still wide with surprise, even though the ceremony was long since over.

I couldn't keep the questions and thoughts from rampaging through my mind, couldn't stop wondering if Sinjin had been telling me the truth earlier, when I'd first told him of his banishment. Maybe deep down in that icy cave of his heart, he was still truly human and capable of caring about someone else. Maybe Sinjin Sinclair could feel love?

Who are you kidding? That voice in my head piped up. *Sinjin is a master of artifice, Jolie. You of all people should know that by now!*

I shook my head, determined to win this argument with myself, determined to find the good in Sinjin. Why, I had no idea—it was almost an automatic reaction. *You saw his expression—you looked into his eyes the same as I did. Are you really trying to tell me that what you saw there wasn't genuine and real?*

It wasn't genuine or real.

You know in your heart of hearts that he's telling the truth. You know he cares about you and always has.

I know I'm not going to fall for it again. I'm not

going to be the naive idiot I've always been. This time, I'm learning my lesson.

Bah! I figuratively waved the voice away and, instead, turned to thoughts of Sinjin's exile. I just couldn't feel good about the decision. Even though almost everyone had agreed on it—well, all the men in the room, anyway—I just couldn't defend the decision. Especially with the Lurker threat ever growing. What did that threat mean for Sinjin? What if the Lurkers discovered him and he had no one to defend him?

Had I just sent Sinjin to his death?

Puhleeze, Jolie! Sinjin is a survivor. You heard Rand, I thought. *He can take care of himself.*

Yeah, but who knows what the Lurkers are capable of? Not to mention what they're planning? Who knows what's in store for us?

Sinjin's punishment was voted on by your counsel, Jolie, and you can't go back now. What he did was wrong, no matter what his motivations were. He pulled the rug out from underneath you and attempted to change the course of your life!

Hmm, that's true.

He tried to destroy everything you knew, everything you cared about! And you're debating whether he deserves his punishment? He nearly separated you from Rand! What the hell is wrong with you?

Thinking about Rand was ultimately what set me straight. Sinjin had nearly destroyed everything I'd worked so hard for—everything Rand had worked so hard for. Yes, what was done was done, and there was no going back.

And this time I would be firm in my convictions.

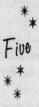

Five

"Damn being announced! I will see her now!"

I heard Varick's voice coming from downstairs, followed by the sound of heavy footfalls and Mercedes demanding to know what the hell was going on. I'd just started brushing my teeth, so I spat out the toothpaste, laying the toothbrush down on the counter as I cupped my other hand and washed the remainder of the paste from my mouth. My heart started pounding in my breast, echoing through my head. I took a deep breath as I tried to fathom what the hell could have upset Varick so badly. I mean, he wasn't the type of person to get irate easily, so something huge had to have just gone down. And that thought wasn't exactly comforting.

I started for the door to my bedroom, but once I was in the hallway, I glanced over the balcony to see Mercedes, Klaasje, and Varick arguing as Trent joined them.

"What's all the excitement about?" Trent asked casually, as if he wanted nothing more than some good gossip.

"You cannot think to burst into the Queen's quarters without first going through me," Mercedes demanded, clearly more interested in propriety than whatever had brought Varick here in the first place.

"Damn your—" Varick started as Klaasje interrupted him, her hands stretched out before her, ever the peacemaker.

"Varick, what happened?" she asked, but her question fell on deaf ears. Apparently, Varick had only one goal in mind and that was to see me.

"I will see the Queen now!" he roared.

"This behavior is outrageous!" Mercedes chastised him as I took the stairs two at a time. I watched as two of my werewolf guards suddenly approached me from either side of the stairwell, obviously afraid that Varick might have lost his mind.

"I am not going to harm the Queen, you bumbling fools!" he railed, and then turned his outraged eyes on me. "You must call an assembly at once."

"What's going on?" I asked, remembering that I was dressed in my pink jammies with red-and-white-striped Christmas socks. I wasn't exactly equipped to receive guests.

"What is going on," Varick started, enunciating every word, "is that twenty vampires in your kingdom have simply . . . disappeared."

"Disappeared?" I responded at the same time that Klaasje inhaled deeply and placed her hand over her heart.

"Holy shit!" Trent said, shaking his head in apparent disbelief.

"Lurkers?" Mercedes asked, her eyes narrowed on Varick as she folded her arms across her chest, still visibly disturbed by his outburst.

Varick raised a brow at her, offering her a duplicate of the frown she'd just given him. "I do not know."

Jolie! It was Rand's voice in my head. He must have felt my apprehension and concern through our bond. *Is everything all right?*

I don't think so, I responded, shaking my head even though our conversation was a telepathic one. *There are twenty vampires missing and Varick has just asked me to call an assembly.*

I am leaving now, Rand's voice was determined. *I will be there momentarily.* He had spent the better portion of the day at Pelham Manor.

I turned to face Mercedes. "Can you alert Odran and Mathilda?" Luckily for me, it had been decided that my panel of representatives would all live in close proximity to Kinloch Kirk for situations such as this one, where immediacy was required.

She nodded. "Of course, my Queen."

"Then I will meet all of you in the library in thirty minutes," I said, and turned around, starting for the stairs again. I mean, it wasn't like I was going to lead a meeting dressed in my pajamas.

"Something must be done—" Varick started, his tone urgent.

I turned around to face him. "Something will be done, Varick, just as soon as my panel is in full attendance."

He said nothing more, so I took a deep breath and closed the door behind me as tears threatened my eyes. I leaned my back against the door, feeling my breath constricting, like a snake was eating me from the feet up.

God, please don't let Sinjin be in trouble, I thought

to myself, terrified that my darkest fears might have just become a reality. The question of whether the vampire disappearances had been orchestrated by the Lurkers was a moot one—the Lurkers were absolutely responsible, of that I was convinced. Why? Because they were our only enemies at this stage of the game. And now all I could do was hope and pray that Sinjin wasn't one of their victims. Yes, on the face of it, it seemed I could reanimate pretty much anyone but I still didn't like the idea of Sinjin . . . dead. And where my abilities were concerned, nothing really was etched in stone.

Exactly thirty minutes later I found myself sitting at the head of the conference table in my massive library, my stomach in knots. I hadn't been able to wipe away my fears about what might have happened to Sinjin. And although I had to remind myself that the chances of him being among the twenty or so victims were slim, it did nothing to allay my concerns. I felt my toes tapping seemingly of their own accord and I tried to concentrate on my panel to take my mind away from the constant onslaught of worry.

Rand sat to my right, Mercedes to my left, Odran and Trent beside her. Varick was at the far end of the table, flanked by Klaasje on one side and Mathilda on the other.

"Thank you all for coming on such short notice," I started in a wavering voice as I glanced around the room. "Varick has some very upsetting news for us, and therefore I will turn the meeting over to him."

I looked at Varick and he nodded as he cleared his throat. "It was brought to my attention at dusk that twenty of the vampires simply disappeared yesterday."

"Crazy, huh?" Trent asked Odran, elbowing him in the side as if to say the news really was that shocking. Odran just frowned down at him.

"What does that mean?" Rand asked at the same time, leaning forward on his elbows.

Varick faced him, his lips in a straight line. "It means there is no trace of them."

"No piles of ash, no bodies?" Rand continued, not paying any heed to Varick's less than polite response.

Varick shook his head, one eyebrow raised. "Nothing. Only minor signs of struggle."

"Do you know who are among the missing?" Klaasje asked with trepidation. And that was when I realized she was as worried about Sinjin as I was.

"Yes," Varick said, and fished into his coat pocket, standing up as he produced a three-by-five index card. He strode to the head of the table and offered the card to me. I took it with a shaking hand and glanced through the list of names, feeling relief beat through me when I didn't recognize any of them.

Sinjin wasn't on the list. Sinjin was safe. And then something occurred to me—Sinjin was no longer a member of my kingdom, which meant his safety was of no one's concern. So not being on this list really meant nothing. I had to swallow down another attack of dread.

"Anyone we know?" Klaasje asked, her eyes wide.

I glanced at her and shook my head, understanding her gist. "No one I am acquainted with. You might know some of them, though." I handed her the card.

I faced Varick again. "Twenty," I started. "Were

they all in the same location when they were abducted?"

Varick glanced at me and shook his head again. "They were in four different territories."

"Boot all happened at the same time?" Odran demanded, shaking his head as he appeared to grasp the situation.

Varick nodded. "As I understand it, yes."

This was how it always was with Lurker attacks. Their M.O. was to attack in random one-offs, but the attacks were fully orchestrated and planned out, exemplified by the fact that they'd hit us in more than one territory at the exact same time. Which had to tell me they'd been scoping out their victims.

"We will need to re-create the scene to fully understand what happened," Mercedes said softly, and stood up, facing Varick. "Were you able to locate anything of a personal nature from any of the victims?"

He nodded and pulled a scrap of clothing from his pocket, which was maybe a two-inch square. It was black cotton, by the looks of it. "This was from one of the households closest to us—a vampire territory in Cambridge, England." He glanced at the cloth as he handed it to Mercedes. "I was told it is a piece of a curtain."

She nodded and accepted it, clasping it in her hand as she turned to face me. "My Queen?"

I nodded and stood up as I realized what it was we were about to do—a re-creation spell that would reveal exactly what had gone down a few hours earlier. Mathilda took her place beside me, and together the three of us touched the fabric swatch and closed our eyes, allowing our magic to unite us as one and open the great gate to our sixth senses.

Probably due to the fact that Mercedes, Mathilda, and I together were like a magic powerhouse, the spell took shape quickly. I opened my eyes to see a white puffy cloud floating right before us, in the center of the table, maybe two feet up. Almost immediately a sound came from the cloud and it began to blink, eventually dissolving into the ether. In its place, colors began to appear out of the air, bobbing around like fireflies. The gentle glows became stronger as the colors began to meld, eventually forming an image of a house.

It was a one-story, nondescript sort of house, and judging from the extreme shadows surrounding it, I imagined it was early evening. As everyone around the table focused on the image more intently, most of us leaning in toward the spectacle, a moving van pulled into the driveway of the house. The driver killed the engine and two burly men jumped down from the passenger door. They strolled up to the front door of the home and in a split second one of them kicked it in.

I could feel the tension around the table as we watched these . . . Lurkers come for our own. I was sure they were in fact Lurkers. Even from watching this reflection of what had happened, I could feel their power—it caused all the hairs on my body to stand at attention. It was a foreign power, a magic dissimilar to our own.

It seemed like five minutes or so lapsed before the "movers" returned, each carrying a plain pine box— about the length and width of an adult male. I felt myself gulp as I watched them load the sleeping vampires into the rear of the moving truck. They didn't bother closing the busted front door and instead hopped back into the front seat. The driver started the engine, and the truck disappeared down the street.

The image made the same popping sound the cloud had and erupted into nothing but thin air.

"They kidnapped them," Klaasje said softly. "They didn't kill them."

"It makes no sense," Trent added.

And that was the truth. It didn't make any sense. In the past, the Lurkers had staged the same sort of guerrilla ambushes, but they had always finished off their victims, leaving piles of ash in their wake.

"Every vampire household should be protected by a were, witch, or fae in the daytime," Rand announced. "Until we have a better understanding of the nature of this threat, vampires should not be left to their own defenses in the daytime."

Varick nodded. "Agreed."

"Why would the Lurkers be kidnapping vampires?" I asked out loud, suddenly afraid for the answer.

For the remainder of the evening, I found myself trying to understand just what the Lurker threat entailed, but it was incredibly frustrating because we still didn't know very much about them. They were an unseen force that just picked off our kind here and there with no real uniformity to their attacks. And since their attacks were so random, it was next to impossible to prepare for any future attacks.

With no ready solution for the Lurker problem, I

decided to focus my energy on the other dilemmas plaguing my kingdom. And currently the biggest plague went by the name of Bella. Something had to be done with her. Either she needed to take an oath of loyalty and become a member of my kingdom or be dealt with in a harsher way. She couldn't remain my prisoner forever.

So with steely resignation, I marched out of my bedroom and headed for the guesthouse just behind Kinloch Kirk. I couldn't even remember how long we'd been holding Bella there. With the whole time-travel thing, my sense of time was completely thrown off. It could be that she'd been my prisoner for days, or even months. Either way, it had been long enough. And, yes, it did occur to me that maybe I should have discussed this visit with Mercedes or Rand or my counsel of representatives, but I dismissed the thought as soon as it reared its unwanted head. As far as I was concerned, this was just between Bella and me.

When I stepped outside my back door, the cold Scottish sea air accosted me with its chill, wrapping itself around my legs as I shivered involuntarily. I folded my arms around myself as I glanced up at the moon. I hurried down the pathway leading to the guesthouse and was greeted by two werewolf guards who seemed unfazed by the frigid air. 'Course, weres naturally have body temperatures that run much hotter than humans, so they were probably as comfortable as I would have been on a warm beach in Maui.

"Hi," I started in an unsteady voice. Then I remembered I was their Queen and should do my best to seem like one. I fluffed my proverbial feathers and stood up straight and tall. "I'm here to see Bella."

The guard closest to me bowed and then nodded, stepping aside. He was huge—as in Odran huge, but unlike Odran, this guy wasn't eye candy. He had a really wide face, covered with moles, and eyes that were too close together, setting off a nose too small for his moon face. But then it occurred to me that he was probably a nice guy, and I was suddenly irritated with myself for noticing his homeliness first.

"If you need us, just holler," he said, smiling warmly.

What a jerk I was.

I took a deep breath and gave him a fake smile, hoping my demeanor was casual. Inside, though, it was another story. Why? Because Bella and I had a long and ugly history. That history was now tainted or tempered with memories from a different past, ever since Sinjin had time-traveled. I couldn't help but wonder if Bella was aware of what had happened. Did she have layered memories like I did? Did she remember how Sinjin had mistreated her, how she instructed me in magic lessons at his insistence? For that matter, did she remember that Sinjin and I had been a couple? I could only hope the answer was no.

I eyed the were farthest from me, another huge guy with long, dark hair and dirty fingernails. (Jeez, did I only notice the negative? Okay, he had nice broad shoulders.) He bowed in greeting and then unlocked the door. I approached it, and holding my hands against the wood, felt the energy reverberating from it. It was similar to what I'd felt when I went to see Sinjin. I closed my eyes and sent the feelers of my mind to inquire as to what kind of spell this was and how I could break it.

It turned out to be a simple charm, and it only took me three seconds to break it. I focused on the darkness of my eyelids and imagined a bright white light usurping control over the charm's spell. As soon as it dissipated into oblivion, I had to wonder why such a weak spell had been cast to hold Bella. As that thought crossed my mind, I ran into the Barrier Ward. Now this one would be a real feat to break.

You can always tell who put a spell in place because charms have a magical fingerprint, and as soon as I encountered this one, I could feel Mercedes' energy all over it. It was bad enough that it was an incredibly strong spell, but given the fact that Mercedes had woven it? Well, that just added to its difficulty. But I was pleased to see it in place because it pointed to Mercedes' thoughtful preparation. The only way we had any hope of keeping Bella behind figurative bars was to employ magic stronger than her own.

I motioned for both guards to back away. "This could get ugly," I said, and frowned, wondering just how ugly it was going to get. "Bella, if you're on the other side," I called through the door, "back away to the far end of the wall."

She didn't respond, but I hoped that she heard me and, more important, that she'd take my advice. I held my hands up to the door until they were an inch or so away and clenched my eyes shut. I imagined energy pouring out of my fingertips and into the depths of the ward, forcing the tightly wound magical threads apart. I could almost hear the gossamer strings ripping apart like Velcro, and my energy suddenly boiled up, overflowing from me as the walls of the ward crumbled and broke away, leaving nothing but the door itself.

I opened my eyes and smiled. My magic was getting stronger every day. A few months ago it would have taken me way longer to break through one of Mercedes' wards, and yet that little stunt had taken me all of thirty seconds. Yep, I had definitely come a long way.

Returning to the business at hand, I inhaled deeply and opened the door with my chin held high. I immediately noticed that Bella was standing at the far end of the living room, her arms crossed against her buxom chest, an irritated expression on her face. I glanced around the room, taking in the comfortable furnishings. For a prisoner, Bella was living the high life.

"What do you want?" she demanded.

I sighed—things with her were never easy. "I'm here to give you an ultimatum, Bella," I started, not wanting to pick a fight but finding it difficult to keep a level tone. "You can't remain a prisoner here forever."

Her left eyebrow reached for the ceiling as she considered me with straight lips. "I'm listening."

I didn't back down or drop my gaze or the rigid resolve of my shoulders. I wasn't going to take no for an answer and I also wasn't here to negotiate. "I want you to take the loyalty oath and become a member of my kingdom. I want you to have your freedom and be an ally, not an enemy."

She didn't say anything right away, but just studied me with her eyebrows knitted in the middle of her face, looking super pissed off. "What's the alternative?"

"Permanent exile," I said immediately. "And in these uncertain times, that wouldn't be a smart choice for you to make."

"What uncertain times?" she repeated, glaring at me as if she desired nothing more than to see the floor open up and swallow me whole.

But I wasn't going to be done away with so easily. "The Lurkers are becoming an ever-growing menace."

"Interesting," she said with a frown, not appearing to take the threat seriously.

I was suddenly struck by the notion that Bella knew more than she was letting on. It was there in her eyes and the way her lips curved up at the ends into something that resembled a smile. "Interesting?" I repeated as I eyed her suspiciously.

"Interesting that the Lurkers don't appear to be what everyone always thought they were," she continued. She was acting like she had a plethora of information up her sleeve.

"What do you mean?" I demanded irritably.

She shrugged, playing aloof, and even added a yawn. She was pissing me off . . . royally. "We've always believed they were just vampire impostors," she started, "but they're much more than that. They are witches, or at the very least, they possess magic."

Now this wasn't exactly new information. I realized that the Lurkers possessed magic when they assaulted me in my dreams, something a vampire could only dream of doing, no pun intended. But how Bella had obtained this information was the million-dollar question. As soon as the thought entered my mind, though, I remembered that she had helped cure me when the Lurkers attacked me in my sleep. It had happened in the virtual reality that was created when Sinjin time-traveled. Was that what she was referring to? If she could remember that, it also meant that she was well aware of the history between Sinjin and me, just as I was well aware of her infatuation with him.

"How do you know this?" I asked, none too gently.

"I guess you could say I've been in contact with them," she said, and then shrugged again, as if she hadn't just dropped an enormous bomb right into my lap.

"You what?" I insisted, my voice cracking with the effort. And that was when I got angry. "Bella, as your Queen, I demand you tell me everything you know about the Lurkers or I will try you for treason."

She smiled at me, a smile that suddenly turned ugly. "I have a few of my own requests before I'll impart any information. And as to you being my Queen, I haven't taken that loyalty oath yet in case you've forgotten. I owe you no allegiance."

I cleared my throat, telling myself to calm down. Getting into a bitch fest wasn't going to help either of us. "Whether or not you take the oath doesn't change the fact that I am the Queen of all Underworld creatures. Whether you support me makes no difference."

She frowned, but said no more. And I realized that this was my window of opportunity—I needed to try and get information out of her without ruffling her feathers. The more I played offense, the more she'd dig her heels in the mud, and that would get me no-where. "What are your requests?" I asked.

"I want my freedom," she responded quickly.

I'd figured as much. "Meaning what?"

"I want the freedom to return to the States and be my own solitary witch."

I shook my head. "You must first become a member of this kingdom."

She nodded. "I will take your silly oath."

I was surprised, but tried not to let it show. She'd always seemed completely opposed to becoming a member of any kingdom, opposed to subjugating her-self to anyone else's rule, especially mine. Why? Be-cause Bella had wanted to be Queen of the Underworld from the beginning. We actually waged war and bat-tled over that exact subject, which was how she be-came my captive. Obviously, she lost.

"Then all you're asking for is to return to your home in California?"

"Yes," she nodded. "That's all I'm asking."

"And you will abide by our rules and laws?" I con-tinued.

She simply nodded again. That was when it hit me—if she had information on the Lurkers, she might be a useful source. "I will grant your request on one condition . . ." I started.

"Which is?" she asked, eyeing me askance.

"You can have your freedom and return to the U.S. only if you work with us against the Lurkers. I want to know everything you know and any new informa-tion you receive." No, I didn't imagine Bella would just willingly hand over any new information. What I wanted—and she was well aware of it—was to put a spell on her that would *force* her to deliver any newly acquired information—whether it be a dream, a vision, whatever.

She was quiet for a second or two. "Deal."

I wasn't sure why, but I hadn't thought it would be so easy to win her over. But any joy in that thought was tempered when I remembered that Bella had admitted she was in contact with the Lurkers. This was information I wanted and needed. "So spill the beans," I said. "How have you been in contact with the Lurkers and what do you know?"

She glanced out the window and seemed to be stalling for time, making whatever she had to say that much more suspenseful. She was like an actress—well-trained in the art of duplicity and disguise.

"I received information by way of a vision from someone who called himself the Supreme Elder of the Lurkers," she said.

I took a deep breath, feeling my heart beginning to pound louder. "Go on."

Her lips tightened and her eyes went a bit wide. Bella was scared—I could read it in her gaze. "He said his kind will attack us. They are preparing now."

"They've already attacked us," I said absentmindedly, recalling the disappearance of the twenty vampires. Then it occurred to me that I probably shouldn't reveal anything to her.

She scoffed at me, waving her hand in my face as if I were an idiot. "This will be a battle, a war between our kind and theirs. The attacks they've waged against us so far are no more than child's play."

"And the Lurker elder told you this?" I demanded suspiciously.

"Word for word," she answered simply.

"When will this battle take place?" I insisted. "And where?"

She shook her head. "I don't know."

It was about as useful as the information Mercedes had collected through her Lurker task force. It seemed we had lots of tidbits of news; in a vast puzzle where our pieces were so small and inconsequential, we couldn't even tell what the puzzle depicted.

"They are in the process of preparing now," Bella repeated. "It is just a matter of time before all hell breaks loose."

"How did you get this information?" I asked. "Was it a vision from your own mind or do you believe it was sent to you? Did the Lurkers actually contact you?"

She frowned. "Yes, they definitely contacted me."

"Maybe they're just trying to throw you off or make us believe something that isn't true." And then something else occurred to me. "Or maybe you're just making this up."

She glanced over at me in surprise, and moments later her look of shock gave way to anger. "I will gladly subject myself to a Liar's Circle," she said. A Liar's Circle was a spell that allowed the charmer to test whether or not someone had pure intentions. It was considered the best trial to decide if a witch was genuine. I closed my eyes and imagined a circle of bright white light surrounding her, then repeated the words in my head several times: *Bella Sawyer, are you sincere?* A bluish light began to usurp the white glow of my circle, which meant Bella was telling the truth.

She had been contacted by the Lurkers, or at the very least, she'd channeled a vision of them.

"Mercedes needs to hear this," I said. "Everyone does."

"I wasn't finished," she said, and frowned at me again.

I glanced at her in surprise. "Go on."

"They want you," she finished.

"What?" I asked, swallowing hard.

She shrugged like the news wasn't a big deal, like it was no sweat off her back. Yeah, 'cause all the sweat was on mine. "The elder said it was the Queen they were after." She glanced at her fingernails, appeared to carefully inspect them for the next few seconds, then looked up at me. "You should do us all a favor and turn yourself over to them."

I decided to ignore that last bit. My mind was entirely stuck on the Lurkers wanting me. Was that the reason I'd been the only one to receive that strange dream of the battlefield and the unattended throne? Probably so. I glanced at Bella again, wondering if she knew more. "Why were they after me?"

She shrugged again. "I don't know."

I felt sick to my stomach just explaining everything Bella had told me to Rand and Mercedes. I didn't know what it meant that the Lurkers wanted me in particular. I mean, I guess it made sense to bring down the Queen first, as the figurehead of the Underworld, but still, that didn't make hearing the news any easier to swallow.

"We need to speak with Bella," Rand said as he

paced back toward me from the far end of the living room.

"You are certain she is telling the truth?" Mercedes asked me, worry evident not only in her tone, but also the strained look in her eyes.

I merely nodded. "I did a Liar's Circle on her, so I know she was."

"We still need to talk to her," Rand continued, now starting for the opposite side of the room. He pushed his hands into his pockets and stopped pacing for a few seconds, glancing at me even though I knew he was wholly focused on his thoughts. I could see it in his eyes.

"She'll tell you the same thing she told me," I said. "She doesn't know why they want me or what they're after, Rand."

Mercedes nodded, but it seemed she was lost in her own thoughts, looking right through me. "I do not like this one bit," she finally admitted. "I can feel magic stirring—something in the air," she continued. Rand stopped pacing again and faced her at the same time I did. Mercedes nodded and strode to the window, the moonlight bathing her in its milky glow.

"What magic?" I asked.

She didn't turn to face me. "Magic that I don't recognize . . . magic that is not born of our own."

"The Lurkers, then?" Rand asked, running a hand through his hair. "You must be detecting their magic."

I felt myself stand up automatically from where I'd been sitting on the couch. Rand wrapped his arms around me and pulled me in. He glanced down at me and I was suddenly suffocated with feelings of protectiveness.

Everything is going to be okay. I heard his voice in my head.

I said nothing, just nodded at him and smiled, wondering if he could feel my doubt through our bond.

"I can feel them stirring and I believe they will act soon," Mercedes said, turning to face us. "I can't get a grasp on anything more."

"Then you must have received the same vision Bella did," I said, my voice sounding hollow.

"Perhaps," Mercedes answered, then sighed in frustration. And frustration on the face of the prophetess definitely didn't give me a good feeling.

"What are we going to do?" I asked.

She glanced at me and frowned. "I do not know."

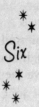

Six

The next day I found myself sitting on the sofa in Christa and John's living room. The house, which was a modest brick two-story, was in the neighboring town of Coldingham, Scotland, a mere ten minutes from Kinloch Kirk. With everything that had been going on recently, I just needed a mental break, some time to focus on something other than the Lurkers, Sinjin, and Bella. And my best friend would provide me with just the hiatus I needed.

As I took a sip of my iced tea, Christa shifted from her position on the floor and rolled onto her stomach, propping herself on her elbows. With her legs in the air, she flipped through *Bride* magazine quickly as she sang in time with Coldplay's "Clocks." I looked around her, at the multitude of wedding books and magazines strewn about like the entrails of some beast.

We were in the midst of discussing wedding colors and invitations. Luckily, the wedding invitations had pretty much been decided on, so all I had to do now was sit through an endless display of four-inch squares of various fabrics in an array of colors. With all the swatches scattered around me, I looked like I'd been sewn into a patchwork quilt. But endless questions on wedding colors aside, I was so grateful to have Christa in my life. She had been by my side through all the ups and downs and the trials and tribulations of my transformation from Girl-Next-Door Jolie to Queen of the Underworld Jolie.

"I like the celadon green, I think," I said, pointing to the third scrap of fabric she held in her hand, next to a bubble-gum pink and a tangerine orange. Celadon green I could handle. Irritating bright pink and fluorescent orange? Not so much. In fact, I couldn't help but grimace.

She glanced at the green scrap and held it up to a silver one, clasped in her other hand, studying them both with a razor-sharp intensity. "You think they go together?" she asked, not bothering to look up at me.

"I think the green goes way better with silver than orange or super-annoying-pink does," I answered with a smile as I started collecting the remaining swatches that littered the floor like a butchered rainbow. I figured she'd narrowed the color choices down to green, silver, orange, and pink.

"Well, I've got to have some pink. You know it's my favorite color," Christa protested as she held up the pink with the green. It actually wasn't as off-putting as I'd imagined it would be. 'Course, at this point I was pretty much over the whole thing. I mean, you can only look at color pairings for so long before you start to lose your mind. And we'd been at this for well over two hours.

"Whatever you want, Chris," I said with a smile. "It is *your* wedding."

"Well, *you* are the maid of honor," she argued with me. "So I do want your input." She smiled broadly at me, kicking her feet back and forth like a restless kid.

"I'm happy with whatever makes you happy . . . but if you force me to wear anything fluorescent orange, I will kill you," I finished, and pointed with distaste at the orange swatch that was now crumpled on the ground in front of her.

She laughed, and something suddenly occurred to me. Christa had been in my store with me the day Rand first walked through the door two years ago, and she'd also been there when Sinjin did the same, after he went back in time to mess with my past. That mystery hadn't yet been put to bed—the mystery of which reality was the true one, the real one. Well, now it was time to find out the answer.

"Okay, I promise not to put you in the orange," she said, smiling up at me as she reached for her *Martha Stewart Weddings* book. She opened the first page, humming as she skimmed it, and moved on to the next. Reaching for her stack of Post-it notes, she started marking pages that apparently deserved a second look.

"Chris . . ." I hesitated, knowing my question was going to sound odd, but I couldn't think of any other way to ask it, so I figured a direct approach was best. "Do you remember the first day Rand walked into my store in L.A.?"

She eyed me before nodding, then dropped her attention back to the book. She was marking off a page with a picture of a butterfly bouquet—butterfly bouquet, as in no flowers, just butterflies on the ends of what looked like nearly imperceptible wire surrounded by a cloud of tulle. It was cute. "Yeah, 'course I do. I remember how we both freaked out about his English accent and how hot he was. Who knew he'd end up being so stuffy?"

I raised my eyebrows at her and then laughed, imagining how offended Rand would be to hear her talk about him like that, although she sort of had a point. Sometimes he could be stuffy, but I assumed that was from his austere English upbringing. I must admit that I still loved him for it, all six-feet-two inches of Rand Balfour stuffiness.

I gulped as I considered my next question. "And do you remember the day we met Sinjin?"

She turned to the next page and inhaled quickly once her eyes feasted on a picture of a table setting completely in celadon green, including the floral arrangements, which appeared to be green roses. And, yup, the accents were in silver. "Wow, Jules, look at this." She studied it for a minute or two, cocking her head to the right and then the left. "You know, you're right; this color combination really looks pretty."

I glanced at it and smiled, but my thoughts weren't on table arrangements. "Yeah, really pretty." I cleared my throat, eager to get an answer to my question, if only to understand how her brain had processed something so implausible. "Do you remember Sinjin walking into the store, Chris?"

She glanced up at me and frowned. I guess she was probably wondering why I was going on about all this when she wanted to focus on her wedding details. She brought her attention back to the book and plucked off another Post-it note, placing it directly in the middle of the picture, like it was awarded Most

Important or something. "Yeah, he got a flat tire—why are you asking me this?"

I took a deep breath, knowing there was one more question I needed to ask, one more piece to this puzzle that I had to find. "Who did we meet first, Rand or Sinjin?" I cleared my throat.

"Why does it matter?" she asked, clearly much more interested in the colors, bouquets, and table arrangements that were splayed around her.

"Um, it doesn't matter," I answered quickly, hoping to sound casual, unconcerned. "I just wondered if you remembered," I added, trying to give my questions a semblance of normalcy. "Was it Rand or Sinjin?"

She immediately opened her mouth, as if she had the answer right on the tip of her tongue, but then shut it just as quickly and glanced up at me. Her expression told me she didn't have a clue. She frowned and shook her head.

"Um, God, who was it? Jeez, is my memory that bad?" Then she was quiet for a little while longer, but it wasn't because her attention was elsewhere, on the upcoming wedding, for example. No, she was genuinely trying to remember. She shook her head. "It's really foggy. How weird! But I literally *can't* remember who came into the store first." Then she faced me again. "Who was it? Do you remember?"

"Rand," I said as I debated whether to tell her about the whole time-traveling saga. I knew it would come up eventually, but so far I just didn't have the energy to divulge it. And I couldn't say I was feeling any more energetic at the moment. "Rand came into the store first," I repeated. "We met him before we

ever met Sinjin." And that was the truth as far as I
was concerned. It was also what I'd convinced myself
to believe. Regardless of what Sinjin did to manipulate time, Rand had come into my life first.

Christa seemed to consider it for a few more moments and then nodded, looking up at me with a
smile. "Yeah, that's right. That's how I remember it
too." She shook her head again. "How weird that I
couldn't remember it before. It was like I thought
they both were first. Guess I'm not getting enough
sleep," she said and laughed. "Sheesh!"

I smiled back at her and couldn't help the anxiety
that suddenly flooded my body. It seemed that every
time I thought about Sinjin, something rebelled inside
of me and made me feel nauseous, sick to my stomach
over what had happened between us and his banishment. I just didn't feel good about the decision, even
now. I couldn't wipe away my fear that he might cross
paths with the Lurkers, as improbable as that seemed.
I mean, Sinjin could be anywhere and the Lurkers
could be anywhere, so what made me think their
"anywheres" might collide?

Christa closed the Martha Stewart book and moved
on to the one just beside it, a, much smaller book that
was black and red. She opened it and then smiled up
at me impishly.

"What's that?" I asked, trying to shake away the
feelings of sickness that lodged in my gut. I felt light-
headed, winded and ill—like I had motion sickness or
something. It was sudden and . . . weird.

She opened the book and scanned a few pages,
pausing for dramatic effect. Then she looked back up

at me and smiled again. That's when I knew something was up.

"Well?" I prompted as I shook my head, laughing all the while. "I can tell the book is naughty just by the way you're looking at me."

She giggled in return and then nodded. "'How to Free Your Inner Sex Diva,'" she read from the cover, only to flip back to the inside of the book almost immediately.

I sighed deeply and couldn't help laughing. "Chris, there's no possible way you could free your sex diva anymore. It's already broken its leash and is halfway down the block."

She giggled again and sat up straight, crossing her legs Indian-style. She began thumbing through the pages before she glanced up at me and read: "'Tip Number Thirty-two: It's all about your nipples. Get in the mood by touching them. Massage them, squeeze them, and roll them between your fingers.'" She looked up at me again and then returned her attention to the book. "'Put ice on them,'" she whispered in a sultry voice.

"Oh my God," I said and rolled my eyes. "What kind of tip is that? What's the point?"

She shrugged. "'Cause it feels good and gets you in the mood."

"Ice?" I repeated. How could that possibly feel good? I exhaled, feeling like my overwhelmed mind couldn't handle any more. I mean, I didn't have the time or the interest to deal with wedding details, so I really didn't have it in me to focus on silly sexual advice. "Can we go back to the wedding stuff?"

"This is important, Jules," she argued, looking at

me like she was a teacher disappointed with her star student. Then she arched a brow and considered me with interest. "I bet Rand would appreciate it."

I shook my head, but I couldn't help but smile. That smile quickly turned into a frown as I realized I was giving in and waving my white flag of surrender. "Okay, read me another one."

She smiled and thumbed through a few more pages, apparently looking for something extra juicy. "Hmmm . . . pubic mound, lubrication . . . um, what else? Ah, here we go . . ." Then she flicked her finger against the page like she'd really found something worthwhile.

"What?" I asked, my tone halfway between resignation and interest.

"Watch yourself in the mirror," she finished, and smiled up at me slyly.

"Watch yourself in the mirror doing what?" I fished. "That sounds pretty dumb."

She frowned at me and then shook her head like I was a hopeless cause and it was a wonder I was even having sex. "Come on, Jules, watch yourself you know . . . titillating yourself, rubbing the ol' kitty!"

"Oh God," I started, shaking my head in disgust even though the idea didn't totally appall me. It was just easier to pretend I had no interest in this sort of thing. Otherwise it would only encourage Christa and that would be like opening Pandora's box. "Why?"

She frowned. "It's supposed to be kinky and erotic, Jules. You need to get in touch with that side of yourself."

I shook my head and just laughed. "So tell me how any of this helps Rand and me in the bedroom?"

She smiled again and slapped the book shut, as if I'd finally asked her the right question. "Because it puts you in the right frame of mind for sex and turns you into a sexual being, a sexual diva . . . like me. I think about sex constantly."

"Trust me, I'm well aware," I muttered. A dull ache began to spread behind my eyes, making me feel light-headed again and nauseous. I gripped my head and leaned back against the couch, closing my eyes.

"What's wrong with you?" Chris asked.

"I just got a killer headache," I said.

"Gosh, Jules, you don't have to be such a prude!" she barked at me. Then she burst out laughing. "Oh my God, I can't believe you just pretended to have a headache to get out of talking about sex with me! Ha, that's supposed to just work on men!"

"No, I really don't feel well," I said, and shook my head, wishing I was pretending.

"What's wrong with you?" she asked, her voice a little more caring.

"I don't know," I said, feeling the ache behind my eyes dissipate as I magicked it away. "I just suddenly didn't feel very good. It was weird." I opened my eyes and faced her again, feeling nausea bubble up inside of me. I magicked it away and felt it disappear as quickly as it had come. "I felt like I was going to throw up."

"Hmm . . . maybe you're getting the flu or maybe you ate something bad?"

I swallowed hard as I realized that the cause might not be so simple. Why? Because I had felt exactly the same way when the Lurkers attacked me in my sleep. I'd gotten incredibly sick afterward, and this was what it had felt like in the beginning—extreme nausea and light-headedness coupled with a developing ache behind my eyes. Had I been attacked again? If so, it had apparently happened in the broad daylight! Could the Lurkers enter my psyche without going through my dreams? Did that mean they were getting stronger?

Jolie, you're totally freaking out for no reason, I told myself. *Maybe Christa is right and you're experiencing the first symptoms of a flu. I mean, when you think about it, you really aren't that sick. You're just a little nauseous.*

But this is how it felt after that Lurker attack, I argued with myself.

Yes, and this is also how it felt the last time you had food poisoning or the flu.

I stood up and smiled down at Christa, trying to appear unconcerned. I mean, there was no use in getting her worried—at least not until I knew what was wrong with me for sure. "I'm going to head home, Chris," I said. "Not sure if I ate something bad or not, but I really feel sick."

She stood up and gave me a hug. "Sure, don't worry about it. And thanks for stopping by and helping me out with everything. It was great to see you."

It was something you would say to someone you hadn't seen in a while. I felt a rush of guilt. I knew it was true. We hadn't been as close lately as in the past. It was mainly because my life had basically become a complete disaster. "Sure, Chris, it's my job," I said, and smiled. "Sorry I've been so busy, but I'm here for you whenever you need me."

She nodded and smiled at me sweetly. "I know how busy you are, Jules, and I know you're stressed out, so don't worry about me."

"Well, don't hold back when you have questions about DJs, food, linens, or your dress," I said, and started for the door, before turning back to face her again. "Especially your dress. I definitely want to be part of that."

"Oh, you'll totally be a part of that, Jules! I mean, you are my best friend—it's like your duty."

I laughed as she walked me to the door, opening it wide while I beeped my silver Range Rover Freelander unlocked. Suddenly seized with the feeling that I was going to throw up again, I hurried over to the car.

I made it as far as the rear door behind the driver's seat before I hunched over on my knees and threw up between my feet.

Later that night, after convincing Christa I was fine to drive home, I went to bed early, still feeling under the weather. I decided that my illness had nothing to do with the Lurkers, so I didn't bother warning anyone. Christa must have been right after all. When I focused my magic on them, the feelings recessed and I actually felt okay for a little while—something I hadn't been able to do when I was attacked by the Lurkers before.

I felt another bout of nausea bubble up inside of me and closed my eyes, bathing myself in white light while I willed the feelings to go away. I felt better as soon as I opened my eyes, but I also knew that the feelings would return in a matter of an hour or so. I couldn't seem to delay them permanently. Maybe I'd been struck with a really strong strain of flu?

Jolie? It was Rand's voice in my head.

Yes?

Are you well? he asked, and I had to imagine that somehow my nausea had transferred over to him through our bond.

Yes, I think I just ate something bad and now I'm paying for it. I tried to remain unconcerned. *Are you feeling the same way I am? I hope you're not sick too because of our bond?*

He didn't answer, but somehow I knew the answer was no. He must have shaken his head or something because the feeling had transferred over our mental connection, slight though it was.

Are you certain it is something you ate? he continued, worry lacing his tone. *And not something more . . . serious?*

Rand's middle name should have been Overprotective or possibly Overconcerned. I laughed and hoped I sounded nonchalant. *Yes, just minor food poisoning or a slight flu. It's nothing my magic can't handle.*

Okay, I just wanted to make certain you were all right, he finished. *I do worry about you.*

That's the understatement of the century, I thought, and laughed.

Hey! Rand thought back.

I laughed again. *I'm fine, Rand, but thanks for checking in on me.*

Very good, he thought hurriedly, and I had to imagine he was busy with his ledgers at Pelham Manor.

He'd been there for the last day, saying he needed to catch up on taxes and other administrative matters.

I miss you, I thought, wishing more than ever before that Rand were with me so I could snuggle against him and fall asleep in his arms, the only place I ever felt truly safe.

I immediately felt an outpouring of love coming from him. *I miss you too, Jolie. More than you know. I look forward to tomorrow.*

Tomorrow Rand would be returning to Kinloch. Currently we were splitting our time between Pelham Manor and Kinloch Kirk, but we spent much more time in my home, because it was my official royal residence. I missed Pelham Manor terribly.

Good night, Rand, I whispered. *I can't wait to see you either. I love you.*

Good night, my love, and feel better.

I closed my eyes, but opened them again when I heard his voice.

Oh, and one other thing, he started.

Yes?

I love you too.

I smiled as I closed my eyes again, hoping the morning would bring not only a new day but a healthier me.

I wasn't sure at what point sleep claimed me, but before I knew it, I was floating in a sea of purple, balmy waves, which carried me farther and farther from the shore. I watched the tuft of land as it faded from view, and before I knew it I was surrounded by nothing but limitless ocean.

"Do not be afraid." The voice was deep and definitely belonged to a man.

I glanced up from where I was floating and looked around, but I saw no one, just the purple of the sea that juxtaposed itself against the pitch-black of the sky.

"Where are you?" I asked.

"Below you," came the quick response.

I looked down but saw nothing but the vast sea, which revealed nothing more than an amethyst void. "I don't understand," I started.

"I am the sea," the voice continued.

"Oh," I responded, not at all surprised that the sea could speak, and was actually quite chatty. Dreams can be funny like that. "What do you want?" I asked, leaning my head back into the water as I stared up into the black sky and watched it fill with twinkling white orbs of light. Little by little the lights began to coalesce into the center of the sky, shining ever more brightly. Then they began to shift until they formed the outline of a man. Even though the man's image was filled with nothing but bright light, based on his outline I could tell he had long hair and a beard, like Father Time.

"We want you, Jolie," the sea answered, but somehow I knew the voice belonged to the glowing man in the sky.

"You want me for what?" I continued.

There was a deep, rumbling laugh that came from the ocean, causing small waves to ripple around me, pushing me this way and that until I started to feel seasick. "Please stop, you're making me sick," I said.

Immediately, the laughing faded away and I was once again floating in a calm sea. "Your sickness is not by our will," the phantom voice announced.

I shrugged, unconcerned, because the nausea had evaporated as soon as the sea stopped laughing. "Who are you?" I asked.

"I am the Supreme Elder of my people, of your people," the voice came back, loud and clear. "You must return to your rightful place beside me and rule as the Queen you were meant to be."

"Who are your people?"

"You refer to us as Lurkers."

I felt my stomach drop, even though I was dreaming. I wanted to be sick. "You are my enemies," I said softly.

"We are not your enemies. And you must take your rightful place as the Queen of your own kind."

"I am Queen of the Underworld," I demanded.

"You are Queen of charlatans," the voice continued, sounding gruff and upset. "You must join us and return to your people and rule as you were intended to." The voice was quiet for a second or two. "You are one of us. You have always been one of us."

And before I could ask any questions, I woke up.

Seven

I was covered in a cold sweat. I could feel the perspiration beading down the small of my back as my heart raced, like an earthquake was rumbling through my body. It was still dark outside and the wind was whipping through the trees, causing the branches to scratch against the windows. I suddenly had the urge to escape, to run through the moors of heather that bordered Kinloch Kirk and just disappear into the cold night air.

Feeling restless, I threw off the duvet cover and stood up, running my hand down the back of my neck and wiping the sweat on my pajama bottoms. I strode to the window and watched the clouds struggle with the moon, trying to obscure it in an effort to hide its luminescence. A gentle rain started, and after a few minutes it gave way to heavy drops that splattered against the glass.

A feeling of dizziness consumed me, and I reached out, stabilizing myself against the back of a boudoir chair as I closed my eyes and willed the feeling to go away. As soon as the dizziness faded, nausea started churning my gut, roiling the contents of my stomach.

Suddenly feeling certain I was going to throw up, I clasped my hand over my mouth and bolted for the bathroom off my bedroom. I made it as far as the sink before hurling. I heaved a few more times until there wasn't anything left and then turned on the water as I tried to catch my breath.

Glancing up into the mirror, I could see my own concern and fear. I was pale—paler than I'd ever seen myself—and the hair around my face was wet with perspiration. I closed my eyes, imagining my mouth filling up with Listerine to eradicate the bitter taste. When I opened them, I tasted fresh mint but was in no way relieved.

Something was wrong with me. But it wasn't a flu or food poisoning. No, something was definitely rotten in the state of Denmark, and now I was convinced that the rottenness had something to do with the Lurkers.

As soon as the thought crossed my mind, my stomach became agitated again and I leaned over, gagging anew. But as before, there was nothing left, so I just choked on my spit as my stomach contorted with pain. After gaining control of myself, I stood up, inhaling for a count of three and exhaling for a count of three.

I'm going to be okay, I said to myself as I pushed damp hair out of my face. *Just breathe, Jolie.*

But that dream . . .

No matter how I looked at it, I had to believe it had something to do with my renewed sense of sickness. Even though the man in my dream had claimed that he played no part in my ailment, I didn't believe him.

Why else did I feel exactly the same as I had after that first Lurker attack?

'Course, you were pretty much on your deathbed the first time, I pointed out to myself. *And you aren't anywhere near as sick now as you were then.*

But I wasn't about to give in so easily. *Maybe it's just because I'm stronger now—my magic is much more advanced than before and I'm harder to take down.*

But the apparition from your dream insisted he played no role . . .

Apparition wasn't even the right name for it, though. No. Whatever I'd experienced couldn't be cataloged as a dream, nor was it a vision. I was convinced that the Lurkers had made contact with me again. But unlike the time I'd had the battlefield dream, the contact was much more precise this time, more exact and bold.

What frightened me most was that whoever had contacted me, whether he truly was a Lurker elder or not, was convinced that I was a Lurker.

And that thought scared the hell out of me.

I pushed away from the sink and hobbled back into my bedroom, watching the rain splatter on the windowpanes as the tree branches appeared to fight against the wind, fighting an invisible enemy that was so much stronger they had no defense and could only snap and break.

What did it mean that this . . . entity insisted I was one of his people? What did he mean when he told me to return to where I belonged and rule as I was meant to?

I closed my eyes against the thoughts swarming

through my head. And then something dawned on me. Something horrible and ugly. Something so atrocious and hideous that I could barely bring myself to consider it.

You are more than a witch, Jolie, my voice boomed within me. *Mercedes and Mathilda both said you aren't what you think you are . . .*

Oh. My. God.

I shook my head, refusing to even consider it, refusing to play host to such a ridiculous and wholly disgusting thought, but I couldn't force it from my head. I couldn't stop replaying the dream. The words of the apparition echoed in my ears: "You are one of us."

What if I'm a Lurker?

How could you be a Lurker? I argued with myself, feeling nausea gnawing at my gut once again. I closed my eyes and willed it away, breathing a little easier once it retreated. *You have no vampiric traits . . .*

But you know now that Lurkers aren't just half-vampires. They possess magic. Maybe they are closer to witches than anyone knows . . .

And maybe they aren't. Maybe I completely misunderstood that dream. And, furthermore, maybe it was just that—a dream and nothing more.

You know that isn't true.

Well, I also know that sometimes things are much simpler than they appear. And you might be working yourself up about nothing more than an upsetting dream, spawned by a flu that you can't seem to shake.

But I didn't have the chance to give it further consideration, because just as the thought crossed my mind, I could hear the sound of heavy footsteps pounding against the wood stairs. Before I could take another breath, my bedroom door burst open.

Rand was standing there, soaking wet.

"Rand?" I started, and suddenly felt anxiety welling up inside me. But it wasn't my own emotions—it was his concern, his worry transferring across our bond.

"Jolie, what's wrong with you?" he demanded as he spanned the few steps separating us and engulfed me in his arms. I shivered against him. He glanced down at me, worry evident in his furrowed brows, and closed his eyes, enveloping us both in heat. He was instantly dry. He pushed me away from him then and narrowed his gaze on me, studying me deliberately. "You're still very ill. You haven't improved."

I felt something constrict in my throat and I knew I couldn't lie to him. Not when he could read my mind and feel my emotions. He had to know the truth—well, most of it. I wasn't about to come out and tell him that I not only had a Lurker encounter, but I now thought I might actually be one. No, that was way too much for him to handle at the moment, and besides, I wasn't even sure I was a Lurker. I mean, who is to say that the man in my dream was telling the truth?

You know he was a Lurker.

Either way, I wasn't going to argue with myself any longer, and I also wasn't going to tell Rand. Not yet, anyway. "I don't know what's wrong with me," I answered, and shook my head, feeling like the weight of the world was on my shoulders. I just needed time and space to think, to figure some things out before I decided what to confide.

Above all, I could think of nothing that would kill Rand's love for me faster than if I turned out to be one of our enemies.

But you have freedom of choice, Jolie, I said, arguing with myself again. *Even if you do have Lurker blood inside of you, it doesn't mean you have to become one of them.*

I didn't feel any relief at that thought, though, because I wasn't sure how things worked. What if becoming a Lurker and turning against Rand and everyone else was like a trigger inside of me that could just be turned on at any minute? What if there was no way around it? What if the destruction of everything I knew was part of my destiny? What if I'd somehow been planted by the Lurkers so they could infiltrate the creatures of the Underworld? What if I were just a decoy? A sacrificial pawn in this game?

But if I were a Lurker, how could I be bonded with Rand? I asked myself. *Only witches can bond with one another.*

I shook my head, determined to stop answering the "what-ifs." There were just too many of them, and I had no answers, only a landslide of questions. There was really no point in even contemplating any of it— not when the questions held no answers. No, once I had more information, I would go to Mercedes. She would know what to do.

"Do you think it's another Lurker attack?" Rand asked, his eyes wide with fright.

I looked up sharply at his mention of the Lurkers, warned that he somehow witnessed my most recent dream or had clued into my thoughts, but there wasn't anything in his eyes that hinted at that awareness. "Maybe," I said solemnly. "But now I can magick away the sickness as soon as it comes, and I couldn't do that the last time I was attacked."

Rand cocked his head to the side and held his palm against my forehead, checking to see how hot I was. "But perhaps your magic was just not strong enough then, and that's why you couldn't treat yourself?"

"Yes, that occurred to me," I said, and nodded up at him with a small smile. Rand enclosed me in his arms again, kissing the top of my head.

"I'm going to find Mercedes," he said, lifting me up into his arms bride-style. He settled me down on my bed and nestled me under the duvet cover. After tucking me in as if I were all of five years old, he sat down beside me.

"Rand—" I started, wanting to talk him out of retrieving Mercedes. I was suddenly afraid that she might be able to detect the thoughts and feelings I was trying to conceal.

"No," he said quickly. "Jolie, I'm frightened for you." He stood up and started for the door, turning to face me once he reached the doorway. "I will return momentarily."

I just nodded and closed my eyes, desperate to shut out the feelings of sickness that were welling up once again. A few minutes later I heard the sound of footsteps and opened my eyes to see Rand again and a worried-looking Mercedes.

"I don't know what is wrong with her," Rand said softly as he reached for my hand, enclosing it between both of his.

Mercedes looked down at me and smiled encouragingly, but I found no comfort in her expression. I was still way too concerned that she might somehow sense or realize that I'd been visited by a Lurker, and worse, that he'd told me I was one of them.

"Mathilda should be here shortly," Mercedes announced, then closed her eyes as she held her palms up to my temples. I watched her lips twitch as she chanted something. Then she opened her beautiful eyes and they twinkled in her face like gems. "I don't sense any type of magical block," she said softly. "I don't detect a magical attack of any sort."

I heard the sound of someone else approaching, and then Mathilda appeared in my line of vision. Mercedes faced her and told her the same thing she'd just told me—she had no clue what was wrong with me.

Hmm, maybe that apparition in my dream was telling the truth—the Lurkers had nothing to do with this sickness, I told myself. Then I immediately forced the thoughts away, still afraid they would be detected.

Mathilda said nothing, but she strode up to my bedside and smiled down at me in a motherly sort of way. I've always liked Mathilda. But right then, I could say I honestly loved her. I loved how she was trying to put me at ease with her soft smile and sparkling eyes. She placed her hands on my cheeks and then moved them down to my collarbone, closing her eyes as she continued down my body, pausing momentarily when she reached my stomach. Then she leaned closer to me and shifted her hands around my belly, only to open her eyes again and nod as if she'd found the source of my illness.

Mathilda backed away then and motioned to Mercedes, and the two of them retired to the far end of the room. I was surprised that Rand didn't follow them. Instead, he leaned closer to me and kissed my forehead. "Everything is going to be fine, Jolie," he whispered. "We will find out what this sickness is, I promise, and we will heal you."

"Rand?" Mercedes said, as she and Mathilda returned to my bedside.

"Yes?" he answered eagerly as he looked up at her, my hand still clasped in his.

"Would you mind leaving the room for a moment?" Mercedes asked. "Mathilda and I need to discuss something with Jolie."

"Leave the room?" he repeated, a scowl marring his perfect features. "No, I will not."

"We need to discuss this with Jolie first," Mercedes insisted, her voice tight and firm, as she crossed her arms over her chest.

"What is wrong with her?" Rand demanded. "I need to know—"

"We will tell you momentarily," Mercedes interrupted, her tone warning him not to argue. Then she reached out and took hold of his arm, leading him to the door. She said something in his ear that was too muffled for me to make out. When he nodded and opened the door, stepping out into the hallway, I knew that whatever she'd said had convinced him to leave.

"I'll be just outside your door, Jolie," he said, giving me a significant glance before he shut the door.

I nodded, my nerves on high alert. Why had Mercedes escorted him out? What did it mean? A sense of fear washed over me. Maybe I was dying and they didn't want Rand to learn about it before I did. I closed my eyes against the panic that started rampaging through me.

"Jolie—" Mercedes started.

"What's wrong with me?" I demanded. "Don't beat around the bush! If I'm dying, just tell me!"

She laughed lightly and shook her head like the joke was on me. "There is nothing wrong with you."

"But," I said, as yet another wave of sickness washed through me, "there has to be something wrong with me." I closed my eyes and willed the feeling to go away.

When I opened them again, I watched as Mathilda took a seat beside me, reaching for my hand. "There is nothing to be afraid of, dear," she whispered.

"Why?" I demanded, still on full alert.

Mathilda glanced back at Mercedes, who was smiling broadly. Mercedes nodded encouragingly, and Mathilda turned back to face me again, a big smile on her face as well. "You are with child."

It took me a good thirty seconds to fully comprehend her words. "What?" I asked, not completely sure I'd heard her right.

"You are pregnant," Mercedes answered, still smiling as she approached us. "Our Queen is carrying an heir."

"How . . . how do you know?" I asked breathlessly, trying to count backward in my mind to the last time I'd had my period. It was due right around now . . . "My period isn't even late yet," I said, having a hard time believing that this sickness could be so benign, and better yet . . . so wonderful. But I couldn't get my hopes up, not yet. "I feel like I'm dying—the same way I felt after I was attacked by the Lurkers."

"You are not dying," Mathilda said, and laughed.

"You just have morning sickness," Mercedes added.

I shook my head again. "Are you sure?"

They both nodded.

"Absolutely certain," Mathilda said, patting my hand encouragingly. "I could feel the energy of the baby within you. She is strong and healthy."

"She?" I asked, then gulped down the sudden flood of happiness that overwhelmed me. "You can tell it's a girl?"

Mathilda laughed. "No, but I am hoping for a princess."

I took a deep breath, my amazement devouring me, and then something occurred to me—something that tempered any joy I was feeling. "But . . . I thought . . . I thought witches weren't able to procreate?"

"Then the father is Rand?" Mercedes asked, probably struck by the fact that I'd said "witches."

I frowned at her, thinking that the answer was obvious. I hadn't even considered that the baby might be Sinjin's, since vampires weren't able to reproduce.

"Yes, of course," I said as the realization that I was carrying Rand's baby dawned on me. I felt another flood of sunshine pouring through me, and couldn't keep the smile from my face.

I was pregnant with Rand's baby . . .

Mercedes' expression had turned serious. "It is not that witches cannot procreate," she said. "They just have a difficult time carrying to term."

The happiness I felt was suddenly snuffed out. I automatically covered my stomach with a protective hand, and right then and there I vowed that I would do anything and everything to keep this baby—my baby—safe. "What . . . what does that mean?"

Mercedes took a deep breath. "It means that you must be incredibly careful."

"Or it could mean something altogether different," Mathilda chimed in as she glanced at Mercedes.

"What?" I demanded.

"Perhaps you will not have any issues at all," Mercedes said, and smiled down at me as if she knew something I didn't.

"Why?"

"Because, as I've always told you, I never believed you to be a mere witch, Jolie. Your power is too strong, your abilities too varied. Perhaps you have proven it by the very fact that you are pregnant."

"And if you have the blood of the fae within you, your chances of delivering this child will be much better," Mathilda added. She was now beaming proudly at the thought that I could be of her own kind. "What is more, we believe that you have been touched by the fae, child."

I swallowed hard, all too aware that the fae might not be in my family tree at all, that maybe this pregnancy added credence to the idea that I was part Lurker.

I can't be a Lurker! I thought to myself. *I'm a witch or I'm fae or I'm both, as Mathilda said . . . I just can't be a Lurker!*

"I . . . I have to tell Rand," I said softly.

Mercedes nodded and backed away. "That's why I sent him away. You should be the one to impart this news, not us."

I eyed Mathilda and could see the worry eating

away at her usually serene expression. She looked over at me and smiled consolingly. "You know he will worry," she said. "Do not allow it to dampen your spirits. This is a joyous occasion."

Then it dawned on me that Rand was definitely going to worry—he'd be a mess because he'd focus on the sad fact that most witches weren't able to carry to term. "But if I really am just a witch," I began, facing Mercedes, knowing she'd give me an honest answer, "could this baby kill me?"

She took a deep breath. "I have seen witches die during childbirth," she answered simply. "But you are not a mere witch, Jolie."

I nodded, trying to take comfort in her words. I only hoped she was right. I watched as Mathilda stood up and started for the door, Mercedes following her. When they opened it, Rand strode inside, his expression broadcasting his concern. Mercedes smiled at him and patted his chest as she walked past him, Mathilda beside her. Rand faced me with confusion as the two of them left the room, closing the door.

I sat up in bed, feeling another bout of sickness, but just smiled broadly.

"Jolie," Rand said as he sat by my side. "What is it?"

I took a deep breath and tried to commit this moment to memory—I knew we would never have it again. "I'm okay, Rand," I started, and took his hand.

"Tell me the truth," he demanded, his countenance rigidly insistent.

I smiled. "I'm sick because I'm pregnant."

There was no expression at all on his face for a few

seconds. He just stared at me blankly, and then his eyebrows knotted and he gulped. "This baby could threaten your life," he said simply.

I shook my head as he stood up and ran his hands through his hair. "Rand, I'm not just a witch," I said softly. "Mathilda believes there is fae in me." I felt the words stick in my throat as I said them, all too aware that I might not be fae at all. "You know I'm more than a witch."

"Then Mercedes and Mathilda do not believe your health will be threatened?" he asked, his gaze piercing.

I nodded, smiling up at him encouragingly. "Mathilda said it is nothing but a joyous occasion." I watched him take a big breath. "Rand, you don't have to worry."

"Then this sickness is nothing more than morning sickness?" he asked eagerly.

I nodded. "Yes, it's just morning sickness," I answered, and laughed in an almost embarrassed way. I mean, here I was thinking I was dying and it was just baby sickness? Yeah, pretty embarrassing. "Everything is going to be fine."

He was quiet for a few seconds as he took a seat beside me and propped his elbows on his knees. He clasped his hands behind his neck and stared at the floor. I didn't say anything, but I was dying to know what was going on in his head. Was he happy? I wasn't getting any indication through our bond.

Please be happy, Rand, I begged.

He lifted his head and faced me with a broad smile. "I am beside myself with happiness, Jolie," he whispered, and leaned over, pulling me into his arms. "I never imagined that I would be lucky enough to be a father," he said softly.

I felt tears filling my eyes, and pushed all thoughts of the Lurkers and my uncertain future from my mind. All I wanted was to live in this moment, to experience the happiness that was consuming me. The idea that Rand and I were going to be parents, that we were pregnant was the only thought to fill my mind. Rand pulled away from me and his eyes shined glassily.

"I love you, Jolie," he whispered as he looked at my belly. He placed his hand on it and smiled. "And I love our baby."

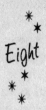

Eight

The next morning I awoke to find my cheek pressed against Rand's naked chest. I blinked a few times and then stretched, sitting up. When I looked down at him, I noticed that he was staring at me with an amused smile on his sumptuous lips.

"How are you feeling?" he asked as he scanned the lines of my body, resting his hand over my belly.

As soon as I thought about them, the feelings of nausea suddenly reemerged and I just shook my head, convinced I was never going to feel good again. "Sick," I said with a small smile, and sighed.

He nodded and brought his fingers to my face, tracing them down my cheek to my chin. "I can still feel your discomfort through our bond." He paused for a few seconds, just smiling at me. "I'm sorry you're so ill, Jolie." Then he closed his eyes, cupped his palms around my stomach, and quietly recited a charm. The nausea immediately faded into nonexistence.

"It won't last long," I said. "But thanks anyway."

"Then we'll keep magicking the sickness away."

But something else occurred to me then. "Do you

think it's okay for the baby for us to constantly charm away my sickness?"

Rand nodded immediately. "Yes, it's perfectly safe."

"How do you know?" I asked, wondering how he knew anything about babies.

"Because magic is only as powerful as its purpose. If your purpose is to relieve your sickness, it does only that. There are no side effects."

Phew. It was a relief to know I could continue treating myself. "Is there anything you don't know?" I asked with a smile. Rand didn't respond, but he cocked a brow and smiled back at me in return. Feeling suddenly restless, I stood up, stretching my arms above my head. Then I walked to the mirror and lifted up my nightshirt, studying my profile. "I think my stomach is getting bigger."

He chuckled and sat up in my bed, his exquisite chest bidding me good morning. This was definitely the best way to wake up—next to the man I loved with all my heart. And of course, it didn't hurt that he was drop-dead gorgeous. "There is no way you would be able to see a difference so soon," he said softly, that amused smile still on his lips. "You look just as thin as you always have."

I glanced at myself again and frowned. It was pretty ridiculous, but I didn't like him referring to me as "thin." I ran my hands down my front to see if my palm could detect a roundness in my stomach that Rand's eyes had missed. Yep, there was definitely something there—it was slight, but definite. I glanced back at him and set my lips in a defiant smirk. "No, I really think it looks rounder and a little more protruding."

Rand laughed again and shook his head, but once his laugh died down, he was quiet as he studied me. He didn't say anything, but there was a heaviness behind his eyes, and I could distinctly feel that something was troubling him through our bond. Yep, something was definitely on his mind—he looked pensive too.

"Jolie?" he said.

I smoothed my nightshirt back in place and turned to face him, anxious to hear whatever was worrying him. "What?"

He cleared his throat and dropped his eyes for a few seconds before bringing them back to meet mine again. "I have been thinking over the past few days . . ."

I wasn't sure why, but my heart sped up—probably because whenever someone says he's been doing some thinking, it's usually not good. "And?" I asked.

He nodded and cleared his throat again, as if the words had somehow gotten stuck on their way out, and then ran his hands through his hair as he always did when he was nervous. "Even though you and I are bonded and therefore married in the eyes of the Underworld, I would prefer it if . . . that is to say, hmmm . . ." His voice trailed off and he took a deep breath before delving in again. "I would quite like us to be . . . married in the eyes of the human world as well." He caught his breath again before quickly adding. "That is, of course, if you consent to be my wife."

I couldn't help the smile that curled my lips—did he just ask me to marry him? In some strange, roundabout, and completely unromantic way, I believed he had. "Rand," I laughed as I shook my head. "You just completely botched that whole thing."

"Botched it?" he repeated, looking even more flustered than he had a few minutes ago.

"Yes, botched it as in you didn't ask me the right way."

He smiled and shook his head, apparently disappointed with himself. "I have never been good at these things."

He stood up then and nearly took my breath away. I had to wonder if I would ever get used to his masculine beauty, and my answer to that was no. He moved to my side, towering over me as he smiled. He took both of my hands and we just gazed at each other for a few long seconds. And then he spoke.

"Jolie, I have always loved you and I will always love you. My heart has only ever belonged to you, and I cannot tell you how happy you make me. There isn't a day that goes by that I don't think of you, and in thinking of you, love you. I want you to be my wife." And then he cleared his throat again, his voice now coming out much deeper and whisper-soft. "Will you, Jolie Wilkins, marry me?"

I felt tears well up in my eyes as I thought about how long I had waited for this moment. From the moment Rand walked through the door of my store in L.A., he had owned my heart. And though it was true that we were bonded—which was, in itself, so much stronger than mere human marriage—my daydreams had only ever been about this moment. I was about to say yes, to scream it so loudly that everyone in the world could hear me, but then something suddenly occurred to me. "Rand," I started, swallowing hard. "Are you sure this proposal has nothing to do with the baby? I mean, I don't want you to think that I have to be married to you just because we're pregnant. Our bond is enough for me."

He shook his head emphatically. "No, this has nothing to do with the baby. I've actually been contemplating marriage for the last few weeks—well, truly, ever since we bonded. Perhaps it seems silly, but there are some human traditions that I still believe in." He shook his head. "Bloody hell, you are right—I have botched this entire thing."

Not sure what he was talking about, I watched as he walked over to my boudoir chair where he'd draped his pants the night before. He fished inside a pocket, and finding whatever he was looking for, walked back to me and reached for my hand.

"I meant to give you this . . . again," he said as he slipped a ring on my finger. When I glanced down, I instantly recognized the antique sapphire. It had been his mother's wedding ring.

When I'd traveled back in time to 1878 and met Rand, he'd fallen in love with me and asked me to marry him. He'd given me his mother's ring, this very one. After my return to the present, however, he and I had gone through many ups and down, and I'd returned it.

"Jolie, I love you with all my heart and my soul. Nothing will ever keep me from you. I promise to love you, protect you, and cherish you forever. You are my second half, my everything."

I smiled and felt tears leaking through my eyelashes as they fell on my cheeks. Rand caught them with the pad of his index finger and smiled at me, his eyes shining. "God, please tell me you will be my wife?" he whispered.

I nodded, feeling like there was a frog in my throat. But realizing that the frog needed to vacate ASAP, I cleared it, forcefully finding my voice. "Of course I will," I said, throwing my arms around his neck. I loved the feel of him as he wrapped his arms around me and pulled me into the cocoon of his body.

I could honestly say I had never known such happiness before—the knowledge that the man I had loved for the past two years loved me in return and that we had our whole lives to enjoy together. Rand cupped his hands over my belly, and I laid mine atop his. We were a family now—Rand, me, and our unborn baby.

Three days later I found myself in the drawing room of Kinloch Kirk with my counsel of representatives in attendance. I had asked Mercedes to orchestrate the meeting because there were a couple of major issues I needed to address. Specifically, we needed to figure out what to do about Bella, and we needed a plan of action for the Lurker threat. And yes, I did plan to reveal my dream, although I was going to omit the part about the Lurker elder implying that I might be one of them. I still hadn't decided what course of action to take as far as that was concerned, so I figured it was better left unsaid. At least for now.

Regarding my engagement with Rand, we hadn't set a wedding date, but as soon as I shared my news with Christa, she insisted that we have a double wedding. What did I think about that? I still wasn't sure, but Rand told me he would be happy with anything that would make me happy. So, with our wedding details anything but organized, we decided to move in together at Kinloch Kirk. Rand said he didn't like the idea of being apart, especially because my pregnancy could prove to be a tricky one. We decided to make Pelham Manor our getaway home when we both needed a break from the trials and tribulations of running the Underworld.

I sat on the sofa, enjoying the blazing fire in the fireplace. With the rain beating against the window and the howling wind, it seemed the perfect backdrop for a ghost story. But it wasn't a night for festive activities. No, tonight was strictly business. After the meeting, Rand and I had decided that we'd return to Pelham Manor for the weekend. 'Course, the rain was coming down so hard, our trip would probably have to be postponed until the morning. That was depressing because I wanted nothing more than to get away.

"Are you comfortable, Jolie?" Rand asked, giving me a concerned look. He had ensured that my spot on the sofa was directly in front of the fire. And, as if that weren't enough to warm me, he'd also draped a blanket around my shoulders. I'm sure I resembled an old, sickly woman—I was just missing the cat. Although I was still sick as a dog, I found comfort in the fact that I was suffering from morning sickness and not a Lurker attack. I continued to magick the nausea away, which gave me about an hour of respite each time.

Rand hadn't left my side for the last three days, and

even now I caught him watching me like a hawk, looking for any possible sign of my discomfort. If he was easily worried before, now he was a nervous wreck. A simple sneeze was enough to put him in a panic.

"Are you feeling well?" he asked, leaning over the back of the sofa to whisper in my ear. "If you are ill, Jolie, Mercedes can chair this meeting without us."

I shook my head. "I'm fine and you need to stop worrying so much." I laughed. "You're going to drive me crazy."

He chuckled. "I apologize. I am just . . . concerned."

I smiled at him and enclosed his hand in my own. "I know and I appreciate your concern."

Mercedes smiled at us before turning to face everyone else in the room. The usual suspects were all present—Trent, Varick, Odran, and Mathilda. But tonight, Klaasje was also in attendance, having replaced Sinjin as my chief protector. Of course, with Rand acting the part of my shadow, she didn't have much work to do.

Speaking of Sinjin, I found my thoughts frequently returning to him. When it was late at night and my sickness kept me awake, my thoughts were restless. I was plagued with memories of Sinjin, and all I could do was pray he was safe and that the Lurkers hadn't found him, wherever he was.

"Thank you all for coming," Mercedes started as she cleared her throat, signifying that everyone should be silent. She gave me a lingering look and smiled. She was excited to tell everyone about my engagement to Rand and our pregnancy. It would be the first subject for discussion. "I would like to begin this meeting with some joyful news."

I felt Rand squeeze my hand, and smiled at him reassuringly over my shoulder.

"We shall soon be celebrating a royal wedding," she announced, beaming at us. There was total silence in the room for a few seconds.

Then Odran let out what I can best describe as a whooping laugh as he slapped his knee in apparent pleasure. "Aye und it 'tis boot bluudey time, man!" he exclaimed as he stood up from the armchair beside the fire to thump Rand on the back. "I woondered when ye would make the moove!"

"Congratulations," Varick said with as little excitement as he could muster.

I noticed that Trent looked irritated and didn't say anything at all. It made no sense. 'Course, he was probably kicking himself for ever treating me so poorly when we first dated. Yep, this was a good lesson for him—treat your girlfriends well because you never know if they might end up as Queen of the Underworld.

"And that is not the only joy we have to share," Mercedes continued as she waited until everyone quieted down. "Soon there will be an heir to grace the halls of Kinloch Kirk," she finished proudly. I heard a round of oohs and aahs and all eyes were suddenly trained on me.

"Aye, this be joyfa news, indeed," Odran said in his deep brogue. He thumped Rand on the back for the second time before engulfing me in a bear hug. Rand frowned and looked like he was one second from pushing the Scottish oaf away from me.

"I canoot wait ta boonce the wee bugger on ma knee," Odran said once he returned me to my spot on the sofa.

I didn't really know what to make of that, so I smiled at him politely and hoped we could move on to news of the kingdom. I didn't care to dwell on personal subjects. "Thank you," I said, and watched as everyone in the room formed a single line in order to personally congratulate Rand and me. "Um . . ." I started, and looked up at Mercedes, who nodded.

"It is customary," she said softly.

"My Queen," Klaasje said as she strode toward me, then gave a slight curtsy. "I am so happy for you both."

I smiled at her, pleased that Varick had appointed her to be my main guardian. She was a strong and able vampire, and seeing her reminded me of Sinjin, something that brought on a sort of melancholic contentedness. "Thank you," I said softly.

"When will you know whether it's a boy or girl?" she asked, black hair framing her beautiful face. Klaasje was classically pretty, with long hair that reached down her back and shining bright blue eyes.

"I don't know," I admitted as Rand cleared his throat.

"Perhaps we will not find out ahead of time," he said with a smile.

"Congratulations to our Queen," Trent said, but he refused to even look at me, turning to face Rand instead. "Congratulations are also in order for the father," he finished, and extended his hand to Rand. He had such a cheese-ball smile, it made him seem like a used-car salesman. Rand smiled courteously in return and shook the werewolf's outstretched hand.

After everyone in the line congratulated us, which took another ten minutes, we were ready to move on to heftier subjects.

"My Queen asked that I orchestrate this meeting because she has agenda items she wishes to address," Mercedes said as she turned to face me.

Recognizing my cue, I started to stand up, but Rand shook his head, indicating that I didn't need to be standing to lead the meeting. Suddenly feeling another bout of nausea, I figured it was better not to argue. "The Lurker threat is growing," I began, as everyone's eyes returned to me. "I paid a visit to Bella a few days ago," I continued. More than a few of them raised their eyebrows in astonishment. "She has been in communication with the Lurkers and has received dream visions from them." I took a breath. "In exchange for Bella's full cooperation and assistance in combating the Lurker threat," I went on, bracing myself for the outpouring of disagreement sure to ensue, "I have granted her the freedom to live in my kingdom."

Everyone seemed taken aback at the news, just as I'd imagined they would be.

"Was that the smartest thing to do?" Trent asked. "Last I heard, Bella definitely was no supporter of you or your kingdom."

I nodded, ready for this. "Bella will never be a true supporter, but if she takes our loyalty oath and submits to the laws of the kingdom, she can help us in our quest to better understand the Lurkers. I see no reason to keep her here as my prisoner."

"I believe she should remain imprisoned," Varick said solemnly. "She is not trustworthy."

"Nay," Odran nodded. "I doona believe this was a good move, mah Queen."

"I'm sorry to admit that I agree with Odran, Varick, and Trent," Rand said, exhaling deeply.

I allowed the naysayers their chance to speak, but once it quieted down, I cleared my throat and addressed everyone in the room. "I have already made a pact with Bella, so none of this is up for discussion at this point," I said resolutely. There were a few raised brows, but judging by the silence, I guessed I wouldn't meet with any more dissidence—at least on this subject.

I took a deep breath, eager to move on to other topics. "The final news I wanted to discuss with you is my dream from the other night, or should I say vision?" I cleared my throat. "I believe it was sent to me by one of the Lurker elders."

I heard surprised gasps from around the room and could feel the heat of Rand's eyes on me.

Why didn't you tell me? His voice sounded in my head.

I wanted to share this news with everyone at the same time, Rand. It is something that threatens everyone.

Jolie—he started, but was interrupted by Mathilda.

"What happened in the dream, child?" she asked, her tone fretful.

"I don't remember the specifics," I started. "But I do know that the person in the dream, who took the embodiment of the sea and then appeared as the outline of an old man in the sky, admitted he was a Lurker elder."

"And what else?" Mercedes prodded.

I swallowed hard. "That was pretty much it."

"That was it?" Trent demanded, a huge smile spreading across his face. "So you're seriously concerned about a dream you had that just happened to be about an old man and the sea?" Then he snickered, apparently patting himself on the back for being so witty.

"It means the Lurkers are getting restless," I snapped at him, before turning to face the others again. "I have been contacted by the Lurkers regularly and now that they have reached out to Bella . . ."

"What did they say to her?" Varick asked, leaning forward.

"She said they were rallying, that a battle between our forces and theirs was pending, and they could attack us at any moment," I said as I felt my voice break with the effort.

"We need to understand why they insist on making contact with you, Jolie," Mercedes said, and studied me. "Did you receive any indication about what their plans are? When they might attack and where?"

I shook my head. "No, I received nothing of the sort. The reason I brought up the dream is that I think it's imperative that all of our forces rally together. I want all creatures of the Underworld stationed together here at Kinloch. I don't think it's safe for us to live separately anymore, not with the Lurkers planning something."

"Where will everyone live?" Trent asked.

"I want you to organize a mass move to Kinloch,

where we'll erect temporary housing on Kinloch's grounds. If the Lurkers attack, we need to be ready for them, and we are much stronger en masse than we are on our own," I answered. And yes, I had given plenty of thought to housing five hundred or so creatures on Kinloch property. I wasn't worried about the issue of space.

Rand nodded and smiled at me with a proud expression. "I agree entirely." Then he faced everyone in the room. "How quickly can each of you gather your factions?"

Odran pursed his lips as he considered it. "Ah will make haste, within ah few days' time," he answered.

"Yep, me too," Trent said.

"I imagine it will take no more than two or three days to gather the vampires," Varick finished.

I swallowed hard and nodded, realizing Kinloch Kirk was about to become a very busy place.

Nine

I was sick again. So sick I couldn't sleep.

I imagined my magic cleansing the nausea from my body and suddenly felt relief. But I still couldn't get back to sleep. I rolled over and listened to Rand's gentle snoring, trying to figure out whether there was a pattern to his inhaling and exhaling . . . raspy inhale for three counts, chain-saw-meeting-glass exhale for three seconds. Realizing sleep would continue to elude me, I stood up and reached for the robe, or dressing gown, as Rand called it, beside my bed. I wrapped myself up and padded across the wood floor, pausing at the large rectangular windows that revealed the crashing moonlit waves below Kinloch Kirk.

Sinjin is somewhere out there, I thought to myself. *Somewhere out in the cold of the night. He's alone, but I hope he's okay.*

God, I hope he's okay. Please let him be okay.

Shivering in the cold air, I wrapped my robe tighter around myself and thought about how much everything was going to change over the next several days. Soon all of the creatures in my kingdom would be assembled at Kinloch—men, women, and children. Although I still thought it was a good idea—we would be stronger as a collective force and more capable of defending ourselves—I also had to wonder if I'd just signed the death sentences of all the creatures of the Underworld. I mean, if we were all gathered in one area and the Lurkers decided to attack, they could completely wipe us out.

Stop second-guessing yourself, my inner voice said. *There will always be a "what-if" to every decision you make as Queen. The decision-making is the important part.*

"Are you ill?" It was Rand's voice and I turned, surprised to find him awake. Stepping out of bed, he stood up and stretched, walking over to pull me into the warmth of his chest. He wrapped his arms around me and we both stared down at the tumultuous sea.

"Yes," I said, and rested my head against his shoulder as we both watched the ocean wrestle with the rocks that punctuated its depths of blue.

"Kinloch is a beautiful place," Rand said softly. He lifted my chin with his fingers as he smiled. "And this is all your doing, Jolie. You never cease to amaze me." He shook his head in wonder. "You have come such a far distance from the girl I first met in your store two years ago."

I returned his grin. "And yet, sometimes I feel I haven't changed much at all—that I'm still just as awkward as ever."

"I hope you never lose that part of yourself," he said with a smile.

I didn't respond—I just continued to gaze out at the ocean, wondering what would become of us, and the Underworld in general. Were we strong enough to stand against the Lurkers? Could we really defeat them? I sighed and figured there was no use in thinking like this—I was just running myself ragged. Instead, I focused on tickling Rand's arm.

"Come back to bed, Jolie," he whispered, and then smiled secretively. "It's chilly out here, and what's more . . . I want you."

I laughed, but shook my head, feeling stressed from head to toe. I couldn't even comprehend sex at the moment. "You seemed very happy in the land of dreams—I'm sorry I woke you up."

"Was I snoring? Is that what woke you up?"

I nodded. "Yep."

"I apologize." He kissed the top of my head. "I was dreaming of Pelham," he said, and his voice took on a nostalgic tone. Pelham had been Rand's best friend and the original owner and namesake of Pelham Manor. When I traveled back to 1878, I met not only Pelham, but also his sister, Christine, and we became fast friends. Thinking of them now left a hollow void in my stomach.

"Whatever became of Christine?" I asked.

Rand held me closer and was quiet for a few seconds. "She lived a long and happy life, married and had children. Of course, I had to move away quite early on, lest Pelham or Christine question me regarding why I didn't age as quickly as they did."

"Where did you tell them you were moving?"

"Ireland, to one of my father's estates." Then he cleared his throat. "Pelham died quite soon after you left in 1878, and Christine moved to northern Scotland with her husband, so I didn't have to maintain the charade for too long."

I nodded and felt my mind slipping back to a time when things were much simpler—a time before I'd had any involvement with the Lurkers, and before Sinjin had time-traveled.

"Do you ever miss those days?" I asked, thinking of how much I missed them.

Rand nodded. "I do and I don't. I miss my friends, of course, but I have always believed in the idea of living in the present. The present holds such riches for me now," he said as he squeezed me around the middle, "that I find myself happier here and now than I ever remember being."

"And you still have Pelham, sort of," I said, reminding him that Pelham's ghost haunted Pelham Manor.

Rand nodded. "Yes, though it is not quite the same thing."

I smiled, but before I could respond, I felt a strong feeling deep inside of me. My heart rate increased, my hands went clammy, and the hairs on the back of my neck stood at attention. The feeling itself was difficult to characterize—something like anger tinged with fear—but it was spreading through my body at an alarming rate. I felt my breath catch as I suddenly went rigid.

"Jolie?" Rand said, noticing that I'd abruptly gone still. "What is it? What's wrong?"

I was about to answer him, when I was struck with a wave of panic. But it wasn't my panic I was witnessing, and since Rand was standing beside me and didn't seem upset, I couldn't imagine it was his either.

"Something isn't right," I told him, and closed my eyes, sending out the feelers of my magic to pinpoint whose discomfort I was receiving.

"Is it our baby?" he asked, sounding panicked. "Perhaps you need to sit down."

I shook my head. "No, it's not the baby. The baby is fine. It's something . . . else entirely."

When he opened his mouth to say something, I shushed him, trying to focus on the source of the fear that still vibrated through me. I clenched my eyes shut more tightly and ordered my magic to expand outward, through Kinloch Kirk, to track down the source of the terror. But when I came up empty-handed, I could only guess that whoever was broadcasting these strong emotions wasn't within the walls of Kinloch. That much was evident or my magic would have located them.

"I don't understand," I said. Then I approached the door, trying to concentrate my abilities more pointedly, to reach out to whomever it was who needed me. I mean, they had to be nearby, right? I couldn't have picked up on something so definite and crisp if the source in question wasn't close.

"Jolie . . ."

And then it hit me. "Bella," I said out loud, and then turned to face Rand, my eyes wide. "Something is wrong with Bella."

"What's wrong with Bella?" he asked, gripping my upper arms. "Did you receive a vision?"

"No, just this bizarre feeling of her fear," I said, and shook my head, because none of it made any sense.

"What could possibly scare her?" Rand asked, his tone suggesting that I might be mistaken.

But I knew better. This was no mistake. "I don't know, Rand, but I sense that she's in trouble." I felt another shard of panic slice my insides and knew that I had to help her. Granted, we had never been close, and were more like enemies than friends, but any way I looked at it, I couldn't leave a fellow creature to suffer through feeling like this alone. "We have to go to her!"

Before Rand could try to talk me out of it, I started for the door. He reached out, gripped my arm and pulled me back, shaking his head. "She's too dangerous, Jolie. I don't want anything to happen to you. I will go instead."

I shook my head in refusal, figuring there was a reason Bella had broadcast her distress to me. 'Course, it wasn't a bad idea to have company, especially Rand's company, since he could kick magical ass. "Let's go together," I said.

Realizing it wasn't up for debate, he just nodded and took my hand as we hurried out of my bedroom. We went down the stairs and toward the rear of Kinloch Kirk. From there, the grounds of Kinloch opened into a courtyard and, beyond that, the guesthouse where Bella still resided. Even though I had emancipated her, she had yet to take our loyalty oath, which was more my fault since I hadn't yet found the time to ensure that she take it. So she was still a captive prisoner until that little ritual was completed.

As we ran outside, I shivered in spite of myself, the cold Scottish gale chilling me to my very core. The werewolves standing guard outside Bella's door spotted us and stepped aside, granting us entry.

The first thing I noticed was how silent her quarters were. "Bella, are you okay?" I called. But no one answered. I turned to face the guards. "Have you heard anything?"

"She's been quiet for the last twenty minutes or so," the first guard said as he glanced at the second, presumably for his opinion.

The second guard nodded before turning to me. "Before that, though, all sorts of strange words were coming out of her mouth. Half of it sounded like gibberish."

"I think being stuck in that room has taken its toll on 'er," the first guard said, while the second nodded in agreement.

Rand went to open the door, but as soon as he touched the doorknob, he received a mild shock, a small blue light arcing up from the knob.

"I forgot to tell you that Mercedes' wards are in place," I said. When I left Bella, I had released a charm that permitted Mercedes' magic to reassert itself.

"Hold my hand," Rand said, extending his own. I didn't ask any questions, I just complied and waited for further directions. "Focus with me and we'll get the wards down that much faster."

Gripping his hand in mine, I closed my eyes and focused on unraveling the net of Mercedes' magic. And just as Rand had promised, together we were able to defeat Mercedes' charm in seconds. I could feel the power slipping away like tiny threads unraveling in my hands until the wooden door was all that separated us from Bella.

Rand took a few steps forward and tested the door-knob, but before opening it, he closed his eyes. He chanted something, probably a divination spell to ascertain whether anything horrible loomed behind the door—like a monster that might already have made lunch out of Bella and was now considering dessert. Detecting nothing, he turned the knob and opened it.

What we saw in there both surprised me and scared the hell out of me. Bella was in a corner of the room, huddled into a little ball, her arms wrapped around her legs as she rocked back and forth, muttering inanely to herself. She looked up at us, but as if oblivious, she focused on a spot above our heads, and then her attention strayed frenetically to other areas of the room before she returned to her knees. As she resumed her incessant rocking, I could see her hair was stringy and wet with perspiration, and her face unusually pale. She looked very sick.

What frightened me most, however, was not that she appeared to be in the throes of a mental breakdown, but that this was Bella Sawyer. Bella had always been fiercely independent, beautiful, and vain woman. She was always dressed to kill, and her snappish and arrogant personality made her a force to be reckoned with. This pathetic puddle of a person cowering before me now in no way, shape, or form resembled the Bella Sawyer I had come to know so well.

"Bella?" I said, gulping hard.

She glanced at me and shook her head, as if she didn't know me. "They are coming," she said softly.

Then she apparently caught the image of something in the room, emphatically shaking her head as tears flew from her eyes.

"Bella! Everything is going to be okay," I said as tenderly as I could. I didn't know what else to say or do. Truth be told, I was still reeling from the disturbing sight of her. "What do you think happened to her?" I whispered to Rand.

His eyes were as wide as mine as he shook his head, sighing deeply. "I don't have any idea."

We both watched as she dropped her head back against her knees and cried out something that we couldn't understand. Then she lifted her head, her eyes following something in the room. I glanced around but couldn't figure out what she was looking at. "Do you see anything?" I whispered to Rand.

"No." Then he took a few steps closer to her. "Bella," he said as he approached. "What is it? What do you see?"

She sobbed, but refused to look up at either of us. She just kept rocking back and forth as she muttered to herself—gibberish, mostly, almost like another language. Rand glanced at me and shrugged. Taking a few more steps toward her, he reached out and touched her shoulder, but as soon as he made contact with Bella, she shrieked, and shrank even farther back in her corner, facing the walls.

"No, stay away from me," she screamed, shaking her head as tears flowed from her eyes. "Don't touch me!" she yelled. "Don't let him touch me!"

"I think she's lost her mind," Rand whispered as he backed away with open palms to show her he wasn't going to touch her again.

I nodded and took a step closer to her, thinking maybe what she needed was a woman's gentle approach. Rand frowned. He obviously didn't want me to get anywhere near her. "Jolie—" he started.

"Please, she might listen to me. Just give me a chance."

Recognizing my iron resolve, he backed away.

I will be here should you need me, he said through our mental connection.

Thanks, I replied with a smile. I watched him back up to the door, where he stood on the alert.

Then I turned to Bella, who was still distraught. Her hair fell in long clumps around her shoulders, and she started winding strands of it between her fingers. Fallen black hairs littered the floor around her like hundreds of tiny snakes. "You have to tell me what happened, Bella," I said in a soft voice.

She glanced at me but still didn't seem to register who I was. It was like she'd been lobotomized.

"They come here," she said softly. "They come here all the time. I am never alone."

"Who are they?" I asked, feeling a tremor of fear shoot down my spine at the mention of "they." I had a pretty good feeling that I already knew who "they" were.

She shook her head and rocked back and forth again as if she hadn't heard me.

"Were they Lurkers, Bella?" I asked.

She nodded, her eyes hollow and wide. Her hair hung in her face, obscuring half of it.

"What did they say, Bella? What did they tell you?" I prodded, needing to learn what she knew and, of course, what the Lurkers had done to her.

"It was him," she said slowly as she scanned the room. She seemed scared, as if we were in danger of being overheard.

"What did he say?" I asked. I could feel the fear welling up inside me as an image formed in my mind. It was the same man from my dreams—the Lurker elder with the long white hair and beard. He breathed power. I closed my eyes to concentrate fully, to absorb every inch of the vision.

"Jolie?" Rand said, reminding me that he was still there. "Are you okay?"

"Yes, I'm getting something," I answered, and looked at Bella. "What did the man say to you?"

"That I must do as he says," she answered, eyeing the room again, recoiling into herself, fear emblazoned on her face. "I am not safe here. None of us are."

And that stuck right in my gut. "Why aren't we safe?" I demanded, swallowing my dread.

"Because they are coming and they are stronger than we are," she said. Then she dropped her face back onto her knees, rocking again. "I have said too much," she cried. "And now I will pay for it." She continued scanning the walls of the room, seemingly focused on nothing. "I'm sorry!" she cried out. "Do you hear me? I am sorry!"

I leaned down and touched her shoulder. As soon as I did, she glared up at me and her eyes went wild, ravenous. "You!" she shrieked, finally recognizing me.

She stood up as I backed away, and then Rand inserted himself between us.

"You are not what you seem!" she yelled at me as

Rand pushed her back. She clawed like a hellcat to get past him. "He was right! You are not one of us!"

"Jolie, get out of here!" Rand yelled at me as he tried to control her.

I wasted no time starting for the door. At the same time, the guards opened it and rushed inside. Seeing Rand wrestling with Bella, they moved to forcefully disable her. Rand pulled away then and exhaled deeply as he looked for me.

"What the hell got into her?" he asked me.

One of the guards followed us outside. "What's happened to her?" I asked him. "And how long has she been like this?"

He shrugged. "It started late last night. She was just in there talking to no one, and then all of a sudden it was like she had lost her flippin' mind. She would cry out and shriek like a crazed coyote."

"Why did you tell no one?" Rand demanded of him, his tone harsh.

The guard shrugged. "She ain't right in the head. Figured it went along with the territory."

I couldn't really say I was paying attention to his response, though, because Bella knew the truth about me. She knew that I was doing my damnedest to hide the truth from everyone else—that I was a . . . Lurker.

Ten

I couldn't stop thinking about what had happened to Bella. And now as I sat on my bedroom window seat, moonlight streaming through the glass and illuminating my otherwise dark room in a milky sort of glow, I felt my head spinning with questions.

How did Bella know I had something to do with the Lurkers? Did the Lurker elder tell her that? Will she tell anyone else?

Then I shook my head—irritated with my own stupidity. *Of course she's going to tell someone else! She's basically a raving lunatic with zero self-control!*

And what did her lunacy mean? Had the Lurkers completely zapped Bella of her intelligence? Was this the way they meant to torture our kind? To drive us to insanity, despondency? And speaking of our kind, how could I, in good conscience, lead the Underworld as their Queen when I was keeping such an extraordinary secret from them? How could I lead my people, when I was nothing more than a charlatan, and maybe worse, their enemy?

You can't, Jolie, I answered myself, feeling my

stomach drop at the prospect. *It wouldn't be right and you know it.*

So what am I supposed to do?

I gulped as I realized the only avenue left to me. *You have to tell someone. You can't keep this bottled up inside you any longer—especially now that Bella knows the truth. If you don't tell someone, it will get out—one way or another.*

"My Queen?" Klaasje's voice broke through the chaos of my thoughts and was accompanied by a timid knock on the door.

I turned from the view—I had been watching the playful breeze dancing sensuously with the heather, tossing it this way and that, filling the air with small purple flowers in the fading moonlight. "Come in," I said softly, feeling exhausted to my very core.

She smiled in greeting as she opened the door and closed it behind her again. She dropped into her customary curtsy, which seemed over-the-top polite, since she was wearing her long black hair pulled back into a ponytail and was dressed in blue jeans and a red sweatshirt that said WATCH IT; I BITE. The deference she displayed suddenly bothered me incredibly because I felt unworthy of it. I was now convinced my heritage could be traced back to the Lurkers. I shook my head. "Please don't do that," I said, and rubbed my hand against my temples, willing the headache behind my eyes to abate. As soon as it disappeared, I exhaled with relief and faced my chief guardian.

Klaasje didn't say anything, she just nodded, smiling slightly, and then approached me. "Rand wanted me to check in on you," she said at last, and I could tell by the expression on her face that Rand wasn't the only one who was worried about me.

"I'm sure I look like crap," I said with an apologetic and halfhearted smile.

She shook her head. "You just look tired."

I smiled at her as I exhaled deeply, wishing I could release all my stress into the air with it. "You can tell Rand I'm fine," I answered. He had spent the evening helping to organize the mass migration of Underworld creatures to Kinloch Kirk. It was the first evening I'd spent solo in over a week, and while I cherished my alone time since it was so scarce, I had to admit that I missed him.

"Are you feeling well?" Klaasje asked, and glanced at my stomach in a worried way.

"The sickness comes and goes," I replied, as even now I could taste the bitterness of nausea churning in my stomach. I had perfected the art of magicking it away, and it vanished almost before I consciously noticed it.

"If you need anything, please don't hesitate to let me know," she said. Then, at the prospect of an uncomfortable silence, she turned on her toes, starting for the door again.

"Klaasje," I said, stopping her. She turned to face me again, her beautiful blue eyes vibrant with curiosity. And I was suddenly so grateful to have her in my life, so appreciative that she and I had become friends. Because truly, I didn't have a lot of friends. Of course, there was Christa, but aside from her . . . I didn't really consider Mercedes my friend. She was just too super human for me to relate to, and Mathilda was like a motherly old woman. Really, the only other person whom I counted as a friend had been Sinjin . . .

"Yes?" she asked, and pushed her hands into her jeans pockets, looking more like a college student than a powerful vampire.

I cleared my throat, not sure how to phrase my question, but then decided to come out with it. "Have you . . . have you heard from Sinjin?"

She immediately colored and dropped her gaze to the floor, which meant she had. "I am not allowed to communicate with him, as you well know," she said softly. "None of us are."

Yes, those were the rules when it came to the exile of a member of the Underworld, but I also wasn't dumb enough to believe that she'd been following them. They were friends, and since they'd both taken on the role of my guardian, they'd become that much closer. I knew it had broken Klaasje's heart when I was forced to send Sinjin away—almost as much as it broke mine.

"I just . . . I just want to make sure he's okay, that he's safe." I paused and waited for her response, but she didn't say anything, just sighed deeply and studied me. "Please, Klaasje, tell me the truth."

"This isn't some sort of test?" she asked, eyeing me suspiciously.

I shook my head—offended that she would even infer such a thing—but given the fact that I was the Queen, I guess I couldn't fault her for it. "Of course it isn't a test. I'm asking you as my friend."

She seemed to light up when I called her my friend, but stayed silent for a few more seconds as the conflict about whether to tell me played out on her expressive face. Finally, she smiled. "I haven't heard from him recently," she started. "But he did contact me, maybe a week or so ago, and he was doing fine . . . then."

Sinjin was safe. I closed my eyes and felt an incredible sense of relief purging much of the stress from my body. I could breathe a little easier.

"I wouldn't worry too much about Sinjin if I were you," Klaasje continued, apparently sensing that her answer had pleased me inordinately. "He's one of the oldest of our kind, my Queen—"

"Please, call me Jolie," I interrupted, hating the distance "my Queen" put between us.

She smiled slightly and nodded. "Jolie. Sinjin could pretty much outwit anyone and everyone. There's a reason he's been around for so long." She took a deep breath. "So don't trouble yourself anymore on his account."

I smiled and nodded, taking mild satisfaction in her words. "Where is he?" I asked.

"Where is Sinjin Sinclair?" Klaasje responded with a laugh as she shook her head in apparent amusement. "Isn't that the ultimate question? Last I heard, he was living in the Swiss Alps, but I'm certain he's moved on since then. Sinjin never struck me as the type of person who wanted to stay in one place." Then she glanced up at me and cocked a brow. "Unless, of course, you were part of the equation."

"What are you saying?" I asked, studying her intently.

She shrugged. "Nothing. Just that Sinjin seemed okay with sticking around when he was your guardian. I never witnessed any of the wanderlust that usually drives him to roam. He just seemed . . . content somehow."

I nodded, not wanting to focus on old memories for fear that they would depress me. Instead, I focused on the fact that Sinjin was safe, and found myself beaming. It was the best news I'd heard all week. "Thank you. I was . . . really worried about him." I paused for a few seconds before something else occurred to me. "Please continue to keep in touch with him."

Klaasje nodded, and I could tell there was something more on her mind, but she seemed hesitant to say anything.

"What?" I asked with a little laugh, encouraging her to continue. "I want us to be friends, Klaasje," I said finally. "And since we're friends, whatever you say to me will be held in the strictest confidence."

She smiled at me in return. "I would like that." Then she inhaled deeply, and though it seemed like she wasn't entirely comfortable with the conversation we were having, continued anyway. "I don't pretend to know what situation existed between you and Sinjin, but obviously, it went awry," she said. Then she took another deep breath, apparently weighing her next words. "And he would probably kill me for telling you this . . ." But her voice trailed off as if she were having a tough time getting the words out.

"Yes?" I asked, wanting her—no, needing her—to continue.

"I think you did the impossible where that vampire's concerned," she finished. Then she shook her head in what appeared to be wonder. The smile on her lips somehow hinted at her past on the great plains of 1875 Texas, taming not only the men around her but the raw wilderness of the land. She emanated the bravery and strength of character that only come through hard experience. I felt like dubbing her "Klaasje Oakley."

But then I focused on what she was saying and scrunched my eyebrows in the middle, completely at a loss. "Did the impossible? What do you mean?"

She nodded, as if realizing she wasn't making any sense. "I just never thought Sinjin had it in him to fall in love with someone."

I frowned and shook my head, not believing a word of it, not wanting to believe a word of it. Why? Because it was a complication I didn't need to add to my life at the moment. "So you're saying you think he was in love with me?"

She nodded. "Yes, I'm convinced of it."

I laughed in a strange, sad sort of way. "Why would you think that? Sinjin is not capable of love." Then I eyed her with a frown. "Self-confessed."

She shook her head, her face a mask of certainty. "That's what he wants everyone to believe, but I don't." She wrapped her arms around her chest and studied me for another few seconds. "And I would chance to say that you don't either."

But I ignored her last comment. "Why don't you believe it?"

"Because he reversed time in order to make you fall in love with him, and that seems pretty desperate to me."

So it was true, then? Sinjin's prime motivation had been to manipulate me into loving him rather than just protecting me? I asked myself.

Well, it's true as far as Klaasje knows, came the response. *I mean, helloooo, it's not like Sinjin is standing here, telling you this.*

Thinking I had a good point, I faced Klaasje again. "Sinjin insisted he did it to protect me from the Lurker threat."

Klaasje nodded. "Yes, that was true too—of course he took his position as protector to the Queen personally and wanted to ensure your safety—but ensuring your safety and putting the moves on you are two totally different things."

I laughed at her choice of words but I firmly decided that I was past the point of caring what Sinjin's reasons were for doing what he'd done. As far as I was concerned, what was done was done and we both were moving on—we *had* both moved on. All that mattered was that Sinjin was safe; and according to Klaasje, he was. End of story. "Well, whatever his reasoning, I'm happy to hear that he's okay as far as you know."

She nodded. "Hopefully, he's keeping a low profile."

I laughed at that thought, although I wasn't sure why. We sat companionably for a moment, and then I said, "I always cared for Sinjin, and it depresses me that things ended up the way they did." I sighed as I thought about it. "I miss his friendship."

Klaasje nodded. "I think you did him the ultimate favor."

"How is that?"

She smiled. "You taught him that he's capable of loving."

* * *

I was sleeping.

I knew it and yet couldn't wake up. It was almost as if something inside me refused to release me from the dream's hold.

Opening my eyes, I felt something wet and itchy against my cheek and pushed up on my elbows, noticing grass below me. It was wet with morning dew and I could feel the heat of the sunlight against my back, warming me with its glorious rays. I yawned and sat up, picking off pieces of grass and flowers from my face and body.

I realized I was wearing a dress I'd never seen before—long, white, and gauzy, with an Empire waist. My hair fell around my shoulders in large sausage curls, and when I looked down at my feet, I noticed that they were bare. Feeling immediately anxious, mainly because I had no clue where I was, why I'd been asleep, and why I was dressed like this, I stood up and checked out my surroundings.

I was on the top of a mountain—more like a mountainous ledge. Behind me, I noticed a tree line of giant pines, and beyond that, nothing but darkly verdant forest. I'd been sleeping on top of a steep cliff, hundreds of feet above a canyon, with nothing but sharp, craggy rocks beneath me. I felt a cool breeze massage my legs, and the skirt of my dress sashayed around my naked skin, tickling me with its satiny hem.

I blinked and suddenly found a man standing right in front me. His hair was as white as newly fallen snow and incredibly long. It fell all the way to the ground, looking as soft as rabbit's fur with a slight wave to it. I tore my attention away from the man's hair and took in his face, which was hard to concentrate on, given his incredibly full and long beard. It was of the same hue and texture as his hair, though it wasn't quite as long—it only reached his knees. He wasn't a tall man, but neither was he short. He was old, though—I could tell as much from the deeply set wrinkles around his eyes and mouth, not to mention the way he limped when he walked—like he had bad knees.

"We meet again," the old man said.

And I recognized his voice as the one that had belonged to the sea in my last dream, in which he'd announced that I was one of his kind, that I was a Lurker.

"I refuse to believe that I'm one of you," I said in a loud voice, the sound echoing through the canyon below me until it seemed like the mountains were screaming at me. "I'm not a Lurker."

The old man laughed with a deep, melodious sound. The mountains laughed with him, the rocks rumbling in agreement. "You know who you are deep down, Jolie Wilkins," he said, his eyes hinting at the wealth of knowledge that existed within him. He reminded me of some old wizard—like Merlin.

I shook my head, not wanting to believe his words. It troubled me that he knew my name. "How do you know who I am?"

He shrugged as he turned to face our surroundings, seemingly grateful for the raw beauty of nature. "I have known you your whole life, child." He said the words with an air of ennui, as if the small talk tired him.

As far as I was concerned, this wasn't small talk. "How is that even possible?"

"Any and everything is possible in our universe, as you well know by now."

I shook my head and stood my proverbial ground. "I am a witch; that is what I know."

The old man nodded and smiled at me—like a smile you give to an unruly child. "You are a witch, yes, but you are more than that." He paused and inhaled deeply, as if savoring the feel of the crisp air in his lungs. "You are more promising and powerful than any of your kind. There is only one other with abilities equal to yours."

"The prophetess?" I said, too quickly, irritated with myself that I'd mentioned Mercedes. I mean, it wasn't like I trusted this dude, so I shouldn't be volunteering any information.

But he shook his head like he wasn't surprised that I'd brought her up. I almost had to wonder if he knew what I was going to say before I said it.

"Your powers far exceed those of the prophetess," he said, frowning. "She is not as powerful as you would assume—merely stuck in time, reliving her life in order to spare herself from death at our hands."

Hmm, so apparently, Merlin aka Father Time, thought Mercedes was still entrenched in 1878 . . . Or maybe he did know the truth and was just playing dumb. Either way, I wasn't about to correct him. Surprises are always good to have in your pocket when dealing with an enemy. "Is that so?" I asked, crossing my arms against my chest.

He nodded and seemed to lose himself as he glanced up at the white puffs of clouds that punctuated the sky. "She is a dangerous woman," he continued, apparently still talking about Mercedes. "I was lucky to lock her in the annals of history, where she belongs."

I swallowed hard—this was the man who had forced Mercedes into the past. It was his fault she'd been there to begin with. It scared me because I'd always considered Mercedes the most powerful being of all, and if this guy had been able to lock her away, he must be even more powerful. "Why is she so dangerous?" I asked, wondering how much questioning I should pursue and whether I should just try to wake myself up. But somehow I didn't imagine I'd be able to do it—at least not until this guy was finished with me.

"She is determined and that makes her dangerous."

"Couldn't someone say the same of you?" I asked as I felt the wind suddenly pick up and throw itself against me full bore, stinging my cheeks.

The old man just laughed, though, and raised his arms as if he was ordering the elements to calm down. When the wind immediately died, I realized he was completely in charge of the scenery around me—it was like everything was just a reverberation of his thoughts.

"You are quick-witted, child," he began. "Yes, I am determined, and yes, I could be considered dangerous . . . to my enemies, that is."

At the mention of his "enemies," I felt something start in my gut—something that felt like fear. It was readily apparent that you didn't want to be this guy's enemy. Not with the sort of power he evidently had at his disposal.

"So if the prophetess is not my equal, who were you referring to?" I demanded.

The old man smiled at me as the scenery around us began to fade, replaced with the image of what appeared to be a woman. She was a mere outline, her long hair flowing in a strong breeze. Her feet were shoulder-width apart, and her hands were grasping a dagger, so I had to imagine she was a warrior of sorts. "You will meet her in time," the old man said. "She is your equal, but like you, she is not prepared, not fully cognizant of all that she is capable. You will find your way together, teaching and learning from each other."

But I refused to believe there was a Lurker alive who could teach me or learn from me. Not when we were enemies. This was just a bunch of guff—a pretty story meant to charm me into believing the old man. Not wanting to give his prophecy any credence, I focused instead on the last time our paths had crossed, when he'd told me I was a Lurker.

"So how do you know that I'm one of your people?" I asked.

He shrugged as if the answer was easy. "I know your bloodline."

"My bloodline?" I repeated. "Last I checked, I was English, Irish, Swedish, and Scottish. No Lurker ancestry whatsoever."

He laughed as if I'd just told a great joke. "You are descended from the original tribe of Lurkers in Gratz, Austria. I knew your parents."

I shook my head and laughed sarcastically. "There you're wrong. My mother was born in 1953 and has nothing to do with witches, warlocks, Lurkers, or anyone else, and my father wasn't any more exotic."

He sighed. "Not everything is as it seems, child."

I was about to question him further but decided against it. I mean, I knew I couldn't trust him.

"I am not your enemy," he said frankly. "In the end, you will have no one to turn to but me because I am your kind."

That thought sunk in my gut like an anvil. "Were you the one who sent me those dreams of the battlefield and the throne?" He merely nodded, so I continued. "What did they mean?"

"It was a sign to you that you must return to your people and rule as you were meant to. Many may die—on our side as well as the side you currently represent. All of this can be avoided."

But I wasn't about to focus on the "returning to my people" crap. Instead, it suddenly hit me that the dreams he'd thrust upon me had nearly killed me. "If I'm one of your people, why did you try to kill me?"

He nodded and then exhaled, long and hard. "It was not my intention. I wanted to talk to you, to get into your psyche, but your walls were too high for me to overcome. I doubled my magic, and in the process polluted you. But that was never my intention."

"Well, it nearly killed me," I answered in a caustic tone.

"As I said, it was not my intention, child. I wanted only to communicate with you." He paused for a second and then smiled at me. "My apologies."

But somehow "my apologies" didn't cut it. No, this man—this creature—had haunted my dreams for months and nearly killed me. Whatever his reasons, they weren't good enough. And that was when it dawned on me that I was not his latest, nor least, offense. "What did you do to Bella?"

The old man said nothing for a while, just breathed harshly before he opened his mouth and spoke. "Bella does not have the constitution to understand our kind."

"So why did you try?"

"We wanted her to deliver a message to you that we want you to be with us, your people, again. But Bella's powers were not capable of accepting our magic. Instead, it addled her mind."

"Addled her mind?" I repeated. "Is that what you call it? Do you know that she's completely bonkers? She's scared to death of you or whoever has been contacting her, and if you want me to even consider talking to you again, you must immediately release Bella from the spell you have over her."

The old man paused for a few moments before speaking, then said, "We have released her, but the damage is done."

I shook my head. "Then you must not be as powerful as you profess."

"That is up for debate," he said snidely, seemingly offended by my criticism. "What I came to tell you, Queen, is that you must return to your people."

I swallowed hard. "I am with my people."

"No," he said fervently and shook his head. I could feel his frustration in the wild wind that started whipping around us again. "If you come to us willingly, we will not attack those you call your people now."

"What?" I repeated, my voice becoming desperate. "Then you *are* going to attack us?"

"If we feel we have no alternative," he finished, then took another breath, turning his predatory eyes on me. "All we ask is for you to take your rightful place beside us, where you belong."

"I am where I belong," I said.

Suddenly, his image began to dissipate before my eyes.

"Wait!" I called. "I want to know why you want to destroy the creatures of the Underworld when you are essentially a part of it! You are vampires and witches!"

But it was too late, the man had already disappeared, the scenery around me melting into a drab brown, pulling the grass, trees, and flowers in with it until it resembled melted caramel.

Then I woke up.

Eleven

I couldn't shake off the dream and go back to sleep. The Lurker elder was completely convinced I was one of his kind, and while I desperately wanted to wake Rand up and tell him everything, I hesitated. Why? Because I was scared to death that this news might destroy everything we now shared. I couldn't stand the idea of what I might see in his eyes—disgust.

You're going to have to tell someone soon, Jolie, I chided myself. *And remember what happened the last time you held out on Rand?*

Yeah, when I realized that I was Rand's missing bond mate from 1878, I had kept it a secret. He had eventually figured it out anyway and what bothered him most was the fact that I hadn't told him the truth.

So aren't you supposed to learn from past mistakes? I asked myself.

Yes, yes, yes! I thought in response. But glancing over at him, I immediately came up with another excuse. *He's sound asleep and I shouldn't wake him up.*

You're going to have to tell him one way or the other, I continued in that know-it-all voice that did nothing but irritate me.

I knew I had to do it soon, but I wasn't about to do it now. A part of me just hoped I could work it out on my own. I wanted something to happen that would prove once and for all that I wasn't a Lurker and that Mathilda was right—I was a witch with a little fae in the ol' gene pool.

Now fervently in favor of not telling Rand, I decided to try to sleep. I fluffed my down pillow a few times and rested my head, closed my eyes, and tried to will myself to sleep. No go.

I tried a few more times but ended up tossing and turning like a boat on a restless sea, the thought of which summoned feelings of nausea in my stomach, which I then magicked away. Once I was ready to voyage back to the land of dreams, it was Rand's turn to keep me awake.

"J-Jolie," he said in a muffled voice as he rolled his head to the opposite side and his brows knotted between his eyes.

I turned to face him, but instantly realized he was still sleeping, his twitching eyelids a sign that he was dreaming.

"I . . . I'm here," he said and then grunted something unintelligible. I just shook my head and laughed lightly.

"It's okay, Rand," I whispered. "I'm here too. Roll over and go back to sleep."

He didn't say anything more, just nodded and rolled onto his side, falling back into a deep sleep. I rolled onto my back and stared up at the ceiling, wishing I could join him. But it was becoming increasingly apparent that sleep wasn't going to happen for me.

I sat up straight, staring at the moon as it streamed in through the curtains that covered the French doors. They seemed to flutter in the breeze, dancing this way and that until they resembled undulating ghosts. Then it dawned on me—the doors were open, and I distinctly remembered closing and locking them before going to bed.

Feeling my heart hammering in my chest, I stood up and was immediately chilled by the cold sea air. I wrapped my arms around my body, wishing I'd worn my long-sleeved pjs to bed. Hurrying to the doors, I pulled them closed just as a scent I knew well enfolded me in its clean spiciness.

Sinjin.

There was something in me that suddenly erupted— something hopeful and happy, because if I could smell Sinjin, that had to mean he was here, right? It wasn't so much a feeling of missing a long-lost lover, but rather, finding a long-lost friend.

I glanced around the room, wondering if Sinjin was still here, but there was no sign of him. Nothing other than the flirtatious dance of the curtains and the lingering spicy scent of men's aftershave. I could feel his calling card as clearly as the cold, which was now wrapping its icy embrace around my body. I shivered in spite of myself and rubbed my arms up and down, trying to ward away the goose bumps. But I didn't return to bed. Instead, I found myself gazing out the window into the blackness of the night as the stars twinkled from above. I couldn't help but wonder when Sinjin had been there and for how long.

Maybe this was all a figment of my imagination? Maybe I'd been worrying about him so much lately that my brain simply pulled a memory of his scent from the Jolie Wilkins archives and put one over on me?

Or maybe Sinjin Sinclair hadn't left my side at all, and had been fulfilling his post as sentry to the Queen from the shadows. That thought brought me an inordinate sense of peace and comfort.

Was Sinjin the one who woke me from my nightmare? Did he somehow force the old Lurker to vacate my dream?

Of course, I couldn't answer either question and, instead, found myself gazing into the dark sea, watching the way the moonlight sparkled on the waves as they crashed onto the beach.

Sinjin, if you're out there, I thought to myself. *I hope you're safe. And if you really were here tonight, thanks for stopping by.*

I cleared my throat.

I miss you.

Just before dawn, when the sky was still a dark blue, I reached my breaking point. I'd tried to get back to sleep countless times but couldn't do it. I'd basically been awake for the past three-plus hours and felt like I might lose my mind if I didn't find something to occupy it.

But what to do? It wasn't like there was much going on at this early hour. But I had to imagine there was one person who might actually benefit from being checked on . . . Bella. Feeling suddenly charitable, I stepped out of my pajamas and magicked myself a pair of jeans, a long-sleeved shirt, and a thick down jacket, knowing I'd freeze as soon as I stepped outside in the early Scottish morning.

I tiptoed to the door and smiled at Rand, who was still deeply asleep. I was so happy about everything that had happened between us. Not wanting to lose myself to a mushy moment—I could tell my pregnancy hormones were in full effect—I closed the door behind me and started for the staircase that led to the guesthouse where Bella was currently imprisoned.

As I hurried through the house, it dawned on me that I hadn't seen the werewolf guards who were usually stationed at my door during daylight hours. But this realization didn't cause me any sort of disquiet, mainly because Rand had taken it upon himself to be my protector. I had to figure that the weres would get disgruntled at some point and go find something else to keep them busy.

Once I stepped foot outside, the cold assaulted me and I slammed my hands into my coat pockets, forcing myself forward. I scanned the vista of the moors on one side of Kinloch and the craggy shoreline on the other and felt fortunate to have this quiet moment alone. Kinloch was going to be in a frenzy when all the creatures of the Underworld were assembled on my property. While I thought I made the right decision, I couldn't help but bemoan the loss of peace that would ensue.

I jogged through the courtyard, and when I reached the path that led to the guesthouse, I was suddenly overcome with thoughts of Sinjin. Was he out there somewhere, watching me at this very moment.

Could it really have been Sinjin in my bedroom?

Somehow—and I wasn't sure why—I desperately wanted to believe it was true and that he really wasn't that far away from me.

I reached the guesthouse and quickly noticed that only one of the werewolf guards was on duty. He glanced over at me and smiled as he dropped into a low bow. "Good morning, my Queen," he said.

"Good morning. What's your name?" I asked, realizing I should have done so long ago. Part of being Queen was earning political points by kissing babies and the like. I had to admit I hadn't been great in that department.

"Brandon James," he replied, grinning from ear to ear. He clearly took pride in his position.

I nodded and smiled, extending my hand. "It's nice to meet you, Brandon." Then I looked at the door, the smile falling off my face as I returned my gaze to him. "How is she?"

He shrugged. "She seems to go up and down. Sometimes she's real quiet-like, an' other times she's a handful."

I nodded. "How was she last night?"

"Quiet. The most quiet she's been in a while."

I tried to exhale my anxiety as I wondered what was happening with Bella. Was her delirium getting worse as the Lurker elder claimed? Was the damage that had been done irreparable? Yes, it was true that Bella and I had never been fond of each other, but I couldn't help but feel sorry for her. It just seemed life had been dealing her some pretty nasty cards, including that she'd loved Sinjin and he hadn't cared for her at all.

"Can I go in?" I asked.

The were just nodded as I started for the door and put my palms up against it to take down Mercedes' wards. I got the barriers down and opened the door to find Bella seated on the sofa with a book in her lap. She looked up at me with an expression of calculated irritation. If her hair hadn't been so messy, I might have thought her wits had been restored.

"How are you, Bella?" I asked with trepidation upon entering. I nodded to the werewolf guard that he could shut the door behind me.

Once we were completely alone, Bella responded, "I am well." Then she jutted her chin out as if to say she had nothing to add to the subject. Or any subject, for that matter.

"What are you reading?"

"None of your business," she snapped, training her angry glare on me again. "I am a busy woman. Why are you here?"

I nodded, not really knowing what to say. She almost seemed . . . normal. Her usual persnickety and unfriendly self seemed to be reemerging. "I came to make sure you were okay—" I started.

She shook her head. "I am more than okay. I'm preparing for my inaugural dinner festivities."

I was surprised, but tried not to show it. I figured it was best to humor her. "What inaugural dinner is that?"

She glowered at me and then lifted her book up, pretending to read it. I might have bought the whole charade if she hadn't been holding it upside down. And odder still, it was *Curious George*.

"My inaugural party for when I become Queen of

the Underworld," she answered without looking up at me, her nose held high.

I felt myself swallow hard as I realized she was just as crazy as she had been a day or so ago.

"Oh," I said, and for lack of anything else to say, started for the door. I figured that Bella was as good as she was going to get.

"He visited me again," she said in a low voice, still pretending to be wholly absorbed in Curious George's adventures at the zoo.

"Who?" I asked.

"He calls himself Luce," she answered. "He's the Lurker elder."

I wasn't sure why, but the thought that the creature who had been plaguing my dreams had a name terrified me. It made him a little too human. What was even more ironic was that *Luce* meant "light."

"What did he say?" I asked.

She shrugged. "He told me to prepare for my inaugural dinner. He said he'd invited all sorts of people and that I should plan on giving a speech. He also promised me a red satin gown and said I would be stunning in it."

I swallowed hard as my anger began to supplant my fear. What he had done to Bella was unacceptable. "I don't think it's wise to trust him," I said.

She eyed me and dropped the book. It fell to the ground with a thud. Returning my eyes to hers, I realized she was livid.

"And why not?" she asked, sounding furious. "Because he wants me to rule, not you? Your jealousy is so transparent."

I shook my head, acknowledging my mistake. I hadn't wanted to upset her, and without realizing it, I'd done exactly that. "No, that's not what I meant," I said.

Bella stood up and her eyes were suddenly wild, wide and bulging. She took a few steps toward me and I watched her hands fisting at her sides. "He warned me about you," she said, and raised a clenched fist. "He said you're a liar and a manipulator and that you're dangerous."

I shook my head again and backed away, suddenly afraid that she might attack me. "None of those things are true, Bella. I want to be your friend."

"My friend?!" she railed. "Of course! You want to be my friend because you seek power! You want to befriend the Queen of the Underworld and then steal my throne again!"

"No," I said, holding up my hands in an attempt to show her that I wasn't her enemy.

"He always loved you!" she yelled, and it took me a few seconds to realize she was no longer talking about Luce, the Lurker elder. Now I was pretty sure she was referring to Sinjin. "He always promised me that he cared about me and that we would be together. He said you were just a pawn, but I knew better."

I figured the best way out of this was to try to defuse her anger, and the only way I knew how was to appeal to her vanity. "No, that isn't true. Sinjin told me he was in love with you."

She shook her head and her hair flew around her face like Medusa's snakes. "Lies! He will suffer for his prevarications, and so will you!" She held up both fists and broke into a nasty laugh, her gaze focusing on something just above my head. Then she looked at me again and her smile got even uglier. "Sinjin is nothing to a Queen, just a mere insect to be trod upon."

I nodded and took another few steps backward, nervous about the fact that she was still approaching me, her eyes reflecting a complete loss of sanity.

"You will see," she continued. "Soon they will be here and then I will be back in power, where I belong."

I didn't say anything, but I felt my back hit the wall. I needed to make a break for the door. That crazed look in Bella's eyes wasn't getting any more endearing. I looked at the door then back at her, suddenly feeling like I was moving in slow motion.

Her eyes went wide again and she vehemently shook her head. "You can't leave," she said, opening her hands, palms facing each other.

"Bella, it doesn't have to come to this," I replied, realizing what was about to happen.

Instead of answering, she concentrated on her palms. A glimmer of light began to shine between them—a bright white light that quickly became orange-red and then red as a ruby.

"Bella," I warned again, just as she lifted her hands and launched the glowing ball of light at me. I ducked and it shattered against the wall, exploding into an array of sparks that popped and fizzed into nothing, seemingly impotent. But I knew well enough that if her ball of light had hit me, it would have frozen me in place and seconds later I would have shattered into a million Jolie Wilkins pieces. I would have disappeared into the ether, never to be heard of or seen again.

"I don't want to do this, Bella!" I yelled, wondering why the guard wasn't interrupting us. Then it dawned on me that Bella had probably issued a charm of silence around the room when I wasn't paying attention.

It was becoming crystal clear that she wanted to destroy me, and in doing so, destroy my unborn baby. That was when I got pissed.

"You are a usurper!" she screamed at me. "I was supposed to be Queen! Luce said so himself, and you stole the throne from me!"

"Bella, drop your hands and step away!" I yelled back, but she made no motion to do anything of the sort, so I was left with no other options.

I immediately surrounded myself with white light, a buffer to ward off any evil energy. My timing was impeccable because two seconds later she flung another orb of glowing red energy that hit me square in the chest. The white light surrounding me swallowed the ball of energy, but I felt my strength wane slightly.

No longer playing games, I held my hands together and imagined a river of electricity raging through me, pouring out of my fingers into the air between my palms. The blue orb glowed powerfully, and not wasting any more time, I hurled it at Bella. It landed in her stomach and she flew about five feet, crashing on her back, after which she was completely still.

Jolie! It was Rand's voice in my head, but I couldn't

respond to him. I didn't dare take my focus away from Bella. Not when I didn't know if I should still consider her a threat or if she was . . . dead.

I approached her and kicked her foot, wondering if I'd charged my orb with too much electricity. I'd just intended to knock her down so that I could buy myself some time and put a spell on her, or get the guard to help me. But maybe my energy was stronger than I realized, because she didn't look good.

Bella still didn't respond, so I sent mental feelers her way to see if she was really dead. As soon as I did, I could feel a slight buzz of energy coming from her and breathed a sigh of relief.

My sigh of relief was short-lived, though, because Bella turned on her side and threw her open palm toward me, tiny fragments of light flying from her outstretched fingers. Before I had the chance to respond, the lights started circling me in a frenzy, like I was in the middle of a tornado. Bella sat up, resting on her elbows as she watched me with a wretched smile on her face.

I felt myself fall to the ground as the lights continued to swirl around me, zapping me of my strength. I closed my eyes, imagining the white light of my shield encircling me, but Bella's power was too much for me, which meant that there was more to this picture than met the eye. Bella was an able witch, but she wasn't as strong as I was, so her power shouldn't have immobilized me in this way.

I tried to fight the power by imagining defensive walls, but it was no good.

"Jolie!" I heard Rand's fists pounding on the door

and I turned to face it. I wanted to reach out and open the door, but I was too weak and just crumpled back onto the floor.

Rand, I need your magic, I thought in my head. *Bella's done something to me.*

There was a silence of maybe two seconds, and then I could feel something welling up within me—fear. Rand's feeling, not my own. There was another set of pounding fists against the door.

I can't break through, Jolie! Rand screamed through my head. *I can't get through whatever spell she's woven!*

Then he pounded on the door again.

"Give me your hand."

I heard a voice and glanced up from where my cheek was pressed against the floor. I saw the old man with the white hair and beard standing before me. He wasn't ethereal like you'd imagine an apparition to be. It was like he was standing there beside me, flesh and blood.

I saw Bella gape at him with shock in her eyes, and then something strange happened. She let out a small gasp and fell to the ground, her eyes wide with fright as she stared at nothing. She was dead. It was as obvious as the fact that I was about to join her shortly.

You did this to me. I thought the words as I glared up at him, too weak to even lift my head from the floor.

"No," he said, shaking his head adamantly. "I am here to save you, but you must take my hand. Time is running out."

I shook my head, or at least I wanted to shake my

head. I was so tired that I had no control over my body. *I don't trust you.*

"You will die if you do not take my hand! Do you understand?" he insisted. "My power is not strong enough for me to stay here much longer."

Who is in there with you, Jolie? Rand demanded, sounding frenzied.

It's a Lurker, a Lurker elder, I thought back. *Luce.*

Stay away from him! Rand railed.

I'm dying, Rand, I thought the words, realizing what I had to do in order to save my child. It was the only option left to me. *I have no other choice!*

Jolie, no! he screamed again, his voice ringing through my head.

Luce's outline was beginning to waver and he started to grow more translucent. I swallowed hard at the same time as I reached out and let him grasp my hand in his.

Twelve

I wasn't sure what I expected when I took Luce's hand, but as soon as I did, I felt a swoosh of air against my face, which caused me to close my eyes. When I opened them, I was no longer in the guesthouse of Kinloch Kirk. Where was I? I had no clue.

That thought scared me to death. No one would know what had happened to me or where I was. At least I'd been able to tell Rand that a Lurker came for me. How that information would benefit me, I didn't know, but it seemed a step in the right direction.

Don't focus on that now, Jolie, I chided myself. *Focus on surviving!*

I took a deep breath and realized I was bent over on my hands and knees. There was green grass below me, which told me I was outside. I glanced to my right, taking in what seemed to be miles of chain-link fence topped with two rows of barbed wire. On both sides of the fencing there was a perimeter of pine trees that towered in the air above me, their dark green contrasting against the brilliant blue of the sky.

I sat back on my haunches and craned my neck to

the left, where I noticed that the chain-link fencing ended in a little white tollbooth (or guardhouse) type structure. Was I in a prison? An unpaved road led up to it and disappeared into an alcove of trees. Standing in front of the tollbooth structure was a man dressed in a gray uniform, armed with what looked like an Uzi. Before him were orange traffic cones, lined up in front of roadblocks that were three feet high and wide. The obstacles would force any persistent drivers through a minicourse in order to slow them down. Talk about high security. Wherever I was, it was apparent that outsiders were meant to stay out and insiders were meant to stay in. Either way, it didn't leave me with the warm fuzzies.

"Welcome to our training center," Luce said, and shock whirred through me at the thought that he had been standing just behind me the entire time. I'm not sure why I was so surprised, considering he was the one who brought me here. He offered his hand to me, his eyes gentle, echoing the same sentiment behind his easy smile. I shook my head, righting myself as I stood up and took a deep breath. The pine scent of my surroundings reminded me of Christmas.

Then I remembered everything. How could Bella have attacked me with a power that should never have been hers? "What happened to Bella?" I demanded, feeling sick to my stomach as I remembered her sightless eyes.

Luce shrugged as if it were of no consequence to him, and started walking away from the barbed wire–topped fence. I had no choice but to follow him. Once I caught up, he turned to face me. "You killed her," he said, "but you did so purely in self-defense."

I shook my head, letting his words sink in. But I knew better. I hadn't killed Bella. Maybe I'd underestimated my final blow, but she'd still had enough life left in her to brutally attack me afterward. She'd died after Luce appeared. That had to mean something. "Her power should never have been enough to do what it did to me," I said, eyeing him suspiciously as I tried to understand who was truly responsible.

Luce didn't respond right away, he just continued moving forward with me by his side. We walked up a grassy knoll, surrounded on either side by more grass and pine trees. Then he paused, facing me earnestly. "It is what it is. Bella is no longer a threat that you need to concern yourself with."

But I wasn't going to let it go that easily. "Why did she seem to think you were going to make her Queen?"

Luce chuckled without humor. "You put too much stock in the words of a lunatic. Who knows what her motivations were? She was sans intellect."

I shook my head, knowing there was more to Luce's story, but also knowing it wasn't a good idea to pry. Now more than ever before I was keenly aware that I was at his mercy. But I wasn't finished with my line of questioning—it seemed like a good idea to learn as much as I could about my enemies. "How were you able to transport me here just by touching me?"

Luce paused and shrugged, and his white hair and beard almost glowed in the sunlight, like an angel's. "I merely relocated us," he answered. But the power involved in such a stunt was hardly simple. It just pointed to how strong he was . . . whatever he was.

"What are you?" I asked, sounding awed, keeping pace with him as he began walking again.

He chuckled, as if my confusion were an award he could wear proudly. "I am an Elemental."

"Does that mean you're a witch?" I asked. Looking ahead, it seemed we were walking toward a forest, and I suddenly felt afraid. I stopped walking.

"No, I am not a witch," he said, giving me a curious look. "What would make you ask me that?"

"Well, I don't know what 'Elemental' means," I said, irritated. "And you seem like a witch to me."

He frowned, as if calling him a witch were the equivalent of calling an Aussie a Brit or vice versa. Well, excuse the hell out of me!

"Elementals and witches are only similar in that they both possess magic," he explained. "An Elemental, especially an aged one, is much more powerful than a witch or a warlock."

"How so?"

"We live longer and are more physically powerful. Our magic is purer."

"How is that possible when you are basically descended from witches?"

He glanced at me with an arched brow, as if impressed that I knew that much about his race. "We are sprung from witches, yes," he started, then took a deep breath. "But similar to your prehistoric man, we became like Cro-Magnon—stronger, smarter, and better able to survive—quite dissimilar to Neanderthals."

Well, one thing I could say about Luce was that he sure had an overinflated sense of self-importance. I harrumphed but said nothing more, figuring any disagreement I voiced would end in a "no, you're not/ yes, we are" argument.

"There were two lines of ancestry for our kind," he continued. "Those who are descended from the humans who were attacked by vampires in Gratz, Austria, and those who are descended from the humans who were attacked by witches."

This part of his story actually stoked the furnace of my memory, because I'd heard it before. Though I knew next to nothing about the two sects of Lurkers, I had been told about their origins. Centuries ago, during a massacre of ordinary humans in the woods of Austria, some of the surviving humans had ingested vampire and witch blood. The resulting offspring were super humans, known as the Lurkers. Well, we called them Lurkers, anyway. Apparently they didn't refer to themselves as such. "Then you *are* descended from witches," I pointed out. "So why do you say you aren't a witch?"

"Because I am not," he said curtly as a breeze embraced us both, lifting my hair so it brushed my cheek. I refastened it back behind my ears.

"If it looks like a witch and acts like a witch . . ." I said with a frown.

He just smiled. "Is a spaniel the same as a wolf?"

I shook my head, realizing where he was going. "No."

"Ah, but a spaniel is the descendent of a wolf?"

"Okay, I get it," I said gruffly, holding my hair in place as another breeze attempted to pull it free. Then something occurred to me. "So, as an elder, you're still a descendent of the original Elementals from Austria?

That is, you didn't experience the beginning of your race firsthand?"

Luce smiled knowingly. "Oh, yes, I lived it myself."

I felt my jaw drop. This had to mean that Luce was centuries old. And that said something about his powers and abilities.

Given his origins, I still wasn't convinced that he was really that different from witches. My skepticism must have shown because he cleared his throat and eyed me speculatively.

He continued with his explanation. "My powers and abilities are quite different from those of the prophetess, for example. And similarly, our citizens of the 'fang' persuasion can walk in the sunlight."

"So they aren't real vampires?" I finished.

"No, quite different. You will learn all of our ways in time."

That was when I remembered the dire predicament I was in. I didn't want anything to do with "in time." "I need to go back," I replied as he stopped walking and turned to face me. I couldn't help the tone of my voice, which sounded hurried and nervous. But even as I said the words, I realized how moot they suddenly were—Luce had me right where he wanted me. There was no way he would just bring me back to Kinloch. I had to find out what he wanted from me, and I needed to be sure any decisions I made were for the safety of not only myself, but my baby. Our survival was at stake.

"In good time," he responded, holding out his arm to me.

Figuring I needed to play the game, I wrapped my

arm in his and allowed him to escort me forward again. "Where are we going?"

"To our community," he answered, glancing at me with arched brows. "Don't be afraid."

"I'm not," I answered quickly, maybe too quickly. I mean, it had to be pretty obvious that I was completely and totally freaked out.

"No one will do you any harm," he said softly.

I didn't respond, focusing instead on the trees ahead as feelings of nausea worked their way through my body. Rather than magicking them away, at the risk of possibly drawing attention to my condition, I just dealt with the sickness and focused on my surroundings. I could see the outline of what looked like homes through the trunks of the enormous pines. As we walked through the darkness of the forest and emerged on the other side, I noticed rows and rows of white, single-room dwellings that reminded me of something you might see on a military base. Each house was the exact copy of the one next to it, and each had a perfectly manicured grass lawn delineated by a white picket fence. People walked to and fro, some disappearing over the horizon of the hills, going God only knew where. All of them seemed busy. I mean, I didn't catch a glimpse of anyone kicking back on their front porch or taking a catnap in the sunshine.

"Are these homes?" I asked, realizing how stupid the question was as soon as it came out.

But Luce didn't belittle me. He just nodded. "All of our people are well provided for. We believe in community. We exist for one another."

That was when it hit me—I was in enemy territory.

I was a prisoner in the Lurker camp and wasn't going to be getting out anytime soon.

You need to learn as much as you can, Jolie, I told myself. *Ask questions and find their weaknesses. You'll never get another chance like this.*

"Where are we?" I asked Luce, figuring it was as good a place to start as any.

He heard me but just shook his head. "Although you are my revered guest, I am certain you will understand my hesitation in revealing our whereabouts. It is highly confidential and very few know our specific location."

I looked around us again at all the white houses, which suddenly looked like giants' teeth. "You mean that the people who live here don't even know where 'here' is?"

He nodded. "That is exactly what I mean."

I shook my head. "Then everyone is being held captive?"

Luce chuckled lightly and then tsked me as if I were completely clueless. "Of course not. They are all here of their own free will." I was about to ask another question, but he shushed me with a shake of his head. "We will have ample opportunity to answer your questions, my Queen," he said, and I couldn't tell if he was patronizing me or not. "In the meantime, if you would allow me, may I use this opportunity to take you on a tour?"

I nodded, figuring I needed to buy myself as much time as I could while gaining as much knowledge about the Lurkers as possible.

Jolie! It was Rand's voice in my head.

Rand. I said his name and relaxed as relief began

welling up inside me. I'd been worried that our mental telepathy wouldn't work here—wherever here was.

Where are you? he asked.

We can't communicate like this, I thought in return, all too aware that Luce could probably listen to my thoughts. *I'm in the Lurker camp and I'm afraid our conversations are being overheard.*

Are you okay? he asked, his voice quaking. *God, just tell me you're okay, and as soon as I get my hands on those fucking bastards—*

I am for now. Rely on our bond, Rand, I said. I wasn't sure if it would be possible for us to relay information without actual communication, but it was all I could think of at the moment.

"What does this tour entail?" I asked Luce, hoping to draw his attention away from what was going on in my head.

He nodded as he led me through the last alcove of cookie-cutter houses and we stepped onto a dirt pathway. It led down a small hill, with massive pines on either side of us. I felt like I was on a tour of a retirement village or something. It just had that sterile sort of feel to it.

"I will explain about my kind—our kind," he finished, offering me a quick smile.

I will find you, Rand persisted. *Do you have any idea where you are?*

No. I swallowed hard, eyeing Luce to see if he could sense that I was conversing with Rand. But he didn't divert his attention from the trail ahead, so I figured my secret was safe. Well, I hoped it was anyway.

Rand, we can't continue talking like this because there's a good chance someone can overhear us, I stressed again. *I will try contacting you again when I'm able,* I finished.

I didn't hear his voice again, so I figured he'd gotten the message. I took a deep breath, feeling the sudden need to cry, but I squelched it. I needed all of my wits about me—I couldn't give in to emotions that would do me no good. I had to be my own wall of fortitude and courage, because I was determined to take this one step at a time—I was going to survive.

"You are most highly esteemed by our people," Luce continued as he smiled sincerely at me. "They have longed for a leader, and now you have finally returned to fulfill your destiny."

"It seems like you're doing a fine job of leading them," I responded, wondering where all this "leader" business was going.

He nodded and pursed his lips. "I need a front-runner, Jolie. I need someone to exist between me and my people."

"You're saying you need an assistant?" I asked, and laughed shallowly.

"No," he said, irritated. "You were meant to return to us, to take your rightful place as figurehead for our people. Well, you and one other."

"One other?"

He shook his head. "You will meet her in time. For now, it is important for you to understand that you are here for a reason and I shall act as your guide."

So he was basically the male counterpart of Mercedes. Although where Mercedes was absolutely honest about her intentions for me to be Queen, somehow I didn't get the same feeling from Luce. It was almost as if he was making up this "leader" stuff just because

I was already a Queen. Sort of like offering me a job while knowing I wouldn't want to be demoted in title or status.

Not knowing what to make of the whole leader business, I said nothing. I could see that the path we were on led to a two-story white building that looked like a white box with a few gray windows. There was no one around, and everything was completely silent, almost as if we were on a set of some sort. "Where is everyone?" I asked.

He smiled. "Keeping busy, no doubt. Each person has his or her own duty."

I said nothing else, trying to shake the feeling that I had somehow wandered into an old *Twilight Zone* episode. "Are you the only elder?" I asked abruptly.

He smiled at that. "No, but I am the elder who possesses magic." *Otherwise known as a witch*, I told myself, almost wanting to smile.

"And let me guess, there's also an elder who represents those who possess . . . fangs?" I said.

Luce chuckled, then nodded. "Though here, their teeth are not their best attribute. We value their exceptional speed and strength."

"What do you call them?"

"Daywalkers," he finished.

"And yourselves?"

"We are the Elementals," he said, and I was reminded of how he'd called himself an Elemental earlier.

"So there are two elders, you and the Daywalker one?" I summed up.

Luce nodded. "Nairn, yes. I will introduce you to her in time."

I wasn't sure why, but I swallowed hard, under Luce's intense gaze. "In time?" I asked.

"She does not interact well with strangers," he finished.

I nodded, filing this information away for future use. Although, I had to wonder if there would ever be a future, since I had no idea what Luce's intentions were. I had to guess, though, that I wasn't on the "to die" list, since he could have exterminated me long ago if that were the case. And that thought did bring me some relief.

Reaching the white building with the gray windows, Luce held the door open for me. I walked in and he followed me. "This is our hospital," he said, looking around with obvious pride. Women in nurse uniforms passed by in an apparent rush, while patients hobbled around. It was a small waiting room with plastic chairs lining each wall. On the far side there was a registration area, where a woman in blue scrubs was smiling at us.

"My elder," she said as she bowed her head to address Luce.

It was the first time we'd come across any other Lurkers, and I couldn't help but gulp. While Luce pretty much looked how you'd imagine a centuries-old elder would look, the rest of the people in this hospital looked exactly like that—people. They just seemed so nondescript, so unthreatening in their busyness.

As I watched the scene before me, a nurse wheeled a handsome young patient past us. Both of them smiled up at Luce, dipping their heads with obvious reverence. They eyed me with surprise, probably since I was a stranger. But I couldn't say my mind was wholly focused on them. Instead, my eyes darted around the room, taking in each of the patients as something occurred to me.

"All of the patients here are young men," I said, not even realizing I'd said it out loud.

Luce nodded then and sighed. "You are quite observant, and your observation brings me to a touchy subject."

He led me down a long corridor, the white tiles of the floor and the twitching of the overhead fluorescent lights about as "hospital" as you could get. We stopped in front of an elevator and he hit the call key. He didn't say anything as we rode up to the second floor, and neither did I.

When the elevator doors opened, he offered his arm again and I took it, letting him lead me down another long corridor. He paused at a nurse's station just outside a door. I peeked through the window and noticed a bunch of beds, but that was really all I could make out.

"How are they?" Luce asked the nurse on duty, a stout woman with a manly face.

She smiled at him, dropping her head, just as the others had. Then she looked at me, wearing the wary expression of a watchdog.

"She is one of us," Luce answered. I felt a chill flow through me at the thought, but I said nothing.

"They are not doing well," she answered. Ignoring me, she added, "As usual."

Luce just nodded and dropped his attention to my arm, which was still looped through his. The nurse stood up, opened the door for us, and we walked inside.

There were twelve beds, each separated by a brightly colored curtain. Lying on each of them were young men who couldn't have been older than twenty-five. Most appeared to be sleeping, their eyes closed. The one closest to us, though, was wide-awake, his eyes blazing with fear.

"It is going to be all right, my young one," Luce said to him as he leaned over and patted the boy's shoulder encouragingly.

The boy didn't respond—he just continued staring at Luce with wide, terrified eyes. His cheeks were sunken, his face so hollow you could see the shadow of his cheekbones. His skin had a grayish tinge to it and he had the overall look of someone who'd been starved.

"He cannot respond," Luce said, sighing deeply as he shook his head in apparent pity.

"What's wrong with them?" I asked, realizing that each of the young men in the room seemed to have the same deathly pallor and withered frames.

"It is the curse of the male Daywalkers," Luce said, then turned his old gray eyes on me. "They never live past their twenty-first birthdays."

And then it all became clear—why Luce was so determined to have me, why he'd come up with this ridiculous notion that I was meant to rule his people. He wanted me to reanimate them. It suddenly also made complete sense why the Lurkers so rarely attacked us—their best soldiers were dying. They had larger numbers than us, but their numbers were steadily dwindling.

"But the Elementals don't have this problem?" I

asked, trying to understand exactly what the situation was.

Luce shook his head. "No, but we are cursed with our own issues."

"Such as?" I asked, figuring I had nothing to lose. I had to admit that I was surprised he'd told me this much so far. He seemed to place a blind trust in me, which was something I hadn't imagined a seasoned elder would ever do. It made me more wary of him than ever, because it was clear that he didn't intend to let me go. As far as he was concerned, I *was* one of his people.

"The Elementals rarely bear males," he finished.

I almost wanted to laugh, but it wasn't really funny, given my position in all of this. "Somehow you found out about my gift," I said softly. "You want me to reanimate your dead."

Luce faced me again and his gaze was fervent, searching. "You were always one of us, child," he said. "Your gift was supposed to be ours, not that of the usurpers."

I wanted to yell at him and accuse him of lying, but I held my temper, figuring it was better to play along and make him think I was buying this. "How are you so sure that they won't just die again as soon as I reanimate them?"

Luce nodded as if he'd already considered this same question. "I am not so sure, as you say. But we will not know until we try, will we?" I didn't say anything, so he continued. "And that brings me to our next subject."

I glanced up at him in surprise, but he said nothing more. He turned to face the nurse who was busily tending to the boy on the cot in front of us. "Where is Number 134?" he asked the woman.

"Number 134" must be one of the patients, and I didn't like the fact that he was just a number to Luce—I glanced down at the row of cots and noticed that one was empty.

"We lost him a mere hour or so ago," the woman answered, her face a mask of indifference.

"Is he in the morgue?" Luce continued.

She nodded, and he turned on his heel, heading for the hallway. I kept up with him. "Let me guess, we're off to the morgue?" I asked.

Luce didn't acknowledge my question, just kept his eyes trained forward as we reached the elevator. When it arrived, he held the door for me again and clicked the button that looked like it would take us down to the basement or, in this case, the morgue.

"I need to know, Jolie," he started, and turned to face me, his eyes yearning. "I need to know if you can help them."

I gulped down an acid response and wondered if I should reveal my gift—if I should reanimate one of their dead Daywalkers. If I did, Luce would never let me go. 'Course, if I didn't or couldn't, he might use it as an excuse to kill me. In this case, I figured it would be better to prove useful, better to be considered an arrow in his quiver than something that needed to be taken out with the trash.

"We are in the process of searching for the missing gene in the Daywalkers," he continued, holding the door for me once we reached the bottom floor of the hospital. I walked outside and waited for him to take the lead again.

"Missing gene?" I repeated.

"Yes, once we can identify that gene, we can cure the Daywalkers of this horrible illness."

"Then you believe that the sickness they succumb to is a problem with their DNA?" I asked as we walked down a dimly lit corridor, then paused outside two double doors with MORGUE painted in black across them.

Luce nodded. "Yes, quite so."

I took a deep breath, suddenly feeling winded and nauseous. But I didn't want to cure myself, since I was still worried he might somehow detect my magic, figuring out that I was pregnant. Who knew? Maybe he was already aware of the fact; but because he hadn't mentioned it, I didn't think he was.

He pushed through the double doors, and I immediately spotted the covered body on top of a steel hospital cart. I felt myself swallow hard. What if I couldn't reanimate the Daywalker? What if my powers were completely useless? I mean, at this point I was convinced that Luce's whole line about me being Queen or leader of his people was a bunch of BS, because he and Nairn were obviously their leaders. Really, he only wanted me for my ability, and if I no longer had that ability . . . I would become a liability—especially now that he'd explained top secret stuff to me and given me a tour of his camp.

I realized then that if I didn't reanimate this deceased Daywalker, I might as well take his place.

I have to do this. I have to succeed.

He lifted the white sheet from over the boy's face and I felt myself recoil. I'd never seen a dead body up close and personal before. Sure, I'd watched people die on the battlefield of Culloden when Rand's forces had gone up against Bella's, but this was different. This was way too close for comfort.

But I had a job to do, and damn it all, I was going to do it. I said nothing—I just approached the Day-walker and tried to calm my frantic heart. I glanced up at Luce, who nodded at me, signifying that I should give it a shot. Turning back to the still form before me, I placed my hands on either side of the corpse's face, reflexively wanting to pull my hands away because he was so cold to the touch. But I forced myself to stay put and closed my eyes, begging my abilities to deliver themselves.

And that was when I was whisked into a parallel plane—a place that existed between the present and the past.

I was standing in the middle of the hospital wing that I'd just left, and as I glanced down the row of cots, I noticed that each of them was occupied, in-cluding number 134. I walked down the row and paused just beside his cot, knowing I would need to wait until the moment when life no longer pulsed through him. But this was the tough part because when the cause of death wasn't traumatic and obvi-ous, it was hard to figure out when to step in. But I'd done it before and I would do it again.

I leaned down until I could detect the faint rise and fall of the boy's chest, could feel his shallow breaths against my cheek. I closed my eyes, and at the very second when I couldn't feel his breath any longer, I opened my eyes and placed my hands on his shoul-ders.

I jolted as I came out of my trance, nearly falling backward in my shock. Righting myself against the counter, I glanced around and saw that I was back in the morgue. Luce was staring at me with surprise. The moment of reckoning was on me. It felt like ages passed as I turned my neck in the direction of the still form lying on the cot.

The boy was blinking wide as his chest rose with the breath of life.

Thirteen

That evening, Luce showed me to my "guesthouse," which was really my prison cell. I mean, I wasn't dumb, I could see through this whole charade. I served a purpose—that's all there was to it. But the good news was that because I was useful, he had no plans to kill me . . . not yet anyway. I had to imagine, though, that the Lurkers were going to continue pushing for the extinction of the creatures of the Underworld, and my next bit of business with Luce was to find out why. But I was leaving that until tomorrow. For now, I was exhausted and had other plans in mind.

My guesthouse was one of the nondescript white buildings I'd observed when Luce gave me his tour. I was at the end of one of the dirt lanes, titled "A Street." Inside, it looked about as inviting as a cheap motel room—white walls, dark brown carpeting, and lighter brown linoleum in the kitchen and entryway. The furniture was all a lackluster off-white and included two sofas, a bed, a coffee table, and a kitchen table with two matching chairs.

"As these are guest provisions, you will not find

food in the refrigerator," Luce said as soon as he'd unlocked the front door and ushered me into the living room. He then smiled apologetically. "We will provide you with your three daily meals."

I glanced around the dreary accommodations and smiled with faux gratitude, reminding myself that it was important to act subservient. "Does the water work, at least?" I asked, thinking that nothing sounded better than a shower.

Luce nodded and then bowed slightly. "Please sleep well. We have much to do tomorrow." I glanced at him questioningly and he added, "I am eager to introduce you to Nairn."

But I couldn't say I shared his excitement. I nodded and watched as he opened the door.

"Today was a great feat, Jolie," he said softly. "You reaffirmed everything I imagined about you. Your power is great. I have never come across someone with your abilities before." I looked away, unable to subdue the feelings of guilt that had been plaguing me since I'd reanimated the Daywalker. I mean, I'd basically brought my enemy back to life and who knew what that meant? Who knew if he'd end up killing one of my people? Hopefully, he'd just die off again soon, since his DNA must still be missing that piece that allowed for a normal life span. I had to assume that was the case, because although I could bring the dead back to life, it wasn't like I could correct their ailments.

At the sound of the door closing, I realized I was alone. Well, as alone as I could be, considering that I probably had guards outside my door. There was undoubtedly also some magical force field in place that would prevent me from using my own powers. Yes, I could have checked—I could have woven a spell that would reveal the strength of the magic aligned against me, but I figured it was better to keep my magic to myself, better to keep a low profile until I knew what I was up against.

For now, I would focus on enjoying my pseudo privacy and getting in touch with Rand. I knew I couldn't trust our telekinetic connection—mainly because I figured that Luce would be able to breach it since Mercedes could. I decided to rely on our bond instead. I wasn't sure what made me think it might work. I mean, I had nothing to go on because it wasn't like I knew much about being bonded. But I also didn't have anything else up my sleeve, and knowing how deeply connected bonded couples were, I assumed it was my best and only option.

My hope was to use our bond to send Rand information without actually thinking the words in sentence form. If I could somehow tune him in to me so he could see what I was seeing, experience what I was experiencing, I had to imagine that he'd be able to figure out where I was and come up with some sort of plan to get me out.

I wasn't sure it would work, and chances were it wouldn't, but it was worth a shot. Besides, what alternatives did I have? None.

Wanting more privacy than the living room afforded, I walked into the bedroom, which was just as unremarkable as the rest of the house. I took a seat on the bed. The blinds were already closed, lending the room an eerie darkness.

Taking a deep breath, I closed my eyes and tried to

reach out to Rand, careful not to think in words, as much as I wanted to. Thinking in terms of feelings and images was actually much more difficult than I would have guessed. After a few seconds I was no better off than when I'd started.

I tried to bring to mind images of things that made me happy, but then I found myself transfixed on the colors of the images—the azure sky above Kinloch, the green of Christa's eyes. When those thoughts merged into thoughts about how to spell each of those colors. I opened my eyes.

Ugh, this is impossible! I railed back at that voice inside my head that had come up with this idea in the first place. *Maybe this whole thing was just stupid! Maybe I'm just going to be stuck here for the rest of my life, however short that may be!*

Jolie, stop it! Don't let yourself go there because you won't be able to come back! the voice responded. *Now stop feeling sorry for yourself and try it again!*

That other side of me went silent, so the Tony Robbins side continued. *They say a picture is worth a thousand words, right?*

Yeah, I guess.

Then use that! Focus on images, on feelings . . .

I sighed, trying to remember a situation that had brought me joy. Immediately, a memory of Rand and me lying in bed came to mind. I could see the outline of his beautiful body, and when he chuckled at something I said, I saw his dimples and could feel happiness welling up inside of me. I remembered being there in person, experiencing every bit of him.

I shut my eyes tighter and focused on that feeling of complete love and trust between Rand and me. I focused on all those emotions that had helped to create our bond. And then I felt those feelings being reciprocated, felt heat burning within me, and suddenly all the images within my head scattered and were replaced with just one. And it was an image of me—I was dressed in jeans and a white T-shirt and laughing at something silly Rand had said, shaking my head at him. I felt my hand—er, Rand's hand—reach out and run his fingers down the line of my face, and I watched myself blush as I dropped my gaze to the floor.

I was in Rand's mind! We were in each other's minds, which meant . . .

It had worked! Our bond was enough.

Now that obstacle number one—finding out whether our bond was adequate enough for us to communicate—was no longer an issue, I addressed obstacle number two—how I was going to transfer information to Rand. Swallowing hard, I decided to start easy. I began with the room around me, staring at the closet door, the bed with its brown paisley comforter, the oak nightstand, the white lamp sitting on top of it. I was trying to allow Rand to experience exactly what I was experiencing. It seemed easier to zone out on everything around me, letting my mind wander.

Once I'd taken in everything the room had to offer, I took another deep breath and allowed my mind to go blank. I was asking Rand if he'd received any of it. At first there was nothing—no response, just the blankness of my own thoughts. But then something happened that threw me completely. The sudden smell of sea salt was thick in my nose. It was as if I were standing on the beach, watching the waves. I could even feel the mist of the ocean air stinging my cheeks, and the soft sand between my toes was so real, I had to verify that I was still wearing my shoes. I knew then that Rand must be standing on the beach at Kinloch, sending me all his sensory experiences. It was working!

At first I just felt happy, then homesickness welled up in me and I wished more than ever before that I was standing with Rand on the shores of Kinloch at this very moment, that I could experience the beauty and tranquillity of my home, our home. I felt something rise up inside of me—hope. It was almost as if Rand were in the room, holding me and promising that everything was going to be okay. I could feel his determination, his love. He was vowing that he would find me, that he would ensure my safety.

I realized then how truly close we were—how our love had bonded us in such a way that we could communicate without words. I felt tears starting in my eyes and I closed them tightly, running my hands across my belly as I promised our unborn child that I would see us out of this mess. I was a survivor, and now more than ever before, I was going to rely on my instincts. I was going to beat Luce at his own game. One way or another, I was going to get us back to Kinloch Kirk.

At the sound of a knock on the front door, my nostalgia abruptly subsided, replaced by a cool sort of calm—my poker face. I stood up from where I'd been sitting on the bed and started for the living room. Taking a seat on the couch, I tried to maintain my calm facade, even though my mind was still racing with everything that had just happened.

"Come in," I called. It occurred to me then that

Luce might have realized what was going on and had decided to put the kibosh on it.

But when the door opened, I saw that my visitor wasn't Luce at all. It was a woman.

"I brought you dinner," she said in a voice that didn't sound particularly happy, the darkness of the night obscuring her features. But what I did notice was that her accent sounded American. And I had to hope that was a sign—that we were in the States. The sooner I could find out where "here" was, the sooner Rand could get me out.

"Thanks," I answered. It was obvious that she didn't intend to step inside, so I stood up and walked toward her.

As soon as I got a good look at her, my breath caught. It was as if every hair on my body stood at attention and I could feel energy coursing over my skin like the pitter-patter of thousands of marching ants. It's hard to explain what exactly happened to me, but it was like I'd been struck with déjà vu. I'd never seen this girl before, but the feeling that I knew her hit me over the head like a sack of bricks.

Realizing I was standing there like a complete idiot, I tried to pull my attention away from her, tried to focus on something else, but no matter how hard I tried, I couldn't stop looking at her face. It was just so . . . familiar. And even stranger, she was staring at me the same way—neither of us saying anything, while the same energy seemed to sparkle off both of us, joining us in some sort of ethereal hug.

"Have . . . have we met before?" I asked, as if my mind were an open book—and she had the power to turn to any page she wanted and read my secrets. In fact, I hadn't even intended to ask her the question—it just sort of broached itself, with a mind of its own.

"No." She shook her head as if she were as much at a loss as I was, then she cleared her throat and took a step back, to put some distance between us. As soon as she backed away, the halo of energy that seemed to join us died down a bit, until it was just lightly pulsating.

"Do you feel it too?" I asked, awed. I didn't consider the fact that I'd completely dropped my defenses—that she was my enemy.

She didn't respond right away, but after a moment she shook her head emphatically. It seemed she was trying to convince herself as much as me. "No," she said at last, then narrowed her eyes at me, pushing the plate of food closer, uncomfortable with the whole exchange. And I couldn't really blame her. "Are you going to take this or what?"

"Oh," I said in surprise, and taking the plate from her, placed it on the table beside the door. I hadn't been hungry before, and now I was even less so. No, my mind wasn't on food. Where exactly it was, I couldn't say. I noticed something in her eyes then that showed me that she was indeed experiencing this strange reaction too. Her reserve somewhat lifted as I approached her—some sort of surprise that was even now causing conflict in her blue eyes.

She lifted her long curtain of light brown hair, streaked with gold, from her shoulders and secured it with a hair tie. I could suddenly see her face more clearly, even in the low light. As soon as I did, my breath caught in my throat.

Oh my God! She . . . she looks like me!

We looked so similar, we could have been sisters, and suddenly Luce's words came back to haunt me: *You've always been one of us.* But I refused to believe for one minute that this girl was related to me. It was far more likely that she had been magicked—a ploy of Luce's to ensure that I believed I was truly a Lurker. The thought allowed me to breathe more easily anyway.

I knew who I was. I was Jolie Wilkins from Spokane, Washington. I'd seen plenty of pictures of my mother pregnant with me, and several photo albums documented my baby and toddler years. Furthermore, my mother was the type of person who believed in bare reality. She would never have kept something like adoption from me—she didn't sugarcoat things.

I am not a Lurker.

I am not a Lurker.

I am not *a Lurker.*

I still couldn't shake away my surprise when I focused on her face again. The more I studied her, though, the more I realized that while the resemblance was definitely there; it wasn't uncanny. Her lips, however, were the same shape, her almond-shaped eyes were the exact shade of cornflower blue, and her pert, upturned nose hinted at the same English and Irish origins that mine did.

"Do you need anything else?" she asked, her voice coming from deep within her throat. I could see from her eyes that she was just as shocked as I was.

"Who are you?" I demanded.

She swallowed hard and then took a deep breath,

exhaling through her nose as she debated whether to tell me. She swallowed again. "Bryn."

"Are you a Daywalker?" I asked, suddenly wanting to stall her, even though I knew she wanted to leave. But I wanted to learn everything I could about her in order to further distance myself, ensuring that we had nothing in common, especially not DNA.

No, she is a Lurker and I am the Queen of the Underworld.

There was just something so familiar about her, and it made her somehow feel safe—like she was the only friend I had in this godforsaken place. Of course the thought was ludicrous because I didn't know this woman from Eve, and she was as much my enemy as Luce. And that was when I returned to my original suspicion—this had to be some sort of stunt Luce was pulling to win me over.

It was all very conniving and very smart.

"God, no!" she said, then laughed at the very thought that she might have something in common with the descendants of vampires. "I have nothing to do with those leeches."

I was surprised by her indignation toward the Daywalkers. Luce had made it seem that everyone here liked one another. But apparently the Lurkers suffered from their own sense of civil discrimination. "Then you're an Elemental?" I asked.

She just nodded, her jaw tight and her body rigid. It was more obvious than ever that she was uncomfortable.

"Bryn is one of our most talented Elementals," Luce said from behind her. She jumped, surprised, then pasted a smile on her face and bowed her head in deference to him, her irritation only visible in the way her lips were pressed tightly together. He glanced down at her and smiled with obvious pride. "She is a healer and one of our finest warriors."

That was when I noticed her outfit—she was dressed all in black: tight, black capri stretch pants and a black sports bra. Strapped to both of her wrists were small knives, and a dagger was strapped to her right thigh. She was about my height—not exactly tall, but average size for a woman. Where I had a softer overall look, she was pure muscle. I could see it in the lines of her arms and her thighs. Her waist was minute even though she managed to have an ample bustline.

They must be fake, I told myself. Either way, she had a figure that most women would die for. And what was even stranger, while recognizing how much she looked like me—and I didn't particularly think of myself as a showstopper—she was beautiful. No, stunning. And she was the type of beautiful that was indisputable. She was gorgeous.

"If you're an Elemental," I said, wanting desperately to understand the Lurkers and how their community worked, "why are you trained in weapons defense?" I was referring to the weapons strapped to her body. "Why are you trained in knives?"

She was about to speak, but Luce took that opportunity from her. She gave him a look of displeasure. "One cannot always rely on magic," he started, smiling at me as if asking how I took my tea. "Having only one defensive strategy is not much of a strategy at all, is it?"

I gulped, realizing any defensive strategy they had

was intended for use against my people. I simply nodded.

"May I return to my training?" Bryn asked Luce, her left eyebrow raised in an expression that resembled exasperation.

He nodded slowly, exhaling as he did.

"We will discuss this later," she said as she stormed away, which gave me a bit of a shock. I mean, I couldn't imagine anyone talking to Luce that way—he just didn't seem the type to allow it. Yet he had with her. Interesting.

I saw now that he seemed uncomfortable, color flooding his cheeks. "She is young and very able," he said, "though she has not yet learned how to rein in her temper." He seemed almost apologetic.

"She's a healer, you said?" I asked, trying to understand just how powerful she was. I wasn't sure why, but I felt the information would prove useful to me at some point.

"She is one of our most powerful, yes," Luce said, a fond smile taking hold of his mouth.

"And yet she hasn't been able to heal the Daywalkers," I said.

The smile fell off Luce's mouth. "She has done wonders for them. She's been able to prolong many of their lives and has saved them from an inordinate amount of pain."

"Hmm," I said, sounding unimpressed.

"My hope is that the two of you together will be able to achieve the impossible—that you will combine your abilities to heal the Daywalkers, once and for all."

I shook my head. "That sounds like an immensely difficult task."

He nodded. "That it is, that it is." But there was something in his eyes that pointed to the fact that he wasn't used to taking no for an answer.

I stayed silent, wanting only to return to the privacy of my quarters so I could puzzle through everything that had just happened and decide on a plan moving forward.

"Are you settled in for the night, then?" he asked. It seemed he was intent on leaving, which was just as well because I couldn't wait for him to go.

I gave him a courteous nod.

"Then I shall see you in the morning, and we will continue our tour then."

"Okay," I said, surprised there was more Lurker camp to tour. The compound hadn't seemed that large on initial inspection.

Luce nodded and with a slight smile turned and walked away.

Wanting only my privacy, I closed the door and exhaled deeply, my mind running wild as I wondered why Bryn had caused such an influx of bizarre feelings in me. Why did I feel like I knew her?

*
 *
  *
Fourteen
  *
 *
  *

Before I went to bed that night, I tried to relay some of the information I had on the Lurkers to Rand. But I quickly realized it was harder to convey memories than to transmit information about what was going on in the here and now.

Based on the feelings of confusion that came to me through the bond, I was not successful. From what I could gather, he only received random bits and pieces of information. I decided to call it a night. Surprisingly, I actually managed to sleep. I'm not sure whether Luce had put some sort of charm on the house, the room, the bed, or me, but if he had, it worked. All that mattered was that I was able to get in some Z's, and for that I was happy. Why? Because today was going to be a big day for me. I was determined to get more answers and pass those answers along to Rand. First and foremost, I needed to figure out where the hell I was.

As soon as the sun pierced through the slats of the blinds, hitting me squarely in the eyes, I sat up. Throwing the bedclothes off, I stretched, reaching for my pants and shirt from the chair back beside the bed. They were the same clothes I'd worn yesterday—I'd slept in my bra and panties.

Once I was dressed, I strolled into the living room and peered through the windows, where I watched the people of Lurkerville hurrying off to their day jobs. I had to imagine all their jobs centered around this compound. Some were going to the hospital, others were probably in charge of security. There had to be some sort of school, and the list went on. It was like a bustling minitown all encapsulated behind a very high, very barbed wire fence.

A knock on the door pulled me from my reverie. I figured it had to be Luce. I went to answer it, and was surprised to find Bryn standing there. She was dressed in her fighting attire and was holding a pile of clothes. She thrust the clothes into my hands without so much as a smile, but did offer me a raised brow when she registered the fact that I was wearing my outfit from the previous day.

"I'm sure you'll be happy to get out of those," she said in a bitchy way then, dispelling whatever sympathy I'd assumed she had for me, looked me up and down. But somehow her less than gracious attitude didn't seem real. It seemed artificial, trumped up, like she was trying too hard.

A few seconds later I was again struck by the feeling that I knew her and, more eerily, that I knew her very well. But I was also convinced that the feelings weren't genuine. It was nothing more than a trick of Luce's magic, an attempt to win me over to their side. The more I thought about it, the more it angered me, and the more resolute I was to ignore it.

"Thanks for the clothes," I muttered, offering her

an identical copy of the frown she'd just given me. Immediately, the frown vanished from her face, replaced with surprise. Why? I had no clue.

"Your breakfast is on the counter," she said hurriedly, and wrapped her arms around herself as if suddenly uncomfortable. "Luce said to let you know that he'll be coming for you in twenty minutes."

"My breakfast is on the counter?" I repeated suspiciously, deliberately ignoring the part about Luce. Glancing back at the kitchen counter, I spotted a tray with juice, coffee, and a covered plate. Anger began spiraling inside of me as I thought about someone entering my private accommodations without my knowledge. "Did you guys just come in while I was sleeping?" I asked in an irritated voice. Granted, I understood I was a prisoner, but a little privacy would have been nice. "I thought I was a 'revered guest' or some such crap."

Bryn seemed surprised by my anger, but smiled at the "revered guest" part. She shook her head. "You're right—you aren't much of a guest. Apparently, you're smarter than you look."

"I look like you," I threw back at her. She swallowed hard but didn't respond.

She shrugged, trying to maintain an air of ennui. But I couldn't help noticing that she still hadn't reacted to my comment about how we looked alike, which meant she was just as aware of it as I was.

Yeah, but who cares, Jolie? That adversarial voice piped up within me. *Looking like someone doesn't mean anything.*

Come on, we look a lot alike!

Okay, so for the sake of argument, let's say you do.

So what? What's the point of it? What are you trying to say?

I'm not saying anything.

Okay then. Shut it!

"Do you always argue with yourself?" she asked, and I felt my chin nearly hit the floor.

"You just . . . overheard me?"

The look she gave me told me she wasn't joking. She just nodded. "I'm a sensitive and you're . . . pretty loud."

"What the heck does that mean?"

She frowned. "That I can hear idiotic arguments that go on in people's heads."

I tried not to think about anything at all, but I was suddenly overflowing with questions. Did all of the Lurkers have this talent or was she the only one? And if she had overheard my self-debate, what other information was she privy to? Had she been listening to me from the get-go? God! What had I been thinking about all this time? I started to think of Rand but immediately stopped myself.

"Did you get any of that?" I asked.

She laughed, then shook her head. "No, this time you did a good job of hiding it."

"So going back to what you said before you started eavesdropping on me," I began, completely not okay with the fact that she could hear my innermost thoughts. It was a sign that I would need to be even more careful. I had to keep the proverbial lid on my mind, because I didn't know who else possessed such a gift. Maybe Luce? If that were the case, I basically had as much privacy as a goldfish in a bowl.

"I wasn't eavesdropping," she said, almost sounding annoyed. "I couldn't keep your voice out of my head. You sounded like two old women bitching at each other, and I couldn't concentrate on anything else."

I frowned again, a bit offended by her comparison of my innermost thoughts to two old hens. "Anyway, what were you talking about when you replied I'm not a 'revered guest'?" I planned to stash all this information for later, when I could figure out what to do with it.

She cleared her throat. "Just that you are not as much of a guest as Luce would like you to believe and, unlike him, I don't think you're stupid enough to believe it."

Strangely enough, what she said somehow endeared her to me because I felt like she wouldn't sugarcoat anything. She wasn't afraid to tell me how it was, warts, moles, blemishes, and all. "So now we get to the crux of the whole matter," I said with a smile. I liked being able to speak openly with her, without Luce's dog and pony show. "What are your plans for me?"

She shook her head. "I don't know."

I raised a brow and just studied her.

"I know you're here to reanimate our dead Daywalkers. Luce means business, so if you know what's good for you, you'll do it."

"And what then?"

She shook her head. "I don't question him. I just obey."

Somehow I didn't imagine that was true, not based on how she'd barked at him last night. Nope, something wasn't adding up, but I could tell she was eager to be on her way, so I knew better than to annoy her.

She offered me a hurried glare that signaled that our conversation was over. "And as to breaking and entering," she started in a highfalutin way, returning to our earlier conversation, "we are Elementals and therefore possess magic." She said it like she was addressing a child. "So, no, I didn't break into your room, I just prepared your breakfast the Elemental way." Then she smiled smugly, like she was impressed with herself.

I said nothing, so she must have figured it was her cue to exit. She turned on her toes and strode away, leaving me to wonder how the hell I was ever going to get out of this place. Not finding an immediate answer, I closed the door and headed to the kitchen area. I uncovered my plate, which contained two pieces of wheat toast, scrambled eggs, and a slice of ham. It looked good except for the ham, which resembled rawhide.

So the Lurkers had magicked my breakfast. I had to wonder what else they'd magicked into it—maybe a truth serum or something equally unappealing. I pushed the plate away and decided I wasn't hungry, even though my stomach growled in protest. Putting the cover back on the plate, I walked into the living room again, throwing myself onto the couch.

I needed information and I needed it now. Knowing Luce could show up any second, I closed my eyes and tried to open my connection to Rand. I needed him to experience everything just as it was, to see what I was seeing. Hopefully, if I kept the bond open long enough, he'd be able to figure out how the Lurker camp was set up, and he would get to see Luce and Bryn. I wasn't going to allow myself to bemoan how I'd already missed out on importing a wealth of information to Rand. There was no use in crying over spilt milk. But now it was imperative for me to make sure our connection was ready before anything else happened.

I noticed an all-encompassing feeling of determination rise up inside me. It was Rand, feeling my intentions. He was ready and willing. I could tell he'd been waiting for me to contact him, that he was resolved to put whatever information I sent him to good use. I smiled as I felt warmth and safety bubble up within me.

I didn't have time to communicate with him, however, because there was another knock on the door. I jumped up immediately, and could feel Rand's concerns about my early morning visitor. I pulled the door open and found Luce before me. Rand's anger and concern raged through me—my brain had apparently introduced Luce as the Lurker elder who had whisked me away to Lurkerville. I tried to swallow Rand's furious feelings so I could focus on Luce. Of all things, I didn't want him to be alerted to our private conversation.

Apparently, completely oblivious—thank God—Luce smiled broadly. I'll say this for him: He was good at playing the part of generous host. "Are you ready to begin your day?" he asked.

I just nodded, finding it extremely difficult to play along, to pretend like I wasn't boiling inside over the fact that these . . . these beings expected me to bring back their dead so they could build a stronger army against my own people! I allowed the feelings to penetrate my very core, just so I could relay them to

Rand. Hopefully he was seeing and experiencing everything firsthand, as I was. As soon as that thought passed through my head, I could feel Rand receiving it, and I knew he was right here with me. "Yes, I'm ready," I said, and started forward, begrudgingly taking his arm when he offered it to me. I could feel the heat of rage brewing within me, and I wasn't sure if it was Rand's reaction or my own.

Luce escorted me out of my temporary housing and down A Street until we hit the main street, which didn't even have a name, probably because it didn't need one. The camp was set up was like a toothbrush. The main street was the handle and A, B, C, and D Streets were like the bristles, running parallel to one another.

We walked past another three rows of homes on B, C, and D Streets, all identical to mine, but while I remembered that the hospital was to the right of the dirt path, now we took a left, walking through a dense curtain of pine trees into an open pasture. Assembled in the pasture were about a hundred or so Lurkers, all dressed in what I presumed was combat-training gear. The women wore tightly fitted pants and sports bras, like what Bryn had been wearing, and the men were clad only in shorts.

Even though the majority of the men were extremely young, twenty or younger, they all looked like soldiers. There was something dangerous and lethal in their eyes. They were like trained automatons. What scared me the most, what I hadn't been quite so aware of on my tour of the compound, was that there were so many of them! Maybe it was because I'd seen so many dying Daywalkers the day before, but I'd formed the opinion that the Lurkers weren't really such a threat after all. Where did it leave them if all of their strongest men died by age twenty-one? Well, I'd been wrong. Dead wrong. And as I took in the scene around me and the pure power emanating from these soldiers, I had to swallow hard.

"Is this your only training camp?" I whispered to Luce, my tone revealing my awe.

He chuckled and shook his head. "This is but one of many."

I swallowed hard. "And are you and Nairn the rulers of everyone or just this camp?"

He glanced over at me and smiled warmly. "We are the rulers of all."

I felt my heart rate increase with fear as I further considered my enemies. They were lean machines and their bodies were incredible—sculpted with sinewy muscle. We made our way through the crowd and I watched everyone turn and bow to Luce. As their eyes studied me, I sensed that some were malicious and others were simply curious. I could only imagine what Luce had told them.

When we reached the mouth of the crowd, Luce took my arm and pushed me to the side. We both watched Bryn emerge from behind the tallest man in the group. She was wearing the same outfit she'd had on before—black yoga pants with a dagger strapped to her thigh and a black sports bra. Two knives were strapped to each of her upper arms. I was beginning to think they were an integral part of her.

She stood in front of the group, and I could tell from the way the soldiers looked at her that she had their respect. But she paid no attention to them. Instead, she took a deep breath and eyed a young man standing to my left. She nodded to him, and he smiled a great big beautiful smile, running out to join her. There was something inside me that broke. I suddenly felt saddened by the probability that this man, or boy really, was a Daywalker and might, therefore, never live to see his twenty-first birthday.

Are you insane? I asked myself. *He's your enemy!*

And then I remembered that Bryn could overhear my conversations with myself, so I silenced my rebuttal and even bit my tongue in the hopes that I wouldn't start talking to myself again. Returning my focus to what was happening around me, I tried to send out my mental feelers to Rand to see if he was experiencing this too. Based on an affirmation that suddenly overwhelmed me, I figured he was.

"Billy is going to be my sparring partner today," Bryn called out. "Watch and learn."

She faced Billy with a smile, leaning forward slightly as she braced herself, her feet shoulder-width apart. She motioned at him to come for her with a little wave of two fingers. And then he rushed her so quickly, I couldn't even see him move. When he materialized behind her, he pulled her up against his body, clearly impressed with himself that he'd caught her.

"Elementals, if you are ever caught unawares by your enemies—and in this case Billy will play the part of my enemy—what power would you use to emancipate yourself?" Bryn asked of the crowd.

"Dissolving," someone called out. I had to assume it meant they could simply disappear right in front of their enemies. Not a bad defensive measure to have . . .

Bryn nodded. "What else?"

"Metamorphosis," someone else called out.

Bryn nodded again. "Into what?"

The man who had answered shrugged. "Something intimidating, something powerful."

"Such as?" Bryn continued, eyeing him. "You will have a split second to make this decision in battle, Samuel, the answer must come to you instantly."

"A dragon," he responded furtively.

Bryn nodded with a smile. "Nicely played." Then she faced the crowd again. "Any other suggestions?"

"Influencing," someone toward the back called out with a laugh. "Force our enemies to fall madly in love with us!"

Everyone in the crowd started rumbling with laughter, but I couldn't say I shared their amusement. Instead, realizing that the Elementals could disappear into thin air, metamorphose into horrible creatures such as dragons, and influence the emotions of their enemies. These were abilities that witches and warlocks didn't have. We *could* take the shape of beasts, but only beasts that occurred naturally. Yes, one member of the fae, Dougal, had been able to transform himself into a dragon, but he had been the only one with such a gift. From what I could gather here, every Elemental had these abilities.

I was suddenly worried. Very worried.

But my concerns were silenced when Bryn's gaze landed on Luce and then moved from him to me. She suddenly stopped whatever she was about to do. I could see anger coloring her otherwise tan complexion, and she said something to Billy under her breath before emancipating herself from him and walking over to us.

"May I see you for a minute?" she asked Luce.

He just nodded, came over and took my hand, then followed her. We marched down the small hill and took refuge behind a large pine tree. Then Bryn closed her eyes, held out her hands, and a burst of light appeared, creating a circle around her. I knew immediately that she was creating a sound buffer so that whatever was said in that circle wouldn't be overheard. Luce maintained his hold on me, which meant he wanted me along for the ride. Once she noticed my presence, she slapped her arms across her chest and looked like she was about to explode with indignation.

"Luce, I ask permission to speak my mind," she said in a stilted tone.

He nodded. "Of course."

Then she took a deep breath. "Without the enemy present."

Luce smiled. "Jolie is not your enemy, Bryn." I didn't like the sound of my name on his tongue. It was too friendly, too close for comfort. And the truth of the matter was, I *was* Bryn's enemy, just as I was Luce's enemy.

She shook her head. "I don't know what lies you're feeding her, but I'm not stupid enough to fall for it." Then she glared at me. "We are enemies."

I frowned at her but bit my lip, feeling Rand's anger surfacing within me. Good, he was bearing witness to everything. My day was looking up.

"I request your company without her," Bryn continued, staring at me like I'd just crawled out of a swamp.

"Whatever you have to say to me can be said in front of her," Luce finished. I couldn't help my surprise, but had to admit I sided with Bryn. I couldn't understand why Luce wanted to include me in everything. This was top secret stuff, or so it seemed. And then I had an ugly thought—maybe he didn't care about what I witnessed, because he planned on killing me as soon as I was no longer deemed useful.

That thought was as bad as if I'd just unleashed the floodgates for a tidal wave. I felt a rise of panic and anger from Rand. I immediately tried to calm him down, but based on my suddenly piqued stress level, I couldn't say I was successful. Instead, I focused on Bryn, wanting to get as much information as I could.

"It's bad enough that she's here in our camp, but for you to bring her to my training session?" she continued, acting like I wasn't even there. "It's unbelievable! We might as well just make her a list of all our abilities!"

"She is not your enemy," Luce repeated, his tone even.

Bryn glared at him again and threw her hands on her hips. "You have taught us that *they* are our enemies since before I learned to walk."

Luce nodded. "Yes, because *they* are your enemies. She is not one of them. She is an Elemental, just as you are."

All of a sudden I was terrified. Why? Because Luce had basically just admitted I was one of them, and I hadn't told Rand myself. I felt panic rise up in my gut and tears fill my eyes. Almost immediately, a wave of calm washed over me. I had the absolute feeling that I wasn't one of them, and I let it crest over me. It was Rand, reassuring me that he didn't believe a word of it. Not for a minute. I wanted to close my eyes and smile, because if he didn't believe it, I didn't have to either.

Bryn narrowed her eyes at me. "An Elemental?" she repeated sarcastically, then laughed. "She's *their* Queen!"

Luce laughed in return. "Yes, yes, I understand your concern, Bryn." He raised his hands as if to shush her. "But let me repeat that she is one of us."

Bryn shook her head and rolled her eyes. "How is that possible?"

Luce laughed again, a deep rumbling sound. Then he quieted himself and faced her. "It is possible, my dear Bryn, because she is your sister."

Fifteen

I didn't know what to say, and Bryn looked like she'd just seen a ghost, so I guessed neither did she. There was complete silence inside of my mind, so apparently Rand had no response either. We were all just stunned into silence. A few seconds later his shock wore off and my body was engulfed with a sudden certainty that I shouldn't trust either of them. Rand was sure they were trying to set me up for something. As much as I wanted to believe that, I couldn't deny that Bryn and I did look alike . . . a lot. And more than that, there were those strange feelings I had about her that hinted at some sort of intimacy between us.

"Excuse me, what?" I finally demanded when I remembered that my tongue worked.

Luce turned to me and laughed lightly while trying to appear understanding. I'm not sure what it was about ancient beings, but they just didn't seem able to portray human emotions very well. He looked like nothing but a charlatan to me.

"Did you not notice the family resemblance?" he asked me, as if my surprise was unfounded.

I turned to face Bryn again. This time the similarities in our eyes, noses, and mouths were so obvious I couldn't understand how I'd tried to explain it away. We were related—it was as clear as the fact that we were the same height, with the same build—granted, she was in way better shape than I was but, hey, I was pregnant!—and similar features. If she were blond and not quite so tan, she'd practically be my clone.

"I can't be related to one of them!" Bryn yelled, and shook her head as if she absolutely refused to believe it. The idea seemed to appall her. But she had to know, as I did, that there was something to it. In her gut she had to know it was true. It was like one of those things you could fight as much as you wanted, but it wouldn't matter, it was an evident fact. I couldn't understand how it was possible, but I believed it.

So if Bryn really was my sister, did that mean I was definitely a Lurker? I felt a wave of anger rising within me, and realized it was Rand. He obviously didn't believe she was my sister, and he was still convinced it was Lurker magic. The feelings roaring through me also told me I wasn't a Lurker and never would be one.

"This can't be possible," I started, remembering my history and my parents' history. I knew where I came from, and it had nothing to do with this compound.

"It is quite possible and also quite true," Luce continued, smiling at both of us, like we were on the Maury Povich show, like we should be embracing and celebrating our reunion as long-lost sisters. Instead, I wished I had a DNA test on hand.

Bryn shook her head again, exhaling. "Why didn't you ever tell me? Why didn't you prepare me?"

Luce turned to face her, his expression sympathetic, but there was also a steeliness to his eyes, something that told me he would be fiercely loyal only to his own goals and desires. There was nothing good about this man. That feeling struck me solidly. I gulped.

"I did not think it my place, Bryn," he answered lightly. "I knew this day would come and I thought it best for you both to learn of your lineage together."

"So, what? Are we twins?" she continued, staring at me with another frown and shaking her head like she felt sorry for herself.

"Quite so," Luce said with a nod. "Although fraternal twins, obviously."

My throat constricted—could it be true?

It might still be magic, I told myself. *She could have magicked herself to look like me.*

She frowned at me. "It isn't magic."

I bit my lip, irritated with myself that I hadn't shielded my thoughts better. I said nothing more, just tried to make sense of the thoughts swarming through my head. How was it possible that I had a twin? And worse, a twin who was my enemy? From the looks of it, Bryn wasn't just any enemy either—she appeared to be pretty high up on the Lurker ladder. Her position as a trainer in combat, her ability to heal the sick, and her sensitivity to thoughts, all pointed to the fact that she wasn't just anyone. Really, it was just my luck that I would have an evil twin.

"Why were we separated?" I asked, deciding to focus on facts. I needed to get all my questions answered, to understand my heritage and what I truly was. Yes, I knew Rand was along for the ride, but I figured now was as good a time as any, and that he'd hear the same things I did, for truth and discovery.

Luce smiled that fake smile that made my stomach turn on itself. "I am certain you have many questions. Let us retire to your accommodations." Then he turned to Bryn and raised a brow. "Bryn?"

She just nodded. When he offered his arm, she shook her head and started off in front of us both, clearly pissed off. Whether she was more pissed off that I was her twin or that Luce had never told her, I couldn't be sure. It was probably a combination of both.

I didn't take Luce's arm either, but I walked beside him as my mind raced with unanswered questions. Rand continued to bombard me with the feeling that I shouldn't trust them, and I could tell that he was now hell-bent on getting me out of here. But as to where "here" was, I still didn't have a clue. And even though Luce had admitted that most of the people in the camp didn't know more than I did, I wasn't about to let that stop me. I turned to face him. "I think it's only fair for you to tell me where we are . . . I mean, if you expect me to take my place as Queen?"

Luce smiled, nodding. "Yes, of course. We are in the forests of the Smoky Mountains."

I gulped. We were in Tennessee then? In the States? Luce's magic had been strong enough to transport us both from Scotland all the way back to the United States? It was a thought that frightened me, so I dropped it, focusing instead on the dirt path that led to the last house on A Street. A house that, by the looks of it, was meant to be my new permanent home.

I felt my stomach acid riding up my throat at the very thought.

Bryn threw the door open and disappeared inside, still outraged. Luce smiled apologetically at me. "She will warm up to the idea, sooner or later."

I nodded, wondering when I was going to warm up to the whole thing myself. I was suddenly overcome again with the conviction that this was all a sham intended to confuse me and win my loyalty. In Rand's mind, it was all just a game, a way to get under my skin and make me doubt myself.

But I couldn't say I agreed with him. Somehow this just felt too real.

I entered my house and quietly took a seat on the sofa opposite Bryn, wondering where Luce would choose to sit. Beside me, as a welcoming gesture, or would he sit beside Bryn, in an attempt to soothe her? He stood in the middle of us both, choosing, wisely, to do neither.

"I am certain you both have questions—" he started.

"How is it possible that we're related?" Bryn interrupted, her voice wavering with her anger. It wasn't lost on me that she refused to so much as glance in my direction.

Luce cleared his throat and nodded, eyeing the floor as if he wasn't sure where to start. Then he looked back at her for a few seconds before facing me again. "Your mother was fae," he began.

I shook my head. "My mother is human," I said before I had the chance to think about it. Had I thought about it, I would have not said anything at all. Immediately I felt a bolt of irritation snaking through me and realized it was Rand. He was reminding me not to impart any information to my enemies. Even if he hadn't reprimanded me, I would have realized the mistake on my own. I needed to keep a lower profile, telling them as little about myself as possible.

Luce shook his head at my comment. "The mother you knew was not your true birth mother."

"How?" I demanded, figuring it was safe to ask that question. It wasn't like I was showing any more of my cards.

"Because you were switched at birth," he finished. I just shook my head, not understanding how that could be. It just sounded so fake, so cliché.

"Who switched me?" I asked.

No, Jolie! I heard Rand's voice in my head.

I shut him down. I had to reinforce that it wasn't safe for us to talk, especially not when Bryn was so sensitive to people's thoughts and could easily overhear us. Luckily, it didn't seem she'd picked up on his voice in my head. Maybe she was too overwhelmed by this newest bomb that had just been dropped in both of our laps.

"I do not know who switched you—"

"Tell us about our mother," Bryn interrupted. Her saying "us" and "our mother" made me guess she was buying into this whole thing. 'Course, she'd been raised to trust Luce all her life, so why would she start doubting him now?

"She was of the fae, as I said—" Luce started.

"Then she was otherworldly?" I threw out there, realizing that if this was true, Mathilda had been right about my fae lineage all along. The thought of

Mathilda made me incredibly homesick. I wanted nothing more than to see her again.

"Yes," Luce admitted with tight lips. "Though your father was one of our kind."

I gulped down instant heartburn, not knowing what to think or say. Rand's feelings continued to flash through me, and for the moment I wanted to simply silence him, to close off the bond so I could consider Luce's words on my own. Rand's constant reactivity to what was going on was becoming a major distraction. What if what Luce was saying was true? What if I'd been half fae and half Lurker all along?

"So you're saying I am partly one of them?" Bryn demanded, sneering at me when she mentioned "them."

"No," Luce said, and shook his head gently. "You have always been one of us, my dear."

"But my mother wasn't," she said flatly, even though there was a question in there somewhere.

I noticed she still refused to look at me. It was like she was physically disgusted that she could be related to someone so low. 'Course, I had to admit that I was pretty upset about any possibility that I was of Lurker stock. Talk about a rude awakening.

"No, your mother was not of our kind," Luce said simply. "The relations between her and your father were strictly prohibited."

"Then he was an Elemental?" I asked, figuring he couldn't have been a Daywalker since Bryn and I both possessed magic; and last I checked, neither of us had incredibly pointy canines.

Luce smiled. "Yes, your father was a very noble Elemental. He captured your mother during a raid." So he must have raided a fae village and taken my mother hostage. Yeah, he sounded like a really noble dude.

"And what, raped her?" Bryn demanded. I almost felt happy she was here, asking all the questions that either didn't occur to me or I chose not to ask. I still wasn't sure what I believed. I felt like I was lost in a dream that I couldn't wake from.

"No," Luce said and sighed. At that moment I realized he would have preferred for it to have been rape. I gulped down the feelings of hatred that suddenly boiled inside of me.

"Then what?" Bryn demanded.

"Your father loved your mother," he said simply, but in that statement was a background story. I could feel it. It was more than obvious that Luce hadn't approved of the union.

"What happened to them?" I asked softly.

Luce shrugged. "I do not know all the details," he said. "Your father eloped with your mother and left us."

Bryn's breath caught in her throat as if that was the vilest thing she could possibly imagine. "Did he become one of them?" she demanded, her voice low, as if the story could only get worse.

"No," Luce said, and I could tell he didn't want to continue telling it. It made me think our father had met with an end that wouldn't put Luce in a good light.

"What happened to him?" I persisted.

"That is a story for another day," he said simply, but his tone was determined. "What I will tell you now is that when we learned your mother was pregnant with twins, we made it our business to stop at nothing to ensure that you were both ours."

I felt something that resembled fear shoot up my spine, and goose bumps broke out across my skin.

"You took us, then?" Bryn asked, seemingly not at all disturbed by that fact.

"Your mother," Luce responded. "We took your mother."

"How?" I started, but he shook his head, making it clear he didn't want to get into the minute details—of how he'd kidnapped our pregnant mother from the fae. And who knew where our father was at that point? Maybe dead. I felt sick all the way to my toes.

"What is important to know is that when your mother went into labor, there were complications, and we did not have the facilities in those days to care for her. Since your welfare was at stake, we were forced to take her to a human hospital."

"Didn't magic work on her?" I demanded.

He shook his head. "No, my magic did not. She was very powerful in her own right, as a fairy, and my magic failed to . . . help her." Then, as he glanced at Bryn again, he resumed his story. "We had no choice—we could not endanger your lives." He took a big breath and exhaled it slowly, as if reliving the stress of those days all over again. "After giving birth to you two, your mother died," he said simply.

But it was a statement that shouldn't have been issued so drily or treated like a minor detail. Now I was anxiously aware that there had to be more to it. Yes, okay, our mother was dead, but it was how she died that now concerned me.

"Then something interesting happened," he continued. "You, Jolie, were switched with another baby in your mother's ward, whether by design or sheer human mistake, I don't know." Based on the way he said it, he clearly didn't believe it was a coincidence. I didn't either.

"Then you're saying I was never my mother's child?" I said, feeling suddenly hollow because it made sense. I had seen pictures of my mother pregnant, but who was to say she'd been pregnant with me?

"Yes, that is what I am saying," Luce finished.

"Then what happened to her baby?" I demanded.

He nodded slowly. "We raised her as our own and she is still among us today."

"She's a Lurker?" I bleated, shock and anger in my tone.

"A what?" Bryn said to me, furrowing her brows. She turned to Luce. "What did she call us?"

Luce looked at her and laughed. "It is their word for us."

"Lurkers?" she repeated, and shook her head, like it was all very strange, and almost amusing in its strangeness.

Luce then faced me again. "She is neither a Day-walker nor an Elemental," he said simply.

"Then what is she?" I asked.

"A human," he answered.

"Then how is she one of your kind?" I continued.

"We have humans who assist us," he finished succinctly. "I believe she provides cleaning duties."

That revelation made me incredibly sad. Granted, I had never been close to my mother, but she had always thought of me as her own. Now that I knew I'd been someone else's child, it just made me feel for her.

What made it worse was that her real daughter, her real flesh and blood, was just a cleaning lady for these bastards. My jaw tightened as hatred filled my body. I suddenly detested Luce for relegating my mother's daughter to such a position—cleaning up after his kind!

"So when did you realize the mix-up?" Bryn asked.

"After it was too late."

"So why not just tell the hospital there was a mix-up or go after Jolie yourself?" she continued. Hearing her say my name struck me as odd. Well, the whole situation struck me as odd because it was so completely . . . wrong, hideous in how wrong it was.

"There were outside forces that intervened," Luce said simply. "And we were unable to locate Jolie or her adoptive mother."

That was when I realized the Underworld had somehow gotten involved in all this. It was a feeling that surged through me, a triumphant one. Somehow, someone had known what was going on, and they'd made sure the Lurkers didn't get me. That someone, I had to imagine, was Mathilda. Why Bryn had ended up in the hands of the enemy, I had no idea.

I realized then that Rand had gone completely quiet on the other end of our bond. It was as if the truth in what Luce was saying had sunk into him too. I didn't even want to think about what that might mean. My fear—that he might forsake me for my connection to the Lurkers—hit me hard.

All of a sudden, anger flared through me and I realized that Rand had received my thought. He rebutted it instantly and filled me with feelings of love and adoration. *He would never give up on me!* That's what he was saying. He loved me and that's all there was to it.

Luce glanced at me and smiled, but the sight of him sickened me. I wanted to hit him until I could force that smirk right off his face. "We have been seeking you ever since."

"And how did you find me?" I demanded, attempting to squelch my anger.

"When we learned there was a Queen of the Underworld, I immediately knew she had to be you."

"How?" I insisted.

"Because I knew children," he glanced at Bryn, "born of fae and Elemental parents would have powers that have never before been seen."

"Then you heard about my abilities?" I asked, referring to my gift for reanimating the dead.

He simply nodded. "I knew you were she and she was you; and I refused to let up until I had returned you to your rightful home."

My rightful home . . . Just the thought made me want to retch out the bile coming up my throat.

Sixteen

I didn't know what to think. I was angry, depressed, and confused all at the same time. I couldn't say which emotion was winning in the race for dominance. Questions and thoughts spun through my head as I tried to recall everything Luce had told me, as I tried to piece it together and make some sort of coherent story out of it. But, really, before I could even hope to do that, I had to accept his words as true, and that's where I was having a tough time. Yes, I could tell Rand still doubted, but I knew I had to make this decision for myself.

Could everything that Luce told us be true? That was the one-million-dollar question. Granted, I was sure that parts of his story had been fabricated, other parts skipped, and still others completely exaggerated. But I couldn't help walking away with the feeling that it was essentially true. Bryn really was my fraternal twin sister, and we had been born from fae and Elemental parents. Most important, the Lurkers didn't want to hurt me, they only wanted to claim me as one of their own.

What did I think about the whole twin sister thing?

I couldn't really say. I mean, from the moment I met Bryn, I'd had the uncanny feeling that she and I were somehow connected. My reaction to her had hinted at intimacy, a mutual understanding. But at the same time it was hard to get the warm and fuzzies when it was obvious that Bryn hated me and, worse, she was a Lurker, and thus my enemy. It was almost like this bitter twist of fate had been designed to test my sanity and my ability to cope.

The one thing helping me to hang on was that Rand finally knew where I was, and I knew he was working on rescuing me. But as I thought about it, doubt began to churn in my stomach. I had to ask myself if I really believed that Luce would announce the location of this Lurker camp so readily, and so quickly. Then I felt a stronger surge of doubt: Rand's.

Jolie, his voice suddenly sounded in my head.

Rand, this isn't safe, I barked back at him as I stood up and closed the blinds in the living room. I felt as if Lurker spies could see into my mind as easily as they could see into the living room. *Someone could be listening.*

I could sense his dilemma. *We have no other choice. I can't communicate through our bond, although I have tried.*

Quickly then, I answered him, already afraid that we were being overheard.

Luce lied to you, Jolie. You aren't in Tennessee and you aren't in the Smoky Mountains.

My anger overwhelmed me. It was now more apparent than ever before that I couldn't trust Luce—he was no good. *How do you know?*

Mercedes was able to perform a Liar's Circle on Luce.

How?

Our bond is strong enough, Jolie, that she was able to use me as a link to you and Luce.

Wow, I thought, my eyes reaching for the ceiling.

At any rate, the Liar's Circle revealed that what Luce told you about your location was a lie.

Anger burned in my throat again. *Then where am I?*

I felt more doubt flowing through me, followed by a sense of helplessness, worry, and determination. *We don't know yet, but I promise we are working on it night and day. There's just too much magic buffering wherever you are—it's basically impenetrable.*

So what do we do now? I asked him, the hopelessness of the situation hitting me hard.

He was quiet for a few seconds and then I heard him sigh. *We continue to try to figure out where you are, and as soon as we do, I'm coming for you . . . we're coming for you.* He paused for a few seconds as more fierce resolve flowed through me. *We're coming for everyone.*

Then there would be a battle! I kept my realization to myself, not wanting to broach the topic over the insecure line. I felt worry saturating my gut—my own. Rand was too busy dealing with his own anger. Nausea worked its way up my throat and I had to magick it away.

I have tarried long enough, and if it's true that someone is listening, we aren't safe discussing this any longer, Rand finished.

I nodded and resigned myself to doing everything I

could to find out where the heck we were. I was going to continue to give Rand as much information about this hellish place as I could through our bond.

Jolie, just focus on yourself, focus on your own safety and protection, he continued. *Whatever choices you make, make them solely on that basis.* He sighed, long and hard. *I will get you out of there soon.*

I love you, Rand. I thought the words and automatically felt an answering of adoration well up inside of me. But while the feelings elated me, I felt tears prick behind my eyes. No one had a clue where I was, and escape seemed impossible, such an improbable feat. But I couldn't allow myself the luxury of moping. I had to be strong—I had to try to figure my own way out of here in case Rand and Mercedes couldn't locate me.

Jolie, don't give up, I told myself resolutely.

And for the first time in a long time, I felt my other side agree. *No, I will never give up.*

There was a knock on the front door, and worry immediately suffused me—Rand's. I tried to calm him down, but it wasn't any good. Strangely enough, as soon as I pulled open the door and found Bryn standing before me, his worry subsided, and I had to admit, mine did too.

"I—" she started, and clamped a hand over the back of her neck, appearing restless and frustrated. "We need to talk," she finished, then pushed past me, showing herself into my house.

"Okay," I said, closing the door behind us. When I turned around, I noticed that she'd already made herself comfortable on my couch.

"You should sit," she said, and motioned to the chair just beside her.

I said nothing. I just took a seat and faced her, faced my sister.

"I'm sure this is as much of a surprise to you as it is to me," she started, and then shook her head, almost angrily. "Surprise doesn't begin to cover it."

"Yeah, I'd say this is one of the bigger shocks of my life."

She nodded. "I . . . uh, I'm not good with this sort of stuff," she started.

"What, being nice?" I asked, and then laughed, helpless to resist the fact that I desperately wanted to reach out to her, to be close to her, to understand our sisterly bond. But as soon as those feelings suffused me, I had to remind myself that she was first and foremost a Lurker.

"I'm sorry about the circumstances," she said. "I'm sure it was pretty crappy to find out that your mother wasn't your real one."

"And what about your mother?" I asked, realizing I hadn't even tried to put myself in her shoes.

"I have always been told that my mother died in childbirth, like what Luce told us. Only I wasn't aware that she was fae. I thought both she and my father were Elementals."

I nodded, silently appreciative of the fact that she and I were even having this discussion. It was suddenly clear to me that Bryn had to be interested in getting to know me better too, which was probably the reason for this visit. "And what did Luce tell you about your father?"

She sighed deeply, running her hands through her

hair as she shook her head in obvious frustration. "That he'd died shortly after my mother did and Luce also believed my father's death was at the hands of your people."

I immediately wanted to change the subject. The best course to maintain the friendliness between the two of us was to steer clear of anything that would serve as a reminder that we were technically enemies. "I know what Luce has planned for us."

She glanced at me and quirked a brow, interested. "Go on."

"I reanimated one of your dead Daywalkers," I said flatly, watching her as her eyes narrowed and disbelief pasted itself across her face.

"You did what?"

I shrugged. "It's my gift. Just as you can heal people and eavesdrop on their thoughts, I can reanimate the dead."

Her eyes went wide and she studied me suspiciously. "I've never even thought that was possible."

I grinned and raised my brows. "If you don't believe me, ask Luce." She frowned and then simply nodded, saying nothing. " 'There are more things in heaven and earth than are dreamt of in your philosophy,' " I said, quoting Hamlet, the very words Rand had uttered to me in the first few days of our acquaintance, when I'd doubted the fact that I was a witch. I was suddenly overcome with a feeling of longing and homesickness. I yearned to see Rand in the flesh, to feel his strong arms around me and to rest my head against the warmth of his chest. But I pushed the feelings down. Now wasn't the time.

"Nice," she said with a small laugh that sounded sad more than anything else.

"Luce believes that together you and I will be strong enough to heal the Daywalkers, to reanimate them and free them of their disease."

She nodded, but didn't seem surprised. A second or two later a familiar expression of suspicion closed over her face and she regarded me snidely. "And you expect me to believe that you'll willingly go along with this?" She laughed cynically. "I know you still consider yourself one of them."

I nodded, unable to deny the truth in her words. If there was one thing I felt I could rely on about Bryn, it was her honesty. She didn't seem to possess Luce's gift of bullshit. Instead she respected only the truth— plain, sterile facts. As strange as it seemed, I suddenly thought that Rand would respect Bryn; they appeared to be cut from the same cloth, only from two completely different colors. But anyway, I was sure that trying to pull a fast one on Bryn would be a waste of time and, moreover, I didn't want to disrespect her by even attempting it. And so I decided to be truthful with her. "I'm just trying to survive."

She nodded and glanced down at her hands, spreading her fingers wide and then scrunching them into fists again. When she faced me, she nodded again. "That's the best thing you can do. As I mentioned earlier, you should do exactly what Luce tells you. I'm sure you think he's this helpless, old, silly man, but he isn't. He's powerful. More powerful than you can ever imagine, and what's more, he's smart and driven. He has an agenda."

It seemed she was warning me, because she didn't

want to see anything bad happen to me. Or maybe I was just extrapolating. Either way, I recognized that I had an opportunity here. Maybe I could ask my sister some of the questions that were still pounding through my mind. Whether she would answer them was anyone's guess. But if I didn't try, I'd never know, right?

I took a deep breath and for the next couple of seconds we just looked at each other, neither of us saying anything. I broke the silence. "How many of you are there?"

Bryn glanced at me and smiled knowingly, like she was completely on to me. "Pass." It was her turn to inhale deeply. "Is there a King of your people too, or are you the only monarch?"

I was quiet for a few seconds, but then I realized I'd have to hand over information if I expected to get any in return. "Just me." She nodded and narrowed her eyes as if to say, *Well? It's your turn.* "How does one become an Elemental or a Daywalker?"

"Elementals are either born from Elemental parents or humans can become Elementals through a ceremony of magic. True Elemental power only comes with age."

I frowned. "You're only thirty."

She nodded and smiled smugly, crossing her arms against her chest as she leaned back into the pillows of the sofa. "I'm considered an enigma . . . as I'm sure you are."

I nodded, unable to argue with her. "And the Day-walkers?"

"Daywalkers are born that way, through the union of two Daywalkers."

I tapped my fingers against my knee as I digested

the information. "So Daywalkers can't turn humans like vampires can?"

Bryn frowned and eyed me. "Daywalkers and vampires have absolutely nothing in common. It's like comparing a spaniel to a wolf."

I laughed, I couldn't help it. "Is that the only comparison you guys know in this place or what?"

She started to frown, but the frown slowly gave way to a smile and then a laugh. "You want to know what's the funniest part about that?"

"Sure," I said, feeling myself drawn to her. I really wanted to like her. I mean, she was the only blood family I had left. And what was more, she *was* likable. She was strong-willed and opinionated, yes, but she was also funny, and I was beginning to see a more sensitive side to her.

"Luce says that bit about the spaniel and the wolf all the damn time and it drives me nuts!" She laughed and shook her head. "I can't believe I actually stole it."

"I can see how it would get on your nerves," I offered.

She stopped laughing, but the smile was still etched on her lips. "So anyway, no, Daywalkers can't turn humans. The only way to create another one is through a Daywalker and Daywalker union."

"Not an Elemental and a Daywalker union?" I specified.

She shook her head. "We have strict rules that disallow us from procreating with one another. We keep our lines strictly separate, otherwise our powers would be highly weakened."

My eyes reached for the ceiling as surprise echoed through me. I wasn't sure why I was surprised, but I was nonetheless. The Lurker way of living was just so foreign to my own. "Luce said it was rare for Elementals to birth males?" I said, broaching the next question on my mind.

"It's my turn," Bryn interrupted, and I merely nodded, realizing she was right. "Does the prophetess actually exist?"

I swallowed hard, not wanting to answer this question. In the back of my mind I could feel Rand affirming the notion. I hadn't realized he was still with me, and knowing he was still there caused a sense of warmth and happiness to crawl through me. I felt much less alone.

Bryn started laughing, and I glanced up at her in surprise. "Your expression was response enough," she admitted, and then nodded. "Interesting."

Irritated at my inability to hide my emotions, I turned to the next question on my list. "So are Elementals born of Elemental parents stronger than humans who are turned into Elementals?"

She nodded again and started playing with her hair and shaking her knee as if she had trouble sitting still. It seemed Bryn was one of those people who was overflowing with energy and constantly needed an outlet. "Humans who become Elementals by way of magic are the least powerful of our kind. Males who are born of Elemental parents are the most powerful, but as Luce told you, they rarely survive."

"How many purebred male Elementals are there?"

She shook her head and stopped playing with her hair. "Pass."

"Are you planning on waging a war against my people?" I asked, my voice tight.

She was quiet for a few seconds and her eyes were hollow, her lips tight. "I think you already know the answer to that one."

I was consumed with thoughts after Bryn left, and I didn't know what to focus on. Realizing that I was also exhausted, I opted for bed. I decided to give my brain the hiatus it so desperately needed so I could conserve my strength for the next day. I exhaled a long breath and started for my bedroom, still feeling the weight of the world on my shoulders. What would tomorrow bring? While I was eager to learn more about Bryn's history and my own, I was nevertheless wary about the source of the information. I wondered how much Luce was coloring the truth, how he was using it to suit his own ulterior motives.

I closed the bedroom door behind me, pulled off the white sweatshirt Bryn had given me, then took off the equally nondescript white T-shirt and the blue pants, which reminded me of hospital scrubs. I piled them neatly over the back of the chair and stared at myself in the mirror. I was wearing only my bra and underwear. I turned to check out my profile and noticed I really didn't look pregnant at all. As soon as the thought entered my head, I felt a bout of nausea again. It was like the baby was reminding me she was most definitely there with me. I smiled as I magicked the nausea away, still studying myself. No, I didn't look any bigger. In fact, my stomach looked flatter than it usually did, and overall it appeared that I'd lost at least five pounds. That didn't surprise me, considering the fact that I hadn't been eating much lately.

'Course, the stress alone had probably caused the weight loss.

I have to be better about dealing with this stress, I thought to myself. For the baby's sake, I had to stay as healthy and worry-free as I could. It was a monumental task that I had no idea how to accomplish.

Just take everything one step at a time, I advised myself.

I turned from the mirror and walked over to the bed. I was about to settle myself in for the night when I had the sudden and distinct feeling that I wasn't alone. I felt the tiny hairs on the back of my neck stand at attention. Something wasn't right—it was an instinctual response and one I'd learned not to ignore.

Before I could take another breath, I heard a swoosh, interrupting the otherwise still air, and felt someone appear just behind me, pulling me into him as he cupped my mouth. I began struggling against him until his scent bathed me in its spicy male cleanness. I stopped my struggle and felt relief flood through my mind and body.

"Poppet, do not scream," Sinjin said.

"Sinjin," I breathed when he pulled his hand away from my mouth. I gripped each of his arms and hugged myself with them, grateful to feel his presence behind me. I didn't even care that I was basically naked because my response wasn't sexual. It was pure joy. I spun myself around and threw my arms around his middle, pressing my head into his chest as I hugged him. I could feel his surprise at first, but moments later he wrapped his arms around me in return.

Then I looked up at him with shock in my eyes. "Sinjin . . . how did you—" I started.

"I tracked you, love," he responded with that devilish smile I adored. He was dressed all in black, as always, and he blended in with the night, indistinguishable from the shadows.

"You tracked me?" I repeated in a whisper, suddenly afraid that my quarters might be bugged.

Sinjin smiled at me again, and all the stress that had been building inside of me dissolved. It was strange because I recognized our precarious position, but there was something about Sinjin's easy coolness that absolved any panic. I took his hand and squeezed it as I smiled at him, so incredibly happy to see him, and to know he was okay.

"Yes, my pet," he said as he grinned down at me. "I have sampled your blood. Do you not remember? I can track you no matter where you are."

Then I realized that Sinjin knew where we were. I closed my eyes for a second and focused on opening the bond with Rand. I knew he wouldn't respond well to Sinjin's presence, but desperate times called for desperate measures. I could immediately feel Rand's awareness flowing through me—the telltale sign that we were connected. I opened my eyes and glanced up at Sinjin. As soon as Rand recognized him, anger flashed through me, but it was immediately tempered by a sense of relief. He had to realize the reason Sinjin was here.

"Where are we, Sinjin?" I whispered.

He ran his fingers down the side of my face and smiled as Rand's anger became almost palpable.

"In the Black Forest of Germany."

"Germany?" I repeated as anger flowed through me like lava. That rat bastard Luce!

I knew that Rand needed to break our connection so he could concentrate on locating the camp, in order to rally our troops and wage battle.

I nodded as I tried to pass on the feeling that I understood, that it was okay for him to leave me. And even though Rand and Sinjin had never been friends, I could tell that he was happy that Sinjin was with me. It actually elated him that there was someone who cared about me and wanted to protect me in this godforsaken place. Strangely enough, I could feel his gratitude for Sinjin pass through me. I recognized it as Rand's peace offering.

Sinjin pushed me away from him and smiled appreciatively as he took in my seminaked body. He reached for my shirt and pants and handed them to me. "Much as I adore viewing your perfect form in the buff, I cannot allow you to catch cold."

"Sinjin—" I started as I threw my shirt over my head and pulled the pants up. I tied the drawstrings at my waist, but realized I had nothing to say.

"We must go."

"Shh," I whispered. "We might be overheard." He nodded as if he understood, then started forward, but I grabbed his arm and shook my head adamantly. "You have to go on without me," I said with as much strength as I could command.

He merely shook his head. "No chance."

He grabbed my arm and pulled me forward, but I bucked against him. "I can't explain why, Sinjin, but I know I will be safe here," I said in a soft voice.

He faced me with narrowed eyes. "You have two options, love. You may either come with me willingly or I shall carry you. I would prefer option one, as it requires less energy on my part."

That was when I realized I wasn't going to win this argument. It was better just to go with him and pull out at the last minute. How was I going to do that? I had no clue, but I figured I'd work it out later. No use wasting time on trivialities.

Even though I desperately wanted to tell Sinjin that Rand was on his way with our legion of Underworld soldiers, I was too worried that someone might overhear us. Yes, I considered writing a note for Sinjin but I figured Lurker magic would also uncover anything written. As it was, I was shocked that no one had discovered Sinjin yet, but it was probably just a matter of time. I looked around the room for anything resembling a nanny-cam, but found nothing. In the meantime I needed to play along with Sinjin and pretend that I would escape with him, for his safety. I wanted him to return to Kinloch and join up with Rand; it would be better for all of us. I, on the other hand, needed to stay here so that Luce wouldn't be tipped off in any way.

And, yes, I was curious as to how Sinjin had breached the security of the camp but I didn't want to break the silence in order to ask.

I threw on my tennis shoes, grabbed my sweatshirt, and followed Sinjin out of the bedroom, taking his hand when he offered it. Rather than going through the front door, he opened a window in the kitchen, which looked out on the bordering forest, and motioned for me to climb through it. Because I had to hurdle over the counter, he bent down, clasping his hands together until they formed a stirrup. I placed the ball of my foot in his hands and braced myself on his broad back. He lifted me over the counter and I slipped through the window. Pulling my legs through, I caught my balance on the windowsill and supported my body weight with my arms. I dropped to the ground below, barely making a sound.

Seconds later Sinjin materialized directly beside me. He smiled, offering his hand again. "Shall we?"

I took it and exhaled deeply, feeling my heart pounding in my chest. Still holding hands, we started down the hill at a quick pace. When we reached the cover of the pine trees, the moonlight couldn't find us through the thick canopy. I felt hope rise within me.

"Thank you, Sinjin," I said softly, momentarily returning my gaze to the forest floor in front of me so I wouldn't trip.

He raised a brow as if he thought it was strange for me to be thanking him. "I deserve no thanks, my Queen. I am your solemnly sworn protector."

I was suddenly infused with guilt because I knew now that everything Sinjin had ever told me was true—it was just this feeling I had deep down in my gut. My protection and safety were always his priority. Regardless of what had happened between us in the past, I forgave him from the bottom of my heart. Once again he'd put his life on the line for me. "I'm sorry," I said softly.

"Shh—" he started, but I shook my head.

He needed to hear this. I had to make him understand. "No," I said resolutely, inhaling deeply. I must have been out of shape because trying to jog and talk at the same time wasn't easy. "I want you to know that I'm sorry for everything that happened." I inhaled again. "I'm sorry I ever doubted you, and most of all I'm sorry for banishing you." I shook my head, hating the words as they left my mouth. "I should have trusted you."

He was now wearing an expression that was hard. "No, you were correct not to."

Exhaustion swept through me—I was just so tired and I hadn't eaten anything in hours. I had no energy. "I don't understand," I gasped, forcing myself onward.

"My motivations were purely selfish," he said, and paused. He grabbed my arm and packed me onto his back in an instant. I wrapped my arms around his neck and my legs around his waist as he continued forward at a much faster clip.

"Don't say that," I refuted.

"I must confess the truth."

"Then why are you here now?" I asked, leaning my cheek against his broad back. I closed my eyes, inhaling his spicy scent.

"For the same selfish reasons."

"How can that be?" I asked.

He stopped running once we reached the barbed wire fence, and he set me back on my feet. Kneeling down, he pulled the bottom of the fence up, where he'd neatly cut a flap in the wire. Then he faced me and shook his head. "I cannot live without you," he said simply. "Yes, it is true that I have dedicated myself to your protection, but that is only because I could never bear to lose you."

I gulped down my skepticism, shocked by the direction this conversation had taken. "Sinjin—" I started as I watched him widen the hole in the fence by bending it back on itself.

"No." He shook his head and stood up. He grabbed both sides of my face, forcing me to look at him. "I begged Mercedes to send me back in time. I ached to win your love, Jolie, because I wanted you to feel for me what I feel for you."

My shock threw me and I was suddenly at a loss. "I don't know what to say," I said softly, shaking my head.

"There is no more to be said," Sinjin answered. "When you bonded with the warlock, I lost my opportunity."

"I've missed you, Sinjin," I offered in consolation. I cared about Sinjin deeply, but I knew I could never be with him as long as I still loved Rand. Rand was absolutely the only one for me. We were soul mates just as we were bond mates.

"Poppet, there is no time to tarry," he said quickly, and pointed to the hole in the fence. "Go."

"I can't go with you, Sinjin," I said resolutely. "You must go without me and help Rand. I can't explain why now, but there is a plan, a master plan." I shook my head as tears flowed down my cheeks. "Tell him I have reinstated you in my kingdom and appointed you my chief protector, my guardian."

He held my face as he shook his head. "Please, poppet. No more of this foolishness."

I held myself firm. "I'm not leaving."

He eyed me resolutely. "In that case, I shall also remain. I will not leave without you."

"Please, Sinjin, you must trust me, I will be fine." I took a deep breath. "But it isn't safe for you here. You have to go before they find you."

As the words left my mouth, the sound of motors suddenly surrounded us. Before either of us could utter another word, we were encircled by at least five spotlights. Sinjin grabbed my hand and lurched forward, as if to elude the circle of light, but the floodlights increased in brilliance until it was almost like looking at the sun. He fell to the ground, screaming.

"Sinjin!" I yelled, kneeling down beside him. I reached for him, but he pushed away from me. He cradled his head between his hands and I could smell the acrid odor of burning flesh. I yelled at the shadows behind the lights. "Stop it! Turn them off!"

Sinjin's skin was smoking, darkening into charcoal as the lights hit him. I glanced up at the lights again, incapable of seeing anything beyond them, and had to shield my eyes against the glare. Again I screamed out, "Stop it! You've won, just stop torturing him!"

Then I could see the outline of someone stepping forward. I scanned the line of her body and rested my eyes on Bryn. She glared down at me, her body silhouetted by the blinding bulbs behind her. "Luce will be quite interested to hear of this," she said drily as she eyed Sinjin with hatred. "Do something with him!" she called out. Then she walked over to me, grabbed my arm and forced me upright.

I watched as the spotlights abruptly dimmed, dousing us in darkness. It took my eyes a few seconds to adjust, and when they did, I saw that Sinjin was still lying on the ground. The Lurkers poured out of the numerous Jeeps on which the spotlights had been mounted. Two Lurker men grabbed Sinjin, dragging him into one of the vehicles.

"What have you done to him?" I demanded of Bryn as she hauled me forward, before throwing me into the arms of two Lurker men, who handled me none too gently.

"It's sunlight," she said simply. She walked away as I turned to look at Sinjin's prostrate figure in horror. Somehow, they had captured sunlight and turned it on Sinjin. Although I knew sunlight would kill him, I could only hope that it hadn't been enough to do the trick.

God, don't let him be dead, I thought to myself.

"He'll wish he were dead," Bryn interjected as she turned to face me. She'd obviously picked up on my thoughts.

At that moment, I could honestly say I held nothing but hatred for my sister.

Seventeen

"Bryn!" I screamed as I pounded on my door for the umpteenth time.

After Sinjin and I were discovered, Bryn ordered the two Lurkers holding me to return me to my living quarters. Then she sealed the house off with a charm so I couldn't escape. What had happened to Sinjin? I had no clue, but I couldn't stop thinking about her last words—that he'd wish he were dead.

I slammed the door with my fists again and screamed, "Luce! Bryn! Come talk to me right now! Dammit!"

Of course, I received no answer. I also tried to reach Rand, both through our mental connection and our bond, but there was no response. My abilities and powers appeared to have been completely shut off. After realizing I was basically alone, that no one was going to come for me, I collapsed onto the floor and began sobbing.

When I heard the doorknob opening, I forced myself upright and dried the tears from my eyes, not wanting anyone to witness my breakdown. When the door opened, I found Bryn standing there.

"What do you want?" she demanded.

"I want to know what you've done with him," I ground out. "Where is he?"

She shook her head. "You would rather not know because you obviously . . . care about him." She said the words with as much disgust as she could manage—like I was despicable for fraternizing with a vampire.

"Tell me, damn you," I said in my most threatening tone.

She leaned forward and grabbed my hand, pulling me outside. "Fine," she said curtly. She yanked on my arm as she started forward. "He's in our lab, where I will gladly escort you."

"Your lab?" I repeated.

She motioned toward a dark green army Jeep parked outside my door. I followed her.

"Get in," Bryn said simply, and I didn't argue. She hopped into the driver's side, started the engine, and peeled out onto the dirt street. She hit the main street and took a right, then a left onto the hillside, the Jeep straining with the change in terrain. She downshifted and took the grassy hillside all the way to the fence surrounding the camp.

"What is the lab?" I asked finally, a little afraid for her answer.

She frowned. "Well, since you're officially one of us now and you've convinced Luce that you're going to make a mighty contribution to our team, you might as well know." She drove alongside the fence for what felt like a few minutes, finally stopping, turning off the engine and jumping out. I followed suit.

"What goes on in the lab?" I repeated. She didn't

say anything, just started up the base of the hill. Again I followed.

Finally, Bryn turned to face me. "I'd rather you see for yourself," she said simply. Then she started forward again and held her hands up, a bright blaze of light flowing from them. "Enter," she commanded, dropping her hands.

The grass beneath us began to glow in the outline of a box, bisected with a line down the center. Bryn quickly stepped back, clearly not wanting to stand inside the lustrous box. As soon as she did, the grass began dissolving, chunk by chunk, and in its wake, the silver of polished steel emerged. When the grass within the glowing box disintegrated, I found myself looking at two steel doors. They slid open, and I could see nothing but darkness inside. Bryn stepped forward, and from the way she appeared to be going down, I could tell she was on a staircase.

"Well, are you coming?" she demanded, turning back.

I nodded, staring down into the darkness. I could just barely make out the staircase, and took the steps carefully, holding on to a railing to keep myself from falling. When I was halfway down, the doors closed above me. Then the room lit up brightly, fluorescent bulbs on the ceiling guiding our way. There was nothing beside the staircase but an empty room. It was strange.

Bryn continued down the steps until she reached a hallway, then paused and faced me. When I caught up to her, she started forward again, without saying anything. I followed her down the long hallway to another solid steel door, where she held her palm in front of a red, glowing box affixed to the wall and the door slid open. Whatever this "lab" was, it was highly confidential, that much was obvious.

She motioned for me to come through the door, and when I did, I entered a large room—maybe thirty feet square. Inside I saw about fifty hospital beds, and lying atop them the young Daywalkers, obviously close to death. They were pale and sickly with tubes and apparatuses strapped to them.

"What is this?" I demanded as I furrowed my brows at Bryn.

She shrugged as I approached one of the beds. I noticed a long tube inserted into the young man's wrist. Flowing through the tube was what appeared to be blood. "A blood transfusion?" I asked.

Bryn nodded, and that was when it hit me. "Oh my God," I said, steadying myself against the wall. I shook my head as memories of a conversation with Luce suddenly pounded through me.

We are in the process of searching for the missing gene in the Daywalkers . . . once we can identify that gene, we can cure them of this illness.

I felt bile rising up my throat, accompanied with nausea that might have been due to the baby, or maybe not. Suddenly, the pieces were falling into place, painting a terrible, ugly picture. I glanced up at Bryn, aghast. "You're transfusing the Daywalkers with vampire blood."

All those vampire disappearances suddenly made sense. The Lurkers hadn't killed the vampires, they'd kidnapped them . . . for this. Bryn didn't so much as blink. She nodded.

"Do the vampires die?" I asked, a shudder working its way up my spine.

"In the long run," she answered in a monotone, and there was something in her eyes that told me she felt nothing for the vampires; they were merely donors, research subjects to be sacrificed in the name of a greater good.

I gulped hard as something else occurred to me. "Is Sinjin here?" I asked, tears burning my eyes.

I was not going to let Sinjin die.

"Is he your vampire?" Bryn asked, her eyes narrowed.

Is he my vampire? The words echoed through me, and my eyes blurred through the flood of tears. I clenched them shut, refusing to cry in front of these monsters. Then I opened them again and glared at my sister.

She is not your sister! I yelled to myself. *Just because you share the same blood doesn't mean she's your sister! She's nothing but a . . . a monster!*

"So are you going to answer the question?" she demanded, her hands on her hips. She'd probably heard me thinking, but I hardly cared. I nodded, unable to find my voice.

She crossed her arms on her chest and regarded me with cold precision. I couldn't read the answer in her eyes—it was almost as if she didn't know.

"He is here."

The voice had come from my right, and I turned to look at the speaker. It was a woman, maybe five-foot-ten, her cherry-red hair pulled back into a tight bun, which made her look severe. Her skin was a translucent white, and her eyes a dark shade of auburn that made her resemble someone living in a dark cave for years, unaccustomed to the light of day. Her eyes narrowed as she studied me from head to toe, apparently disapproving of what she saw.

"Who are you?" I demanded.

She raised a brow as if I were stupid for asking, as if I should have recognized her the moment I saw her. And the truth of it was, I did know who she was; I'd known as soon as I set eyes on her.

"I am Nairn," she said simply, but the very weight of her name caused the room to go silent, and I could feel my heart rate quickening. When she moved her mouth to speak, I could see tiny fangs, like little, pointed Chiclets.

"If you lay a hand on him—" I started, my eyes burning with rage.

She threw back her head and laughed. But there was nothing happy in it—it was meant to disparage and belittle me. It was as if she were shocked that I would dare speak back to her, much less threaten her.

"If I lay a hand on him, then what?" she demanded finally, her eyes piercing. I noticed that Bryn was silent, though I could feel something coming from her. It seemed she was warning me not to excite Nairn, but the strange part was that it was purely a feeling I was receiving. When I looked at her, I got no indication of it at all, which made me half wonder whether I'd imagined it.

"If I am to be one of you," I said to Nairn, refusing to be intimidated—I wouldn't back down, not with Sinjin's life on the line, "then I want him freed."

She laughed again, but this time didn't make as big a deal out of it. "You are too late."

My entire being deflated and my stomach roiled as I tried to process her words. My mouth dropped open as tears again blurred my vision. I squeezed my eyes shut but it did no good; tears were flowing from my eyes before I realized I was standing there, sobbing. "Is he . . . is he dead?" I asked.

Nairn faced Bryn, her expression was unreadable. "Take her to him so she can see for herself," she said snidely. Bryn nodded and approached me, and if I hadn't known better, I would have said there was pity in her eyes.

"Where is he?" Bryn asked Nairn.

The Daywalker's jaw was tight. "Room B4."

Bryn said nothing more. She just walked out of the room and started down a corridor. I followed her, my heart hammering in my ears, keeping time with the sound of our footfalls against the shiny, tiled floors. We passed rooms on our left and right, and though there were windows at the top of each door, I kept my gaze fixed on the tiles below me. I didn't know why, but I was incapable of looking anywhere else. It was almost as if there was just too much to absorb.

God, is Sinjin dead? Could it be possible that my vampire is dead? I squeezed my eyes shut against the possibility and focused instead on the shiny floor, counting the tiles as I stepped on them.

They're killing vampires, they're killing my people. I now wondered about all the vampires who had gone missing over the years. We had located bodies for some of them, which were reduced to piles of ash, while others simply vanished without a clue. I had to imagine the answer was now facing me—the Lurkers had been using them to heal their sick and dying. But they obviously hadn't been successful, because Luce had said they were still trying to find the proper gene. So what was the point?

Bryn stopped suddenly outside a door and I nearly walked into her. Feeling my heart in my throat, I finally looked up and saw B4 staring down at me in bold type. It was the moment of reckoning. Was Sinjin alive?

God, please let him be alive!

"If it's any consolation," Bryn said as I faced her with red-rimmed, hollow eyes, "this wasn't my doing."

I took a deep breath, hating her words even as she mumbled them. She was one of them, even if another Lurker had slain Sinjin, she was just as responsible too. "It's no consolation," I said truthfully.

She was silent as she scanned her palm against a black box that appeared to be the door's locking mechanism. It beeped twice, and she reached down to open the door. I felt like we were moving in slow motion as we entered the room. Again my eyes scanned the tile floor, moving up to the cot in the center of the room, half hidden by a light blue hospital curtain. My eyes shot to the still form lying on the cot. All I could see was an outstretched arm on which the skin had been burned to a dark crispness—charred black. Lodged in his wrist were two tubes, blood flowing through both. The first led into a machine just beside the bed, and the other terminated in a translucent rubber bag hanging beside the machine. The bag was maybe two feet long and a foot wide. It was three-quarters full.

They're draining him! I said to myself, catching a scream in my throat.

I tore forward and yanked the blue curtain back, gasping out in pain when I saw Sinjin. He was black all over, owing to the sun-strobe lights they'd turned on him when we attempted to escape. It almost looked like he was covered in a layer of soot, but looking closer, I realized it was scorched skin.

"Sinjin," I whispered.

He immediately opened his eyes, the ice blue of his irises shining against his blackened skin.

He was alive!

I had no idea how or why, but he was still alive. I stifled the urge to throw my arms around him. Instead, I bent over and forced a smile, lightly running my fingers down the sides of his face. My tears splashed on his crispy skin and he blinked against them.

He opened his mouth to speak, but his voice was gravelly and barely a whisper. I leaned down farther, unable to understand him at first. He barely whispered in my ear, "I am sorry."

I pulled away and shook my head, tears falling abundantly now. "No, Sinjin," I said, hating that this was his own way of saying goodbye to me. "You can't leave me now. You have to hold on. I need you."

He swallowed with great difficulty and his agony was visible; every second was causing him more pain. Anger surged through me as I eyed the tubes penetrating his flesh, and then I lashed out, yanking them from his wrists. Blood spurted all over the cot, onto Sinjin, the curtain, and me, but it mattered little.

"Enough!" Bryn yelled from behind me as she

stepped closer. "You've seen what you asked to see, now let's go."

I bit my lip. "I'm not leaving," I said, trying to rein in my emotions.

"Don't make me do this the hard way," Bryn responded, gritting her teeth. Her warrior determination and discipline were evident in her eyes.

I laughed. It was a cynical, ugly sound, but I was tired of playing the Lurkers' game. They'd hit me too close to home now. It was time to fight back. I didn't give a damn that I would be fighting my biological sister.

Family hour was over.

I stepped in front of Sinjin to protect him with my body. I placed my feet shoulder-width apart and closed my eyes. I imagined a protective white screen of healing light around the two of us, though I had no idea if it would work since he was vampire and witch magic didn't ordinarily work on vampires. But I was more than just a witch, so I had to believe that it would. Seeing the white sheen of the protective bubble around us, I closed my eyes again and took a deep breath, calling on my power, my magic.

"Don't do this, Jolie," Bryn said in a low voice. "I don't want it to come to this."

I opened my eyes and saw that she'd taken the same stance I had. The white sheen of her protective orb glowed exactly the way mine did. I guessed our powers were equally matched.

"Are you going to allow us to leave?" I asked.

She shook her head, which spoke volumes. "He is done, Jolie. You have to think of us now, and your new life."

I shook my head and laughed acidly. "You mean nothing to me. You are my enemy first and foremost, not my sister; and I will not let you threaten the people I love."

Then something happened that neither of us was expecting. An alarm went off, sounding throughout the hospital. It reminded me of an air raid in a World War II movie. I could see flashing red lights in the hallway accompanying the siren's wail. Bryn now wore an expression of panic, her eyes wide.

"We have to go!" she yelled, dropping her arms in a gesture of surrender.

"What is it?" I demanded. "What the hell's going on?"

She shook her head and I could see fear in her eyes. "The camp has been breached."

A warm sensation arose from deep within me. I knew what it had to mean—Rand. It was Rand who had breached the camp. He was coming for me.

"It's not safe to stay here!" she persisted as she approached me, reaching out to take my hand.

I pulled it away and didn't make any motion to leave. "I won't go without him," I said, glancing back at Sinjin as I tried not to think about the fact that he just looked so . . . dead.

Bryn glared at me, but I held up my hands and threatened her with my energy orb, which was seconds from exploding between my palms.

"Jolie, don't be stupid. He's too far gone."

I stood my ground. As long as there was the smallest sign of life in Sinjin's body—and there still was—I would never leave him.

"If you won't come with me for your own sake,

then do it for your baby," Bryn said in a harsh voice. I felt my stomach drop.

She knew? But how? How did she know?

"I'm a sensitive," she said impatiently as she eyed the hallway again. Her eyes settled on the throbbing red light that pulsed spasmodically, then she faced me again. "I knew as soon as we met."

The alarm continued to blare and the red lights of the hallway seemed to flash with more urgency and frequency, but maybe it was just my imagination.

"You have to come with me now, Jolie," she said again. "Everything in here will self-destruct, and if we don't get the hell out, so will we."

I knew I couldn't move Sinjin and he wasn't strong enough to save himself. "I won't go," I said again. "I won't leave without him."

She shook her head. "Damn you to hell!" she swore as she started for the cot, taking a deep breath and glaring down at Sinjin. "I can't fucking believe I'm doing this."

She reached for a scalpel on the counter and held it up just as I grabbed her arm. "What are you doing?" I demanded.

She stared at me. "What I never thought I'd be doing in a million years," she answered, and extricated herself from my grip, holding the scalpel to her wrist. She jabbed the blade into her skin and pulled back, making a clean slice. Blood spurted from the wound, and Bryn held her wrist to Sinjin's seared lips. She took a deep breath and told him, "Drink, you bastard."

I was shocked that Bryn would do such a thing— risk her own life, if what she said was true about this place self-destructing, in order to ensure my survival. Maybe she wasn't as bad as I'd originally thought.

But now was not the time to think about that. Instead, I watched while Sinjin latched onto her arm and started sucking her blood feverishly. He appeared to be getting stronger with each swallow, his drinking more determined. She pulled away from him, but he held her in a viselike grip. "You're going to have to pull him off me when I say so," she announced with fear in her eyes. "He's going to try to drain me. He won't be able to resist the bloodlust."

Something seemed to occur to her then, as she narrowed her eyes at me. "And don't think you'll be able to get out of here without me. There's only one escape route, and you don't know it."

She thought I might let Sinjin drain her on purpose! "I wouldn't let him kill you," I said softly, surprised the thought would even cross her mind.

Bryn said nothing. She was studying Sinjin carefully to determine if he'd had enough of her blood. "He's almost there," she said softly, her mouth tight, and I could see that he was hurting her. "Now!" she said as she pulled her arm away from him. Just as she'd expected, he reacted violently and lurched for her. She fell, and I threw myself on top of Sinjin, but it was like trying to hold back a train. The blackness of his skin chafed off on my hands. In horror, I realized that the blackness was coming off of him like a crust, replaced with the Mediterranean tone of his beautiful skin.

"Get off me, you fuck!" Bryn yelled as she kicked against him. But Sinjin had her between his legs, his eyes glowing red with bloodlust. She was right. He couldn't control himself and would certainly kill her. I threw myself against him again, but he brushed me aside and dove for Bryn's neck. She went into auto-pilot and karate-chopped him in the side of the neck. He just chuckled and held her on the ground by the throat.

"Sinjin!" I screamed, pounding my ineffectual fists against his back.

"Grab the syringe!" Bryn yelled, eyeing the counter. Just as she did, Sinjin gripped her head and yanked it to the side, burying his face in her neck. She screamed out as I reached for the syringe. I smashed it into his back, pushing down before he could reach around and shove me out of the way. I bumped into the cot, but immediately found my balance again as I faced my sister.

In a second Sinjin's body went slack and he fell on top of her. I pushed him away from her and watched as he rolled to the side, now sleeping like a baby. Then I saw the gaping red gash on her neck. "Oh my God," I said as I reached for her.

Bryn shook her head and took a deep breath, clos-ing her eyes as her lips twitched. She held her hands above the wound, and I could see white light glowing beneath her fingers as she instantly healed herself. In a few more seconds she sat up and the bite vanished. She shook her head and glared at Sinjin before getting to her feet.

"Help me," she ordered as she leaned over, grab-bing one of his arms. I took the other arm and to-gether we dragged him to the door.

"How long will he be like this?" I asked, struggling with his weight.

"A few more minutes," she answered. "But we don't have a few more minutes."

She turned the doorknob and pushed the door open with her foot as we wrestled with our heavy load. We pulled him through the hallway until we came to a T. Rather than going left or right, Bryn paused in front of the wall and scanned her wrist across it. Immediately, a section of the wall recessed back and opened like an invisible door. Inside there was a small room. She propped Sinjin against me and stepped in. There was a clock on the wall, which she studied momentarily, the seconds disappearing as the clock counted our remaining time.

"Dammit!" she yelled. She turned toward a large square structure that dominated the inside of the small room. On the other side was what looked like another hallway, leading God only knew where.

"What's wrong?" I demanded, buckling under Sinjin's weight; he seemed to be growing heavier by the second.

"It's the countdown mechanism," she said. "It's further along than I thought." She grabbed Sinjin's arm then, hoisting him back onto her shoulder, and we started toward the steel box. "We're going to have to get in it," she told me, and huffed and puffed as she hefted Sinjin's weight. I was doing my own huffing and puffing because the vampire wasn't light.

"What's happening?" I inquired when I found my breath.

"This place is about to blow, and we're going to go with it unless we can get in the shed. So stop talking and start hauling this oaf!" She paused outside of the steel box and leaned forward, running her wrist across the locking device of the steel tank. The tank itself was probably nine feet tall by ten feet wide. It beeped and the door slid open.

"On the count of three," she said.

I nodded and on "three" we heaved Sinjin forward. We managed to push him into the steel box, where he landed on the floor. Bryn jumped over his legs and I was quick to follow. Then she grabbed the inside handle of the door and pulled it tightly shut. She ran her wrist across the locking mechanism on the inside and it beeped closed, sealing us safely inside.

I opened my mouth, about to ask her what the hell was going on, when I felt the box begin to quake back and forth. I lost my balance and nearly toppled into Bryn. She grabbed my shoulder and righted me.

"Get on the floor!" she screamed, and threw herself down at the same moment I did. I covered my ears with my hands as explosions rang through the air. The box felt as if it were being tossed this way and that, like we were riding a cork through a turbulent ocean. On the floor, I noticed two enormous bolts in the steel, which must have been holding the box in place, otherwise we would have been launched to Kingdom Come.

I wasn't sure how long the box rocked back and forth or how long the explosions continued to echo through the air, but as soon as it was finally silent, I turned to face Bryn.

She calmly smiled, shaking her head as she said, "Don't say I never did you any favors."

Eighteen

After another few long moments of silence, I figured the destruction was over. Bryn was staring at me with the same pensive expression, as if both of us were waiting for the other to make the next move.

"What do you think?" I asked as I felt my heart rate slow down.

She shrugged but her eyes were still wide. "I think it's over, whatever 'it' was."

I nodded and started to stand up, leaning against the steel wall to get my balance. Then I glanced at Sinjin's still form lying on the floor. He looked like he was sleeping, but as I eyed him, I noticed that his fingers were beginning to twitch. I watched his lips tremble in sync with his twitching fingertips. "I think he's waking up," I said, looking up at Bryn. "What was in the syringe?"

"Charmed blood," she answered as she studied Sinjin in a detached way. She looked up at me again and, noticing my expression of wonder, explained, "It's a way to freeze them for a few minutes." She looked down at him and exhaled, shaking her head, no doubt still shocked that she'd just saved one of her enemies. "Yep, he's coming out of it."

Sinjin opened his eyes and blinked a few times, apparently surprised to find himself encased in a steel box. He was on his feet in the flash of a second and his startled eyes rested on me and then Bryn. Before I could say boo he had Bryn by the throat, her legs suspended in the air as he held her against the wall.

"No, Sinjin!" I screamed, hurling myself against him.

I could see the confusion in his eyes as he studied her. Even though his fangs were fully deployed and ready to sink themselves into her carotid, he hesitated and appeared to be restraining himself.

She glared at him, but I could tell she was afraid. "Get away from me," she seethed in a voice that was cold and calculating, albeit somewhat muffled, given the fact that his hand was wrapped around her throat.

Sinjin just continued to study her intently. Then he licked his lips as if recalling her taste. "You look and taste like Jolie."

Bryn wrapped her hands around Sinjin's, trying to loosen his hold around her neck, but it was futile. He finally loosened his grip, apparently to allow her to breathe. She inhaled deeply, relief flooding her face, then focused on him again and frowned. "That's because I'm her sister, you moron!"

As soon as she said she was my sister, even more surprise flooded Sinjin's face, followed by that devil's smile I was so relieved to see again. He still made no move to release her. Instead, he looked at me and raised a brow. "Is this true?"

I nodded. "Yes, Sinjin, it is," I said, taking a deep breath.

"Poppet's sister," Sinjin said and chuckled, shaking his head as he took Bryn in. He apparently liked what he saw because he licked his lips again.

"Stop looking at me like that, dickhead," Bryn spat out.

Sinjin threw his head back and erupted into a hearty chuckle. "The very same vivacity."

"Hey," Bryn said, turning to face me. "Can you tell your 'friend' to put me the hell down?"

I glanced at him and shook my head. "Sinjin, she just saved your life." And although I had to swallow my pride, I looked at Bryn and said, "Thanks for . . . what you did."

"She saved my life?" Sinjin asked. His eyes were piercing and deadly when they returned to Bryn. "As I recall, she was attempting to kill me only moments ago." I assumed he was referring to the sunlight barbecue.

I nodded, but didn't get the chance to speak. Bryn took it from me. "And I wish I'd succeeded!" she railed at him. She was still kicking out with her legs, trying to get him to release her. He just pushed the weight of his body into her middle, which instantly stopped her.

"Interesting," he said, eyeing her bust.

Bryn shot daggers at him with her fiery eyes. "Let's get one thing straight, bloodsucker, the only reason I did what I did was to get my dumb-ass sister out of the building before it blew up around us." She narrowed her eyes as if zeroing in on her adversary. "And I have no freaking idea what she sees in you."

I didn't even flinch at the name-calling. I was grateful to her, because for whatever reason, she *had* saved Sinjin from dying. As far as I was concerned, that was all that mattered.

"And you allowed me to feed on you?" Sinjin continued. He looked amused now, as if toying with her, playing a game of cat and mouse.

Her lips were tight, her jaw even tighter. "Well, it wasn't like I could ask her to do it, considering the fact that she's pregnant."

I felt my stomach drop as Sinjin's gaze landed on me. His surprise instantly gave way to hurt as he asked me, "Pregnant?" in a hollow tone.

I sighed, long and hard, but before I could respond, he released his hold on Bryn and she fell to the ground. Righting herself immediately, she pushed away from him and started for the door to the steel cell, rubbing her throat as if it pained her.

"We don't have time for this crap," she said, shaking her head at me, careful to ignore Sinjin. It was more than obvious that she was afraid of him. "We need to find out what the hell just happened."

That was when I realized Bryn had no clue that Rand and my people had come for me, much less that war was on the horizon. The battle was brewing. She apparently hadn't read my mind as well or as often as I'd guessed. Knowing she was still first and foremost my enemy, I said nothing. I decided to keep that particular bombshell to myself.

Bryn scanned her wrist across the face of the steel door locking mechanism and it responded immediately. She pulled open the sliding lock and pushed the door open. I heard her gasp in horror when she took in the wreckage outside. The lab was gone, and in its place there was a huge pit that went at least five feet into the ground. It was singed black, and all sorts of refuse littered the enormous hollow. Pieces of concrete, furniture, and paper were scattered in the wind. It looked like a meteor had crashed into the earth right in front of us.

"It's all gone," Bryn said as she looked around in utter disbelief. She leaned down to use the edge of the steel box as support, and dropped herself into the pit. "Everything we've worked for. Gone."

Suddenly realizing she wasn't alone, she took a deep breath. Then, facing us both, her expression hardened. Before she could address either of us, however, a huge flare lit up the night sky behind a patch of pine trees that stood about fifty feet away. It was a magic cloud, bathed in all the colors of the rainbow. Somehow, I knew it was Mercedes.

Bryn watched the blaze with surprise, then her eyebrows furrowed and she turned to me with an expression of shock and suspicion. "They've come for you," she said simply.

I just nodded as Sinjin materialized behind Bryn and grabbed her by the arms, pulling her into him. At that moment all three of us knew she was no friend of ours, regardless of the fact that she was my sister. She was a Lurker. And now, since we were at war, she was our prisoner.

She tried to fight Sinjin, attempting to free herself from his hold, and then closed her eyes. I was immediately reminded of the self-defense lessons she'd been giving to people in the camp. She was in the process of metamorphosing or dissolving or something equally bad for Sinjin. And all I knew was that I wasn't about to let that happen.

I focused on her and imagined all my power roaring into her, sucking her abilities into the center of my being, disarming her, as it were. I could feel her power flowing into me. It was as if I'd been struck by lightning—my entire being seemed to buzz with the intensity of her power. Luce was right; Bryn and I were incredibly potent and, together, I had to imagine we would be almost unstoppable.

"Enough!" she screamed, winded as she drooped forward. "You're going to freaking well kill me!"

I swallowed hard and opened my eyes. I didn't say anything, I just watched her glare up at Sinjin as she panted. "I should have killed you when I had the chance," she seethed.

He chuckled in response. "Hindsight is always twenty-twenty, is it not?"

I hopped down into the pit, since there wasn't any way around it. Sinjin had already forced Bryn halfway through the crater when she collapsed. "Are you all right?" I asked.

"Yes!" she railed back at me. "I just have no energy left, thanks to you!"

Relieved that she wasn't seriously injured, I watched Sinjin reach down and heft her over his shoulders as he started forward again. Another blast of light lit up the night sky. The closer we came to the edge of the crater, the louder the sounds of screaming and fighting. Growls of werewolves, the gnashing of teeth, and the squealing of otherworldly creatures provided the soundtrack to the explosions of magic that rained all around us.

Rand! I thought, no longer caring who could hear me. *Where are you?*

But there was no response. I closed my eyes and concentrated harder, sending out the feelers of my bond to figure out where he was and if he was all right. But I could feel nothing.

Rand, please answer me!

Still no response. It was as if our telepathic bond had been destroyed. I felt my heart drop. Something hollow and panicky started brewing within me.

Is he alive? Is he hurt? Why isn't he answering me? God, what if something happened to him?

But I refused to dwell on the what-ifs. I had one goal in mind and that was to survive. I had to keep my baby—our baby—safe.

"You will never be one of us," Bryn said as she eyed me angrily.

I shook my head, shocked that she could even think I wanted to be. "I never wanted to be one of you and I never will want to," I spat back at her.

She was silent then, perhaps realizing it would be best for her to keep her mouth shut. As we worked our way through the crater, around the piles of rubble and refuse, the sound of fighting and flashes of light became more frequent and much louder. We reached the end of the pit and found ourselves faced with a wall of dirt and debris. With Bryn held to his shoulder, Sinjin grabbed my hand and pulled me into him. A moment later we materialized on the opposite side of the crater. We were still ensconced in the snug harbor of the forest, hidden from the battle that raged on around us.

I felt my stomach tightening as I witnessed what

was happening. We were outside the open pasture that led to the dwellings of the Lurkers—to A, B, C, and D Streets. As I scanned the perimeter, it seemed that almost every house was ablaze. A third of them had already been burnt to the ground. People ran this way and that, screaming as they fought among one another, some falling to the ground as others pressed forward. Chaos reigned supreme, and I didn't know where to look because there was so much carnage around us.

"I have one favor to ask," Bryn suddenly said from her position above Sinjin's shoulders. Her eyes were wide and there was something in them that hinted at a deep sorrow. "Let me save our children."

I gulped hard. I had forgotten there were children in this compound. Of course there were. There was no way I could deny her that request, not when I was carrying my own child within me.

"How will we find them?" I asked.

"They live in Building 100," Bryn answered. It struck me as odd that the Lurkers would separate children from their parents. But I was relieved, in a way, because it would make the job of locating them easier.

"I can walk," she said, glaring at Sinjin. He dropped her on the ground unceremoniously, and after a few seconds of flailing around like a newly born giraffe, she was on her feet, staring daggers at him. Then she faced me. "We need to evacuate them into the storage facility, which is belowground."

I turned toward Sinjin. "I won't let any children die, Sinjin," I said simply.

His expression was hard. "I am your protector. Therefore, wherever you go, I go."

I just nodded, taking it to mean that he would assist me, us. I nodded at Bryn. "Let's go."

She started forward, but before she could take a step, Sinjin gripped her arm, turning her to face him. His face was stony, unreadable. "Let me make something quite clear to you," he said, his voice icy cold. "If you so much as trip, I will end your existence."

She glared at him, hands on her hips and fire in her eyes. "Understood." She turned around, but he gripped her arm again, forcing her to face him again.

"I have not finished," he continued. "I have no regard for familial ties. As far as I am concerned, I am my Queen's protector. I view you as nothing less than a threat to her well-being. If I see you so much as look at her askance, you are finished."

Her hands fisted at her sides. "And as I said before, I understand English." Then she shook her head as she mumbled, "Fucking vampires."

Sinjin's mouth lit up in an amused smile. He nodded, his eyes raking her in a lascivious way. Leave it to Sinjin to find time to ogle a beautiful woman, never mind the circumstances. "Lead the way," he ordered.

Bryn was silent as she started forward, careful to remain in the shelter of the trees. She ran from one tree to the next, with me and Sinjin trailing behind her. When we reached the point where the line of trees ended, she turned to us both. "We need to get to the Jeeps," she said. "It's too far for us to go by foot."

"Where are the Jeeps?" I asked, but Sinjin shook his head.

"Too risky," he said.

Bryn glared at him. "Did you hear a word I just said?"

He returned the glare. "I did." She opened her mouth as if to further lambaste him, but he interrupted her. "Where is the building located?"

She took a deep breath and glanced at the rise of the hill just ahead of us. "It's about a mile or so beyond that hill. We'd have to get through . . . that," she finished, pointing to a throng of people in the middle of the pasture. They were all engaged in battle, and blasts of light continued to brighten the sky.

"Can you materialize that far?" I asked Sinjin, knowing he was wondering the same thing. As a vampire, he could materialize and dematerialize from place to place, but he couldn't go far, usually maxing out at around twenty feet.

"It will be a stretch," he said solemnly.

"Where are the damned Daywalkers when you need one?" Bryn said, and glared at him. "They could easily handle that and then some."

"Yeah, but the trouble with them is that they can't even survive past drinking age," I spat back, irritated that she was doubting Sinjin's abilities.

"Ladies, ladies," the debonair vampire said with a charming smile. Then he faced Bryn and with a practiced grin reached out and grabbed her arm, pulling her into him none too gently.

She pushed away from his chest and frowned up at him. "Watch it," she muttered.

"I am watching it and then some," Sinjin responded, seeming to enjoy nothing more than taunting her.

She rolled her eyes. "I can't wait for the day when you and your kind are extinct!"

"Enough!" I said, and shook my head, not wanting to deal with the two of them. We had much bigger issues at hand. "God, would you both give it a break?!"

Sinjin smiled down at me. "May I?" he asked, offering his other arm. I nodded and accepted it. "Very well, then," he said, and I felt the wind whip against my face as he swept us through the air. It only lasted a few seconds, but it felt like we were flying. When I opened my eyes, the ground was solidly beneath my feet and we were on the other side of the hill.

But our new location also put us in the thick of battle, surrounded by Underworld creatures and Lurkers. Sinjin hadn't been able to materialize far enough away. He pulled me into him as a were fell backward with a knife in his chest. Beside him, a Daywalker ended a vampire's life. Bryn had already started clawing and pushing her way forward, pivoting to miss the claws of a werewolf who had ambushed her.

"It's through here!" she screamed as she continued forward. Sinjin grabbed my arm and forced me on as he took hold of Bryn's arm too. Then we were flying again—manipulating time as we flashed through the air. When we landed, another nondescript white boxy-looking structure rose up in front of us. I assumed it was Building 100 as soon as my eyes took in the two-story structure. And then I saw a blaze erupt to one side. The firestorm blew out chunks of cement and glass. I covered my head with my hands, and Sinjin threw his body over mine, my guardian to the nth degree.

"Are you all right?" he asked in a breathless voice.

"I'm fine," I said as I pushed him away from me and stood up, watching Bryn run for the building.

"No!" she screamed as she approached the blasted section, which appeared to be a kitchen area of some sort. A stove was still intact in the far corner of the room. The blast hadn't been that huge, otherwise the whole building would have disintegrated. All it had done was take out one wall.

"Bryn, no!" I started after her, afraid she might be running toward her death. Granted, she was a Lurker, but she was also my sister and I couldn't deny my connection to her. I got to her and grabbed her arm as another eruption sounded, this time on the opposite side of the building. She turned to face me, her eyes wide and her face pale. "What's happening?" I screamed, shielding my ears against the blast.

Bryn shook her head as she pushed away from me. "All of the buildings are self-destructing, but the children could still be in there!"

She started running forward again, and I turned to Sinjin. "I will go," he said simply. He pushed me toward the crest of a small hill, indicating that I should take cover below it. "You stay put," he said, his expression warning me not to argue with him.

I watched as he turned in Bryn's direction and followed her. They both disappeared into the building, and I was struck with the thought that it might explode with both of them inside. And what was more, it was doing absolutely no one any good for me to be hiding there like an idiot. I stood up and took a deep breath, knowing what I needed to do.

I took the ten or so steps separating me from the building and jumped over the rubble of the kitchen wall. Once inside, the cloud of dust and debris from the initial explosion was almost too much for me to bear. I covered my mouth with my upper arm, finding it difficult to breathe.

I heard the cries and screams of children and felt myself go into autopilot as I lurched forward, up a rickety staircase. The previous explosion had compromised the entire structure and now it groaned and creaked under its own weight. At the top of the stairs, I could make out Bryn at the end of the hall. She was surrounded by about eight children of various ages. She was carrying a crying toddler in her arms and ushering all the children toward the staircase I'd just come up. Sinjin suddenly burst through a door directly before me, a child over each of his shoulders and three more holding on to the back of his shirt.

"Are there more in there?" I yelled to him.

Seeing me, he frowned and seemed about to reprimand me, or worse. His focus was entirely on my safety. I shook my head emphatically. I wouldn't allow him to think of me, not now.

"Are there more in there?" I screamed at him, and he nodded. Not wasting any time, I threw myself past him, into a bedroom. It was so dark, it was almost impossible to see. I closed my eyes and charmed myself into clearer vision—the equivalent of night goggles.

I saw the two small children huddling in the corner

of the room. In front of them, a large beam had fallen from the ceiling.

"Come on!" I screamed to them, holding my arms open wide. "I'll carry you!"

Neither of them moved forward, so I pushed through the debris, stepping over a destroyed desk, only to narrowly avoid walking into another beam that was hanging from the dilapidated ceiling. When I reached them, the look of fear on their faces crushed me. I wanted nothing more than to gather them in my arms and promise that nothing was going to happen to them, that they would be safe.

Another blast suddenly shook the whole building, and I had to stabilize myself against the wall. One of the children screamed as the beam came crashing down, with the other child directly in its path. I held up my hands, imagining a deflection globe surrounding the child. The beam bounced off the orb and slid to a rest just beside the child.

"Nicely done," Bryn said, appearing beside me. I glanced at her and smiled, then climbed over the beam and leaned down, reaching for the child closest to me. She wrapped her arms around me as I lifted her out, and then reached for the other child. The boy said nothing, but his wide eyes told me he was scared to death. The sound of the ceiling creaking grabbed my attention and Bryn's.

"It's not going to hold much longer," she said, motioning for me to hurry the hell up. I quickened my pace over the rubble in the room, holding on to the little girl in my arms as tightly as I could. I could hear Bryn just behind me when a sudden blast knocked me off my feet. I hit the ground hard, the little girl falling on top of me. She shrieked and started crying again.

"It's okay!" I screamed, and pushed to my feet, leaning over to check on Bryn, who had also fallen. "Come on!" I shouted at her as more explosions sounded from outside.

"My foot is stuck!" she yelled back and pushed the little boy forward. "Get the kids out of here!" Bryn turned to try to free her leg, which appeared to be wedged between two beams and the wall. She held her hands together as if to use her magic, but another rumbling quake interrupted her, forcing her to use her hands to protect her face against an onslaught of debris coming from the ceiling.

"Bryn!" I called out, and knowing she could die in here, hesitated.

"Go!" she yelled. "I'll use my magic to free myself!" Realizing I had to get the children to safety, I grabbed them, and once they were nestled in my arms, the little boy shielding his eyes against my shoulder, I bolted for the door.

Sinjin met me. "Where is she?" he demanded.

"She's stuck!" I said in a panicked voice.

He instantly dematerialized. I had to hope he was helping Bryn, because I needed to get the children outside and away from the building, which was about to crumble into nothing. I turned to face them. "Hold onto each other and don't let go. I'm going to get us out of here!" Then I started down the rickety staircase, praying it would hold up long enough. At the bottom, I glanced behind me, pleased to see that they were following me. Once we hit the ground floor, I started jogging for the door, glancing behind me to make sure they were still there. When we made it through the rubble and out into the night air, I felt relief flash through me until I realized that Sinjin and Bryn were still inside.

Another explosion hit the kitchen area again, and I forced the children as far from the building as possible, huddling over them as they shrieked in terror. I watched in shock as the entire structure seemed to wobble and then cave in on itself. The second floor fell into the first in a billowing cloud of dust and debris.

"Sinjin!" I screamed, feeling sick to my stomach.

In a split second, Sinjin appeared just outside the collapsed structure, Bryn in his arms. Her foot was bloodied where the beam had pinned her, but other than that, they both looked okay. I glanced at the children and back at Bryn again.

"Is this all of them?" I shouted to her.

She nodded, but there was still worry on her face.

"What about the storage facility?" I asked, wondering if it was safe to take the children there, whether it might self-destruct too.

Bryn shook her head and there was panic in her gaze. "It's not safe either. Nothing is. This whole place is going to blow!"

"What?" I shrieked. If the whole camp blew up, it would take all my soldiers with it, us included and . . . Rand. I shook my head against the prospect. I could not let that happen! "There has to be a way to stop it!" I screamed. "How do we stop it?"

But Bryn shook her head as if it were out of her control. She was quiet as she seemed to struggle with what to do. "It's Luce!" she yelled just as another building adjacent to the children's building exploded into a mass of shrapnel.

We huddled over the children but luckily were far enough away that no one was injured. I glanced up at Bryn again, frowning. "Luce? Why would he do this?"

She shook her head. "If the compound is threatened, it's better to destroy it than give up our secrets."

"And all your people?" I asked.

She shook her head again. "I don't know."

I didn't have time to consider why Luce was planning to blow the whole camp up. All I knew was that I had to get to Rand and Mercedes. Somehow we had to stop him.

Nineteen

Moments of utter terror and panic can be strange. It's almost as if your mind goes on hiatus—it can't process everything that's going on around it, so it enters a strange dreamscape where everything is slowed down to a snail's pace.

As I stood there, I took in the battle raging around me. I was still far enough away that I was safe from the chaos. Behind me was empty forest—the skeletal outline of the trees seeming to offer shelter from the storm of the battle. I swallowed hard as I watched what appeared to be hundreds of our legion meeting hundreds of our enemies. It looked like two different-colored blankets of soldiers meeting together as one, only to end up a patchwork of Lurkers and Underworlders.

The night was a chaos of screams, clanking metal, explosions, and bursts of magic. At the sound of hollering, I turned and watched two of my weres drop to their knees, their clothes shredding and falling off their shifting frames. Their muscles rippled as their skin turned into fur and their rib cages expanded, the sound of fracturing bones splintering the air. To my right I could see a Daywalker bracing himself for their attack. The weres leapt at the Daywalker and managed to wrestle him to the ground, descending on him like rabid dogs. The Daywalker gripped one wolf by the throat and threw him, the wolf landing with a yelp about fifty feet away. The other one wasn't quite as lucky. The Daywalker ripped into the wolf's throat with his bare hands and separated his windpipe from his neck. I glanced away from the gruesome attack, unable to witness any more.

"We are not safe here," Sinjin said as he looked between Bryn and me and the children, who were standing behind us. It did seem like the throng of soldiers was edging ever closer to us—they'd met in the middle of the camp and were now fragmenting outward.

"Back away," Sinjin demanded, and lifted Bryn when it was apparent she would have trouble hobbling to better cover. Apparently, her ability to heal herself was delayed, owing to the fact that I'd zapped her of her strength earlier and it still hadn't completely returned. I huddled the children together, lifting those who were too young to understand, and once we were under the cover of the trees, my breath caught in my throat. A creature had suddenly materialized in front of us. I shoved a few children behind me as Sinjin and Bryn positioned themselves by my side, Bryn favoring her injured foot. The three of us made a wall between the children and the beast. The creature had simply appeared out of nowhere, and now it stood maybe ten feet away. It was on all fours, but was like no beast I'd ever seen in nature. Its entire body was covered with red scales and its eyes glowed white. Its nostrils were wide and flaring, and as it pawed the air, I noticed talons on its hands and feet. It turned toward Bryn and seemed to somehow recognize her. As soon as it did, it aimed its furious gaze on Sinjin and me.

"Tell it to go away, Bryn," I said in a steel voice. "Tell it to retreat."

"I can't," she said, sounding frightened. "Once an Elemental metamorphoses, he loses all rational thought."

"What does that mean?" I demanded.

"It means the creature is going to want blood, and won't care if it's your blood or mine."

"What the bloody hell is it?" Sinjin asked, his face twisted with confusion.

"It's an Elemental, Sinjin," I responded.

"A what?" he demanded, which was when I realized Sinjin knew nothing about Elementals or Daywalkers. He just knew them collectively as Lurkers.

"It's a Lurker, Sinjin, but it possesses magic."

It was my way of saying, *Keep the hell away from it!* but apparently Sinjin didn't get the message. He disappeared, then reappeared directly in front of the creature. Pulling back his arm, he pummeled it with ferocity, his fangs glowing in the moonlight. But it didn't even faze the creature, which lashed out with its snout full of sharklike teeth. It caught Sinjin's upper arm and pulled away, blood trailing from its mouth. Glancing at Sinjin in shock and horror, I could see the blood gushing from his ragged wound. But the brutal attack didn't even make him wince or falter. The wound began mending almost immediately, sewing itself together as if with invisible hands.

I turned to check on the children, afraid that they

were witnessing the horrible ordeal, but Bryn had diverted their attention to the trees behind us, asking them if they could see the pixies in the branches. As I glanced behind me, I could see the flickering of lights between the trees and had to wonder if Bryn had magicked the supposed pixies. Relieved, I brought my attention back to Sinjin and watched him open his mouth to reveal his fully extended fangs. He ripped into the creature's neck, but the beast just kicked out and sent him sprawling into a tree. The children gasped, and some screamed when he hit the tree. Bryn managed to escort them away from the creature and farther into the forest, hobbling as she did so.

I glanced back at Sinjin. In a split second he materialized in front of the Elemental, wrapped his hands around the thing's neck and simply snapped it. The lifeless carcass fell to the ground as Sinjin dusted himself off. The only reminder that his arm had been wounded was his ripped sleeve.

Turning to look at Bryn, I saw that her eyes were on me. "Well, apparently your Elementals aren't quite as strong as my vampires," I said in a snide way.

She raised a brow. "That was a human Elemental, not one of our strongest by any means."

I didn't say anything else, not wanting to reflect on the fact that it had been a weak Elemental. I looked over at the battlefield, trying to figure out if my side was prevailing. There was so much going on all around me, I had trouble focusing. But then my gaze settled on two women standing to my left, and I recognized the one closest to me as one of my own, a vampire. The woman she was sparring with was a Daywalker—I could tell by her tiny fangs. But small fangs or not, she was a force to be reckoned with. She was quick, almost faster than my vampire, and pivoted around the smaller woman until she looked like a ballerina on fast-forward.

My vampire seemed unsure on her feet. It was clear that she was unaccustomed to such an opponent, and she almost appeared clumsy as she avoided some fist falls and was pummeled with others. The Daywalker was stronger than the vampire, and seemed far from exhausted. The vampire, on the other hand, was tired and getting more and more clumsy. Pretty soon it was apparent that the Daywalker was toying with her, just postponing the inevitable. I felt my palms grow clammy—I couldn't just stand by and watch. I had to do something.

"There's nothing you can do," Bryn said flatly, and I realized I wasn't doing a good job of hiding my thoughts. Dammit, I'd have to be way more careful whenever she was nearby.

"Well, I'm also not going to let that—that woman just toy with her when it's clear they aren't evenly matched."

Bryn frowned and then shrugged, seemingly unconcerned. "All is fair in love and war, right?"

"What does that even mean?" I threw back at her.

"It means it is their fight," Sinjin said calmly, watching the two women. "And furthermore, I will not allow you anywhere near them. It is too dangerous."

Even though I had it in mind to argue, by the time I returned my attention to the combatants, my vampire had been reduced to a pile of ash, which was in the process of being blown into obscurity by the wind. I was too late. I felt a cry catch in my throat as my people continued to fight our enemies and buildings continued to self-destruct around us.

I needed to focus on finding Mercedes. Now. She would know what to do. But the problem was I had no idea where to find her. I closed my eyes and relied on my sixth sense, sending out mental feelers as I imagined the supreme witch of all witches in front of me.

Find her, I said to myself. *Mercedes, where are you?*

With my eyes still clenched firmly shut, I suddenly saw her. She was standing on the crest of the hill just on the west side of A Street, adjacent to the house in which Luce had held me prisoner. I opened my eyes and turned to face Sinjin, whose gaze had already settled on me.

"I have to go to Mercedes," I said quickly.

He nodded and took a few steps toward me, as if to say he was going with me. That was when I realized our quandary. Someone had to stay behind to protect the children, over a dozen of them now in our charge. But I wasn't about to relegate Bryn to that position. I still wasn't convinced she wasn't playing some part in this whole thing. "Sinjin, I need you to stay behind and make sure the children are safe," I said softly.

He firmly shook his head. "You are my priority, my Queen."

Just as I was about to argue, Bryn glanced over at us. "Let me find someone suitable."

Sinjin nodded, showing his support for the idea. Bryn started looking around as if searching.

"The redhead," she said abruptly, pointing to a woman who was three people deep in a mob of soldiers. Sinjin nodded and grasped her arm, allowing her to use him as a crutch. Then they disappeared, materializing through space, no doubt. I checked behind me to ensure the children were all present and accounted for, then took a deep breath, anxiously awaiting Sinjin's and Bryn's return.

A few minutes went by before I could see them on the horizon again. They were accompanied by the redheaded Lurker. She was dressed in training combat gear, so I assumed she was a soldier. Her hair was in disarray and blood and dirt smeared half her face. Sinjin was holding her arms behind her back with one hand and supporting Bryn with the other.

"Do not attempt anything," Sinjin said to Bryn, narrowing his eyes at her.

She nodded, then faced the redheaded woman. "Rhonda, I need you to take the children the back way through the compound until you get to the gatehouse. Once there, tell Hanz that I directed you to take one of the vans."

"What about you?" Rhonda asked her, glancing at Sinjin. "Will you be safe?"

"Do not worry about her," Sinjin responded, his tone icy. "Just do as you are instructed."

The redhead glared at him. Sinjin smiled in return.

"And if the vans are all gone?" Rhonda demanded of Bryn.

"Then you can walk until you find another means of transportation," Bryn said. "Give me your hand."

But before Rhonda could so much as move, Sinjin grasped Bryn's hand himself.

"Rhonda won't get far with Hanz unless she has my blessing," Bryn said through gritted teeth.

Sinjin released Bryn's hand and Rhonda took it, staring at Sinjin with undisguised anger. Bryn closed her eyes as she traced something in Rhonda's palm, which lit up and glowed in what was now dark night. It looked like a circle with a line through it. Then she opened her eyes and dropped the other Lurker's hand.

"What was that all about?" I asked suspiciously.

Bryn frowned as if she didn't appreciate my tone. It was more than obvious that she didn't trust me, so I guessed we had that in common. "It's my signature so that Hanz, the guard at the gate, immediately recognizes Rhonda." Then she faced Rhonda again. "Okay, Plumhoff, when you get to the gate and get everyone in the van, go as far away from the compound as you can."

"Understood," Rhonda said. "Where do you want me to go?"

Bryn faced Sinjin and me. "Breisgau is straight down the A5 and the closest city to us. They should be safe there."

"My Queen?" Sinjin said, allowing me to make the final decision.

I looked at Rhonda and Bryn and nodded.

Rhonda inhaled deeply and said, "You be careful, boss." She gave Sinjin and me a parting glare, as if she hated the idea of leaving Bryn in our care.

The three of us watched as Rhonda picked up the two youngest children and started forward with the others. They all disappeared over a valley in the grassy landscape. I hoped she wouldn't have any trouble getting to Breisgau.

I took a deep breath. "We have to find the prophetess," I said to Bryn. "She's the only one who will know how to stop this place from blowing, taking your people and mine with it."

Bryn nodded, then pursed her lips as she regarded me angrily. "I am only assisting you because I don't want to see everyone destroyed."

"Whatever your reasons, we don't have time to discuss it now."

Sinjin offered me his arm at the same time as he grabbed Bryn's upper arm. His expression said she better not try any funny business with him. He flashed a devil's smile at me. "Where is the prophetess?" he asked.

"At the end of A Street," I answered, and closed my eyes, preparing for Sinjin's brand of air travel. The swoosh of wind across my face didn't even make me flinch, and when I opened my eyes a second or so later, I found we were nearly at the end of the dirt cul-de-sac of A Street. Another blast of air across my cheeks signified the fact that Sinjin was now closing the gap. I opened my eyes and noticed all the buildings had been completely flattened, and nothing remained but burnt-out craters where homes had once stood.

That, however, wasn't what captured my attention. We had found Mercedes, all right, but apparently so had Luce. The two were standing on top of the hill at the end of A Street, facing each other. They were surrounded by a circle of blue flames that arced up every once in a while in a great show of light and sparks. Although five feet separated them, it was obvious they were engaged in battle. Each had a hand raised in front of them and an intense look of concentration.

I couldn't tell who was winning.

"That's why the camp hasn't imploded yet," Bryn

said in a soft voice, shaking her head in apparent understanding.

"We have to help her, Bryn," I implored. "We have to make sure this camp doesn't blow, or else every one of us is going to die."

She hesitated, and I realized again that she was, first and foremost, a Lurker. She'd spent the last thirty years of her life being brainwashed, and fully supported Luce. I could see it in her eyes.

I took a deep breath. "I have to help Mercedes," I said to Sinjin.

Sinjin nodded and tightened his grip on Bryn's arms, as if to say she wasn't going anywhere. I smiled in silent understanding and started forward, knowing what I had to do. Mercedes needed me, and I hoped that together we could defeat Luce.

When I was ten feet from them, I gulped down my fear, afraid of Luce's power. I mean, I had no clue how powerful he truly was. But given that Mercedes was a force to be reckoned with too, I ignored my doubts as I approached them. Neither of them even noticed I was there. They were too wholly focused on each other. I closed my eyes and unleashed the power within me, allowing it to flow through my entire being until my skin tickled with magic and every hair on my body stood on end. Then I opened my eyes and concentrated on projecting my power into Mercedes. I imagined filling her up with my magic. As soon as I made figurative contact with her, the circle of flames that had burned around the two of them suddenly pulled me into its center. Instantly, I was overwhelmed with the feeling that something was wrong.

When I saw Mercedes, I understood why. As soon as my power entered their circle, Mercedes had fallen to the ground, unconscious. Well, I *hoped* she was only unconscious. That was when it hit me—this was what Luce had been hoping for; Mercedes had just been a prop. Luce had orchestrated their power play, knowing that I would come to her defense, and now he had me exactly where he wanted me.

"What have you done to her?" I screamed at him.

He stood there in all his glory, his white hair sailing around him as if he were underwater. "Her power could not rival mine," he replied. "Now make your decision wisely," he added, meaning I could fight him or join him.

"I will not allow you to destroy my people!" I shouted, wanting to cut to the chase. I was never going to join the Lurkers, and it was past time that he realized that.

He shook his head. "You have proven to be such a disappointment."

Then he raised his hands toward me and I was suddenly overcome with a dull ache spreading through my body. Soon that dullness became an all-out throbbing that seemed to center in my middle, pumping pain through me.

And then it hit me that he might be harming my baby. I clenched my eyes shut and called on all the power inside of me to fight him, to crush the tentacles of pain from my body. I could feel a glow building within me, repelling Luce's power. And then a sense of calmness surrounded me, and I felt no pain at all.

I opened my eyes.

"Give them up, Jolie," Luce said evenly. But his

voice was ragged. My resistance had depleted some of his energy.

"Give who up?" I demanded.

"The people you call your own. You are not one of them. We are your true family."

I shook my head. "The creatures of the Underworld are my true family," I insisted.

Luce tsked me as if I were idiotic. "Your side is losing, my dear," he said in as sweet a tone as he could muster, like he was trying to be my father. "Your wolves, witches, vampires, and fairies are no match for the Daywalkers or Elementals."

Six separate images suddenly appeared in the air directly before me—against a backdrop of misty clouds. I focused on one and recognized that it was a dreamscape of the battle raging in the camp—I could see an Elemental fighting one of my witches. The Elemental threw a fire orb into my witch, thrusting her backward. When she hit the ground, she erupted into an inferno of flames and rolled back and forth frantically, trying to put herself out. But it was no use. The fire raged out of control, spurred on by Elemental magic, and the witch succumbed. I felt my stomach drop as I glanced at the next cloud and the next, realizing they were all projections of battles. Somehow I knew that they were all going on at that exact moment. The more I watched, the more I realized Luce was right. The creatures of the Underworld were not as strong as the Lurkers.

"Jolie, no!"

I heard Rand's voice behind me, but I knew better than to turn toward him. Luce would use the opportunity to blast me with his magic. I concentrated on opening the bond between us, thus fortifying our power. Together we would be much stronger. Immediately, I felt Rand's response, and his side of our bond reaffirmed our connection, our mutual understanding.

I would never give in to Luce, or anyone else for that matter, even if he was right and our soldiers were dropping like flies. All anyone had was his or her own fight, and I wasn't going to allow Luce to win this one.

I held out my hands again, throwing my power, now joined with Rand's, into Luce. Of course, Luce pumped up his power too, and was suddenly much stronger than he had been. I realized that his last demonstration had been little more than a warm-up—a way of judging how much juice he'd need to defeat me.

Don't give up, Jolie, I heard Rand say in my head. *Together, we can bring him down.*

I just focused all my power, all my magic, everything I had, into Luce. I could feel Rand's abilities feeding into me. But it wasn't enough. The empty space inside of me was growing at a faster rate than Rand could refuel it. I could feel my defenses weakening as exhaustion started to claim me. I scrunched my eyes tighter and imagined an orb of glowing light surrounding me as well as Rand. It was a defensive measure to create a buttress against Luce's magic so I could focus on refueling my figurative magic tank.

I didn't have time to fully regroup before Luce attacked me with another onslaught of magic—sending heat flaring through me. I felt like I was being stabbed with thousands of knives. I focused on my orb, trying to strengthen it, but another blow of heat disabled me.

Luce's power was emptying me, and I dropped down to my knees, no longer able to stand. Was this what he'd done to Mercedes? Since she was still sprawled out on the ground next to me, I had to imagine it was.

Out of the corner of my eyes I watched Sinjin lash out against Luce, as if trying to take him unawares. As soon as he entered the fiery circle around us, however, he started shaking violently, as if being electrocuted, and he had to take a step backward. He tried again, but the same thing happened. The circle was impenetrable, which meant that I was on my own.

Jolie! Rand screamed through our bond.

But I couldn't respond. I couldn't draw my attention away from Luce. Suddenly, I could no longer feel Rand's power. It was almost as if his supply had been cut off. At the same time, Luce's magic had gone quiet as well. I watched in horror as Luce lifted Rand into the air. Rand struggled to free himself, continuing to bombard Luce with an onslaught of his own magical defenses, but they paled in comparison with Luce's power.

"Let him go!" I screamed, pain seizing my voice.

And then I felt something angry and protective start to stir within me. Gritting my teeth, I allowed my power to flow into Luce, in full attack mode. He took a few steps back and his assault on Rand stalled as Rand fell to the ground. He didn't move. But I couldn't devote any attention to him because I was once again on the receiving end of Luce's magic. His attack had doubled in strength.

Still too weak to stand, I pushed up onto my knees. I felt Luce's power draining every inch of me, but I couldn't feel any pain—refused to feel any pain. There was something powerful inside of me, and it would not back down. I wavered a bit before finding my balance.

Forcing myself to my feet, I approached Luce, holding both hands up directly in front of me, using them like a shield to ward off his attack. I continued walking toward him, some inner force compelling me forward, telling me that I could defeat him. I couldn't give up, not now.

I clenched my eyes shut and willed my power to double up on itself, throwing everything I had into him. But there was no response. I opened my eyes and discovered that Luce was gone. It was as if he'd disappeared into the air, or maybe the night had swallowed him.

I took a deep breath and suddenly felt completely exhausted. I fell to my knees again, bending over as I braced myself with my hands. My light-headedness was seriously impeding me, and I took a few seconds to steady myself to ensure that I wouldn't pass out. I opened my eyes once the feeling recessed and looked for Rand, who was lying prostrate on the ground. I crawled over to him. My heart was lodged in my throat as I gripped his face and leaned down. I placed my ear next to his nose to determine if he was still breathing.

He was.

Relief bloomed inside of me. I closed my eyes as I held my hands above his heart, pouring some of my energy and power into him through our bond.

"Jolie," he said softly, and I opened my eyes, smiling down at him as tears began to choke me. "What happened?" he asked.

I shook my head. "I don't know," I said softly. Then I felt Sinjin behind me. He lifted me up and pulled me into his arms.

"Are you injured, my Queen?" he asked with a look of concern. I watched his gaze meet Rand's, but neither of them said anything.

I looked up into Sinjin's ice blue eyes and nodded. Even though I tried to smile, all I could think about was the carnage and massacre I'd observed in Luce's cloud images. "Get Mercedes," I said simply, and Sinjin nodded.

He set me down beside Rand as he approached Mercedes' collapsed form.

I watched Sinjin lift her. "Is she alive?" I asked in a hollow voice.

He looked at her, then nodded. "She is breathing."

Relief flooded through me, but it was short-lived. I remembered with a jolt that the Lurker camp was about to implode on itself. "How do we stop it from blowing?" I demanded of Bryn, who was still standing in the spot where Sinjin had left her. She was gazing around in apparent shock, not saying or doing anything.

"He's gone," she replied simply.

"What does that mean?" I demanded.

She shook her head as if she couldn't make sense of anything that had just happened. "Whatever was going to happen has happened," she said finally.

Then I realized I couldn't hear fighting anymore—there were no more magical bursts lighting up the sky, no war cries or howls coming from the weres. I started down the street so I could get a better visual. Everything was dead silent. But the longer I watched, the more casualties I could see—in the form of lumps on the ground. I glanced up and noticed an outline of people along the horizon. Most were limping or carrying others, but they were all slowly approaching us. As they came nearer, I realized that they were my own people. As for the Elementals and the Daywalkers? I had no clue.

One of our werewolves approached me with a shocked look.

"What is it? What's happened?" I demanded.

The were shook his head, as if he didn't even know where to begin. "They all just . . . disappeared. Right there in front of us. We were fightin' and then they . . . disappeared like the air swallowed 'em up."

At the sound of footsteps, I turned around and faced Sinjin and Bryn. "What does this mean?" I asked her.

She refused to answer. I didn't know if she was keeping it to herself or if she just didn't have an answer for me. I had no clue why she hadn't disappeared with the rest of her people, but was grateful all the same because Bryn was now my prisoner.

Taking a deep breath, I turned around and found Rand smiling down at me. And that was when it hit me. The battle was over for now. The Lurkers had given up, and maybe that alone made us the victors. At that point I didn't even think it mattered.

I smiled at Sinjin. "Rally our soldiers," I ordered. "And tell them we're going home."

Twenty

As I stood in my living room and admired the view from my windows, I had never been happier to see the beauty of the craggy coastline of Kinloch Kirk, to witness the puffins flying in and out of the hillside, feeding their babies. The heather appeared even more purple against the bright blue of the sky, and the ocean air refreshed me with its bold saltiness.

I was home.

"You wished to speak with me, my Queen?" Mathilda's voice pulled me from my thoughts, and I turned to face her, smiling as she held her arms out and I rushed into them. Mathilda, as the oldest of the fae, had waited out the battle in a fae village near Kinloch Kirk.

"I am so happy to see you," I said, and kissed her cheek. It had only been a matter of hours since the battle, and even though I was exhausted, questions about my lineage continued to plague me. Enough that I had decided to solve it here and now.

"Are you well?" she asked, still smiling.

"I'm fine, Mathilda," I said, and motioned her toward the couch. She took a seat, and I sat down beside her, holding her old and weathered hands in mine.

"And Mercedes?" Mathilda continued.

I took a deep breath. Mercedes had come very close to death. Luce had done his utmost to drain her of all her powers, and even though she was alive, it was going to be a long road to recovery. "She's lost the use of her powers," I said softly.

Mathilda nodded. "I have seen similar cases before. We will buffer her with our own power each day until she is well enough to develop her magic again."

I nodded and took relief in her words. I mean, I knew Mercedes was eventually going to improve, I just wasn't sure if she'd regain all her abilities. And that was a sobering thought—as long as I'd known Mercedes, I'd always been amazed by her abilities, by her magic. And yet Luce had made such short work of her.

Really, there was nothing more I could do for Mercedes, and worrying about her wasn't going to do anyone any good. All I could do was hope that Mathilda was right. I returned my attention to the subject that had been plaguing me. "Mathilda, I want you to tell me about my birth parents," I said, my tone hopeful.

Mathilda's expression fell and she looked surprised. She glanced down at her old fingers as if she wasn't sure where she should begin her story. When she looked up at me again, her eyes were glassy. "The Lurkers told you?" she asked.

I nodded and explained everything Luce had said to me, including the part about Bryn being my sister . . . and now my prisoner. She was being held in the guest quarters of Kinloch Kirk, where Bella had met her end. I wasn't sure what would happen between Bryn and me. Even though we were sisters, there was a rift between us that seemed irreparable. From the moment I'd taken her as my POW, she refused to speak to me. And furthermore, she insisted that she would forever remain true to Luce. Even so, I continued to hold out hope that someday we might mend the gap between us and just be . . . sisters.

"Your mother was my grandniece," Mathilda started, and at the look of surprise on my face, she took my hand. "She was a lovely girl, Jolie, so similar to you in appearance and character."

"What was her name?" I asked, my voice sounding hollow, pained, as I fought to understand who my mother was.

"Keila," she said, and her eyes took on a faraway expression, as if she were remembering my mother when she was still alive. After a few seconds Mathilda seemed to return to the present and she smiled at me apologetically. "She had the great misfortune of falling in love with a man not of her own species."

"Then it was true, my father was a Lurker?" I said, my voice sounding stony.

Mathilda nodded. "Yes. There was a raid on one of our villages and many of the fae were killed. Others were abducted, and Keila was one of them."

I sighed deeply, realizing Mathilda's account paralleled Luce's so far. "Luce told me that my father fell in love with my mother while she was his prisoner."

"Yes," Mathilda said with a sweet smile. "Your father was quite taken with Keila." Her eyebrows arched as she turned to another thought. "It was perhaps six months before we saw Keila again. When your father fell in love with her, the others rejected them and they sought shelter from us. Of course we willingly took them in. We believed your father to be a good man."

"Even though he'd raided your village?" I asked, surprised.

Mathilda nodded. "Your father begged our forgiveness, said he had atoned for his ways. And in the end we believed him. People have it within themselves to change, to atone for their mistakes." She took a deep breath. "Your father and mother lived happily among our kind for perhaps a year. When your mother learned she was with child, your father was so excited, Jolie. I remember his smile as if it were only yesterday."

I ran my hand across my stomach, reminding myself of my own baby and the fact that I too would be a parent. And a feeling of deep contentment welled up inside of me. There was nothing I'd ever wanted more than to be a mother, and a wife to Rand. "Go on."

"Your father died shortly thereafter."

I felt the breath catch in my throat as a feeling of deep sadness settled in my gut, replacing the balmy happiness I'd felt only moments before. "What did he die from?"

Mathilda shrugged. "No one knew for certain. It was quite a mystery, though I have always been certain that he was killed by the Lurker elder."

"Luce," I said out loud, hating his name on my lips. She nodded. "Of course I have no proof, but it seemed a strange coincidence for the poor young man to die when he was so very happy."

"And my mother?"

Mathilda nodded as if reminding herself of where she'd left off in her story. "Shortly after your father's death, your mother was overcome with such sorrow that she simply went mad. She became a threat to herself and to you, her unborn child."

"To us," I corrected, thinking of Bryn. "There were two of us, Bryn and me."

Mathilda nodded and frowned as she shook her head. "Yes, two." She paused for a moment. "I never did realize Keila was pregnant with twins. How foolish of me not to have checked."

"It's in the past now, Mathilda," I said sincerely, realizing it disturbed Mathilda, deeply by the looks of it.

She offered me a smile, but it was sad, bereft. "One day Keila wandered out of the fae village and I never saw her again. She simply disappeared."

"And that must have been when the Lurkers found her," I finished. Mathilda simply nodded, and I faced her again, needing to ask the final question in this tangled web, needing to understand why I was just now hearing this story. "Why didn't you tell me?"

She sighed, long and hard, but didn't look at all surprised. "During the time your mother was with us, I received a series of visions proclaiming that the progeny of your father and mother would be incredibly gifted. I realized I couldn't allow the Lurkers to claim you for their own. Through fairy magic, I was able to locate you, and when I learned you were born

in a human hospital, I simply switched you with another baby."

"And the Lurkers never found me," I said softly.

She nodded, her lips drawn into a tight line, her jaw
rigid. "I was quite careful to disguise you throughout
the years, child," she said, sounding pleased with herself. But then, it was clear she had pulled off a pretty
amazing feat—hiding me from the Lurkers for over
twenty years . . .

"So you always knew where I was?"

She nodded. "I kept a strict watch over you."

I'd been a pawn in this battle between the Underworld and the Lurkers from the moment I was born.
It was a strange thought. And even stranger was the
idea that I'd never had the slightest inkling about it.
"And no one else ever knew about this?"

Mathilda gulped, apparently uneasy with this part
of her story. "No. You were my secret and mine
alone."

"Why?"

She cleared her throat and glanced down at the
ground as if this next bit of information was hard
for her to divulge. Then she looked up at me again
and her eyes were fearful. "I acted without the blessing of the King."

"Odran?" I asked, surprised, because I knew that
Odran adored Mathilda and vice versa.

Mathilda shook her head emphatically. "No, this
was long before Odran's reign. King Lucan was not
the benevolent King that Odran is. He wanted to
maintain separation between the fae and the other
creatures of the Underworld, and he strictly forbade
me from getting involved in what he considered for-

eign affairs." She paused for a second or two, biting her lip as if her story still bothered her as much now as it had then. "But I could not ignore you, Jolie. I knew that I had to protect you, and ensure that you didn't fall into the hands of our enemies, even if it meant acting against the orders of my King."

"What would have happened to you if he found out?" I asked, surprised to hear that she'd broken a law. If Mathilda was anything, it was a law-abiding fae citizen.

She swallowed. "I could have been put to death for my transgressions." She paused and took a few deep breaths. "Once Odran took the throne, it seemed the story had taken on a life of its own, and I was afraid to tell him, afraid to tell anyone."

"Odran never would have faulted you for it," I said softly.

"No, but by fairy law I could still have been punished for breaking my vows to my King, even though another had taken the throne." She paused for a few moments. "And by then, I thought it better to keep the secret to myself."

I nodded, understanding her reasons and by no means faulting her for them. It was all thanks to Mathilda that I was standing here today. Without her interference, who knows what would have happened to me? "Thank you, Mathilda, thank you for what you did."

She beamed at me and there were tears in her eyes. "I always knew you were someone special, someone who would lead our people to prosperity and unity. And I was right, Jolie. I was right."

* * *

Now fully aware of my history, I felt somehow content. And the fact that I was part Lurker? I couldn't say it mattered much. Because in my own mind, my parents were like Romeo and Juliet. Doomed from the very beginning, they both died for the most noble cause imaginable—love. Honestly, I didn't even consider my father a Lurker. No, I considered him to be one of my own kind. And that was when it occurred to me that the only other person who was also a byproduct of my parents' love was my sister.

I will do everything in my power to make amends with Bryn, I told myself. We *were* blood, and I wanted to make sure we became the sisters our parents would have wanted us to be.

I stepped out of the shower and after toweling myself off got into my jammies, noticing the gentle rain now pelting my bedroom windows. The moonlight reflected against the drops, and they looked like diamonds clinging to the glass. I unwrapped the towel around my head and, grabbing my comb, started for my bed.

"Jolie."

It was Rand's voice, followed by a gentle knock on the door. He knew I'd been expecting him, so he didn't wait for a response. He just turned the doorknob, opening the door. He had showered as well, although the trauma from the battle still decorated his face and body in bruises and lacerations.

Seeing him, I couldn't help the heat that bubbled up within me. I wasn't sure if it was my reaction or his or maybe both of ours.

"How are you feeling?" he asked, opening his arms

for me to rush into them. His hand encircled my stomach as I rested my face against his chest.

"Exhausted," I admitted.

I giggled as he lifted me into his arms and carried me to our bed. Setting me at the foot of it, he pulled the duvet cover aside, then hoisted me into his arms again and nestled me among the pillows. He sat behind me, and taking the comb from my hand, started separating my wet tresses, combing through each of them.

"I've reinstated Sinjin," I said calmly, wondering how Rand would take the news.

He was quiet for a few seconds but didn't stop combing my hair. "I must admit that Sinjin's actions of late have surprised me," he finally said.

"How so?"

Rand cleared his throat. "I did not think it possible that the vampire could act out of anything other than selfishness, but it seems I was wrong on that count."

"I think you were," I concurred.

He chuckled. "While I will never call Sinjin 'friend,' I see nothing wrong with you reinstating him."

I glanced back at him, my eyes wide. "Wait, what was that?" I asked, dropping my mouth in a wide circle as I pretended to clean out my ears. "I must have bad hearing because I could have sworn Rand Balfour just admitted that Sinjin Sinclair wasn't such a bad guy."

Rand chuckled again and lightly pinched the top of my butt. "I wouldn't go that far, smart arse."

I felt the laugh escape my lips as I leaned back against his chest. I was relieved that there was a lull in the storm and that our battle with the Lurkers was over, for now anyway. I had no doubt that Luce and Nairn were regrouping, working on their next attack against us, but I was happy not to worry about it for the moment.

"What are you thinking about?" Rand asked, and shifted my hair behind my ear, running his finger down the side of my face.

"I was just thinking about how happy I am," I said in a soft voice. "I mean, I know it sounds crazy, since who knows what's going to happen with the Lurkers . . ."

"We know much more about them now, Jolie, and that can only benefit us. They aren't the unknown threat they once were." He inhaled. "And knowledge is power."

That much was true. I now knew what the Lurkers' weaknesses were, and that information was priceless. Now we could prepare ourselves for a threat we finally understood.

"Jolie, I nearly lost my mind when you were in Luce's camp," Rand whispered. I started to respond but he shushed me. "I just want you to know how much I love you, how much I've always loved you."

I pulled away and turned around, facing him. Reaching out, I took his hand. "I love you too, Rand. You're the only person in this entire world that I want to be with, that I want to grow old with."

He smiled and brought my hand to his mouth, kissing it. "You know it's funny, but the day I walked into your store in Los Angeles years ago, I had this uncanny feeling that I was somehow coming home."

I gave him a curious look. This was the first I'd ever heard of it. "You did?"

He nodded. "I didn't understand it at the time of course," he said, a nostalgic smile lighting his lips. "I just remember looking into your beautiful blue eyes while you held my hands in your reading room, and I thought to myself, this just feels . . . right."

I closed the gap between us, lying down on top of him as I rested my head against his. I didn't say another word, just listened to Rand's gentle breathing while reflecting on the fact that while I'd never before fully accepted my role as Queen, I accepted it now. Now, I hungered to be the Queen my people needed.

Despite my mixed-blood heritage, I was first and foremost Jolie Wilkins. I was a girl who had never really thought much of herself, but with the teaching and love of a warlock and the companionship of a vampire, I'd come to realize just how capable I was. Now I was strong, courageous, and powerful. I was a loyal friend as much as I was a loving partner. I was a mother and a leader.

Jolie Wilkins, Queen of the Underworld . . .

Yep, it had a nice ring to it.

Did *Something Witchy This Way Comes* bespell your heart? You won't want to miss any of Jolie Wilkins's adventures! Read on for a sneak peek at the earlier books in the series, *Witchful Thinking* and *The Witch Is Back*.

Witchful Thinking

Jolie thinks she's seen it all, but life continues to spring surprises. The latest shocker? She's just been crowned Queen of the Underworld. Jolie may possess a rare gift for reanimating the dead, but she doesn't know the first thing about governing disparate factions of supernatural creatures. She can barely maintain order in her own chaotic personal life, which is heading into a romantic tailspin.

First there's sexy warlock Rand, the love of her life, from whom Jolie is hiding a devastating secret. Then there's Sinjin, a darkly seductive vampire and Jolie's sworn protector—though others suspect he harbors ulterior motives. As the two polar opposite yet magnetic men vie for Jolie's affection, she must keep her wits about her to balance affairs of state and affairs of heart. Overwhelmed, under pressure, and longing for love, Jolie decides it's time to take charge—and show everyone that this queen won't take jack.

"So, no more ghostly encounters?" Christa, my best friend and only employee, asked while leaning against the desk in our front office. She was referring to the fact that the previous evening I'd seen my first ghost.

I shook my head and pooled into a chair by the door. "Maybe if you hadn't left early to go on your date, I wouldn't have had a visit at all."

"Well, one of us needs to be dating," she said, knowing full well I hadn't had any dates for the past six months.

"Let's not get into this again . . ."

"Jolie, you need to get out. You're almost thirty . . ."

"Two years from it, thank you very much."

"Whatever . . . you're going to end up old and alone. You're way too pretty, and you have such a great personality, you can't end up like that. Don't let one bad date ruin it." Her voice reached a crescendo. Christa has a tendency toward the dramatic.

"I've had a string of bad dates, Chris." I didn't know what else to say—I was terminally single. It came down to the fact that I'd rather spend time with my cat or Christa than face another stream of losers.

As for being attractive, Christa insisted I was pretty, but I wasn't convinced. It's one thing when your best friend says you're pretty; it's entirely different when a man does.

And I couldn't remember the last time a man had said it.

I caught my reflection in the glass of the desk and studied myself while Christa rambled on about all the reasons I should be dating. I supposed my face was pleasant enough—a pert nose, cornflower-blue eyes, and plump lips. A spattering of freckles across the bridge of my nose interrupts an otherwise pale landscape of skin, and my shoulder-length blond hair always finds itself drawn into a ponytail.

Head-turning doubtful, girl-next-door probable.

As for Christa, she doesn't look like me at all. For one thing, she's leggy and tall—about five-eight, which is four inches taller than I am. She has dark hair the color of mahogany, green eyes, and rosy cheeks. She's classically pretty—like cameo pretty. She's rail skinny and has no boobs. I have a tendency to gain weight if I eat too much, I have a definite butt, and the twins are pretty ample as well. Maybe that made me sound like I'm fat—I'm not, but I could stand to lose five pounds.

"Are you even listening to me?" Christa asked.

Shaking my head, I entered the reading room, thinking I'd left my glasses there.

I heard the door open.

"Well, hello to you," Christa said in a high-pitched, sickening-sweet, and non-Christa voice.

"Afternoon." The deep timbre of his voice echoed through the room, my ears mistaking his baritone for music.

"I'm here for a reading, but I don't have an appointment—"

"Oh, that's cool," Christa interrupted, and from the saccharine tone of her voice, it was pretty apparent this guy had to be eye candy.

Giving up on finding my reading glasses, I headed out in order to introduce myself to our stranger. Upon seeing him, I couldn't contain the gasp that escaped my throat. It wasn't his Greek-god, Sean-Connery-would-be-envious good looks that grabbed me first, or his considerable height.

It was his aura.

I've been able to see auras since before I can remember, but I'd never seen anything like his. It radiated from him as if it had a life of its own—and the color! Usually auras are pinkish or violet in healthy people, yellowish or orange in those unhealthy. His was the most vibrant blue I've ever seen—the color of the sky after a storm when the sun's rays bask everything in glory.

It emanated from him like electricity.

"Hi, I'm Jolie," I said, remembering myself.

"How do you do?" And to make me drool even more than I already was, he had an accent, a British one. Ergh.

I glanced at Christa as I invited him into the reading room. Her mouth had dropped open like a fish's.

My sentiments exactly.

His navy-blue sweater stretched to its capacity while attempting to span a pair of broad shoulders and a wide chest. The broad shoulders and spacious chest in question tapered to a trim waist and finished in a finale of long legs. The white shirt peeking from underneath his sweater contrasted with his tanned complexion and made me consider my own fair skin with dismay.

The stillness of the room did nothing to allay my nerves. I took a seat, shuffled the tarot cards, and handed him the deck. "Please choose five cards and lay them faceup on the table."

He took a seat across from me, stretching his legs and resting his hands on his thighs. I chanced a look at him and took in his chocolate hair and caramel eyes. His face was angular, and his Roman nose lent him a certain Paul-Newman-esque quality. The beginnings of shadow did nothing to hide the definite cleft in his strong chin.

He didn't take the cards. Instead he just smiled, revealing pearly whites and a set of grade A dimples.

"You did come for a reading?" I asked.

He nodded and covered my hand with his own. What felt like lightning ricocheted up my arm, and I swear my heart stopped for a second. The lone red bulb blinked a few times then continued to grow brighter until I thought it might explode. My gaze moved from his hand up his arm, and settled on his eyes. With the red light reflecting against him, he looked like the devil come to barter for my soul.

"I came for a reading, yes, but not with the cards. I'd like you to read . . . me." His rumbling baritone was hypnotic, and I fought the need to pull my hand from his warm grip.

I set the stack of cards aside, focusing on him again. I was so nervous, I doubted any of my visions would come. They were about as reliable as the weather anchors you see on TV.

After several long uncomfortable moments, I gave up. "I can't read you, I'm sorry," I said, my voice breaking. I shifted the eucalyptus-scented incense I'd lit to the farthest corner of the table and waved my hands in front of my face, dispersing the smoke that seemed intent on wafting directly into my eyes. It swirled and danced in the air, as if indifferent to the fact that I couldn't help this stranger.

He removed his hand but stayed seated. I thought he'd leave, but he made no motion to do anything of the sort.

"Take your time."

Take my time? I was a nervous wreck and had no visions whatsoever. I just wanted this handsome stranger to leave so my life could return to normal.

But it appeared that was not in the cards.

The silence pounded against the walls, echoing the

pulse of blood in my veins. Still, my companion said nothing. I'd had enough. "I don't know what to tell you."

He smiled again. "What do you see when you look at me?"

Adonis.

No, I couldn't say that. Maybe he'd like to hear about his aura? I didn't have any other cards up my sleeve . . . "I can see your aura," I almost whispered, fearing his ridicule.

His brows drew together. "What does it look like?"

"It isn't like anyone's I've ever seen before. It's bright blue, and it flares out of you . . . almost like electricity."

His smile disappeared, and he leaned forward. "Can you see everyone's auras?"

The incense dared to assault my eyes again, so I put it out and dumped it in the trash can.

"Yes. Most people have much fainter glows to them—more often than not in the pink or orange family. I've never seen blue."

He chewed on that for a moment. "What do you suppose it is you're looking at—someone's soul?"

I shook my head. "I don't know. I do know, though, that if someone's ailing, I can see it. Their aura goes a bit yellow." He nodded, and I added, "You're healthy."

He laughed, and I felt silly for saying it. He stood up, his imposing height making me feel all of three inches tall. Not enjoying the feel of him staring down at me, I rose too and watched him pull out his wallet. I guess he'd heard enough and thought I was full of it. He set a hundred-dollar bill on the table in front of me. My hourly rate was fifty dollars, and we'd been maybe twenty minutes.

"I'd like to come see you for the next three Tuesdays at four p.m. Please don't schedule anyone after me. I'll compensate you for the entire afternoon."

I was shocked—what in the world would he want to come back for?

"Jolie, it was a pleasure meeting you, and I look forward to our next session." He turned to walk out of the room when I remembered myself.

"Wait, what name should I put in the appointment book?"

He turned and faced me. "Rand."

Then he walked out of the shop.

The Witch Is Back

Funny and feisty witch Jolie Wilkins is back—or rather, she's back to her humble beginnings. Propelled into the past to her old Los Angeles fortune-telling shop, Jolie has no idea she possesses extraordinary powers, and she definitely doesn't remember becoming Queen of the Underworld. But at least she has two incredibly sexy men vying for affection: Rand Balfour, who looks very familiar, though Jolie can't place his gorgeous face, and Sinjin Sinclair, who is tall, dark, and perfect . . . except for the fangs.

Yet despite her steamy love life, Jolie can't shake the sense that something is not quite right—like she's stuck in a déjà vu gone terribly awry. As both men race against time—and each other—to win Jolie's heart, the fate of the Underworld hangs in the balance. And Jolie's decision can either restore order or create an absolute, drop-dead disaster.

When the phone rang at ten minutes to seven, I wasn't surprised. Nope, I figured that Sinjin Sinclair, the most handsome and charming man who had ever stepped into my life, had probably just come to his senses and realized he didn't want to take me out for dinner after all. Maybe he'd suffered from a slight brain freeze the night before when he'd been awaiting roadside assistance at my tarot-card-reading shop, and that was why he'd asked me out.

So when he phoned to say he was lost, I was

surprised—not so much that his navigational skills were lacking but that he actually wanted to go through with this. Okay, I know what you're thinking—that I must look like a troll, or something equally heinous . . . Well, I'm not a troll by any stretch of the imagination, but I'm also not the girl who stands out in a crowd. I'm more the girl next door—or at least I live down the street from the girl next door.

Okay, I'm probably being a little too hard on myself because I have been told that I'm attractive and I know I'm smart and all that stuff, but I'm still nowhere near Sinjin Sinclair's league.

But back to the phone call. After Sinjin said he would be at my door shortly, I hung up and then stood in the center of my living room for a few minutes like a space cadet, gazing at the wall until I'm sure I looked like a complete and total moron.

But while it might have appeared that nothing much was going on in that gray matter between my ears, appearances can be deceiving. Thoughts ramrodded my brain, slamming into one another as new ones were born . . . *What am I doing? What am I thinking? What do I possibly have to talk about with a man as cultured and refined as Sinjin Sinclair? Moreover, how am I going to eat in front of him? What if I choke on an ice cube? Or I sneeze after taking a mouthful of salad and spray carrot chunks all over his expensive clothes?*

Jolie Wilkins, calm down, I finally said to myself, closing my eyes and taking a deep breath. *You are going to go on this date, because if you don't, you're never going to forgive yourself. And, furthermore, Christa will most definitely murder you.*

I inhaled another deep breath and forced myself out of my self-inflicted brain coma, staring toward the mirror as I took stock of myself for the umpteenth time in the last hour. Christa, my best friend and self-proclaimed fashion advisor, had left twenty minutes ago after chastising me about my current getup. Yes, she'd tried to force me into what amounted to shrink-wrapping, complete with stiletto heels that were so narrow they could double as weapons. Then, after that attempt had failed, she'd tried to get me to go with a flame-red corset dress that was so tight, I couldn't walk—and breathing was out of the question. So yes, I'd defeated the raunchy-clothing demon but I couldn't say I felt very good about my victory.

I sighed as I took in my shoulder-length blond hair and the fact that the curl Christa had wrestled into it only minutes before was already gone. It could be described as "limp" at best. My makeup was nice, though— Christa had managed to talk me into a smoky eye, which accented my baby blues, and she'd also covered the freckles that sprinkled the bridge of my nose while playing up my cheekbones with a shimmery apricot blush. She'd lined my decently plump lips in a light brown and filled them with bubble-gum-pink lipstick, finishing them with a pink gloss called "Baby Doll."

There was a knock on my front door, and I felt my heart lurch into my throat. I took another deep breath and glanced at my reflection in the mirror again, trying not to focus on the fact that I was anything but sexy in a black amorphous skirt that ended just below my knees, black tights, and two-inch heels. Even though my breasts are decently large, you couldn't really tell in my gray turtleneck and black peacoat.

Maybe I should have listened to Christa . . .

Another quick knock on the door signaled the fact that I was dawdling. I pulled myself away from my reflection and, wrapping my hand around the door-knob, exhaled and opened it, pasting a smile on my face.

"Hello," I said, hoping my voice sounded level and even-keeled, because the sight of Sinjin standing there just about undid me. A tornado was rampaging through me, tearing at my guts and wreaking havoc with my nervous system.

"Good evening," the deity before me spoke in his refined, baritone English accent. His eyes traveled from my eyes to my bust to my legs and back up again as a serpentine smile spread across his sumptuous lips.

"Um," I managed, meaning to add a *How are you?* to the end of it, but somehow the words never emerged.

Sinjin arched a black brow and chuckled as I debated slamming the door shut and hiding out in my room for the next, oh, two years, at least.

"You look quite lovely," he said, with that devilish smile as he pulled his arm forward and offered me a bouquet of red roses. "These pale in comparison."

My hand was shaking and my brain was on vacation as I reached for the roses, but somehow I did manage to smile and say, "Thank you, they are really beautiful."

The beauty of the roses didn't even compute, though—my overwhelmed mind was still reeling from the presence of this man. *Man* didn't even do him justice; he seemed so much more than that—either heaven-sent or hell's emissary.

He was wearing black, just as he had been the night before. His black slacks weren't fitted, but neither were they loose—in fact, they seemed tailored to his incredibly long legs. And his black sweater perfectly showcased his broad shoulders and narrow waist. Even though his body and intimidating height would have been worth writing home about, it was his face that was so completely alluring.

Sinjin's eyes should have been the eighth wonder of the world. They were the most peculiar color—an incredibly light blue, most similar to the blue-green icebergs you might find in Alaska or the Alpine waters of Germany. They almost seemed to glow. His skin was flawless, neither too pale nor too tan, without the kiss of a freckle or mole.

His hair was midnight black, so dark that it almost appeared blue. Tonight it looked longer than I remembered. The ends curled up over his collar, which was strange considering I'd only met him the day before and I could have sworn he had short hair. But the strangest thing about this enigmatic man was that I couldn't see his aura . . .

I've been able to see people's auras for as long as I can remember. An aura is best described as a halo-type thing that surrounds someone—it billows out of them in a foggy sort of haze. If someone is healthy, his or her aura is usually pink or violet. If someone is unwell in some way, yellow or orange predominates. I had never before met anyone who didn't have an aura at all or whose aura I couldn't see. And what surprised me even more was the fact that I hadn't noticed his missing aura the first time I'd seen him . . . Of course I had been pretty overwhelmed by his mere presence—and that dazed feeling didn't seem like it was going to go away anytime soon.

"May I escort you?" he asked as he gave me another winning smile and offered me his arm.

I gulped as I tentatively wrapped my hand around his arm, trying not to notice the fact that he was really . . . built. Good God . . .

"Thanks," I said in a small voice as I allowed him to lead me outside.

"Are you forgetting something?" Sinjin asked as he glanced down at me.

"Um," I started and dropped my attention to my feet, attempting to take stock of myself.

Shoes are on, purse is over my shoulder, nerves are present and accounted for . . . the only thing I'd forgotten was my confidence, which was currently hiding beneath my bed.

Sinjin stopped walking and turned around. I followed suit and noticed that the door to my modest little house was still open—gaping wide as though it was as shocked as he was that I'd forgotten to shut it.

"Oh my God." I felt my cheeks color with embarrassment. It had to be pretty obvious I'd completely forgotten how to function in his presence. I separated myself from him and hurried back up my walkway, shaking my head at my inattention. Anxiety drumming through me, I closed and locked the door behind me.

"Shall we try this again?"

I jumped, shocked that he was suddenly right beside me. I shook the feeling off, figuring that he must have been trailing me all along. But still, there was something . . . uncanny about it, something that set off my "Spidey" senses. I blamed it on my already overwhelmed nerves.

"Yes," I said with an anxious laugh as he offered his arm again and I, again, took it. This time we made it to the curb, where a black car awaited us. So angular it almost looked like a spaceship, it was the same vehicle he'd been driving the night before when he'd gotten a flat tire and had asked to use my phone. He opened the door for me and I gave him a smile of thanks as I seated myself, glancing over at the steering wheel where I recognized the emblem of a Ferrari.

A Ferrari . . . seriously?

I had to pinch myself. This just wasn't real—it couldn't be real! I mean, my life was composed of TV dinners and reruns of *The Office*. My only social outlet, really, was Christa. Men like Sinjin Sinclair with their impeccable clothes and stunning good looks, driving their Ferraris, just didn't figure into the Jolie Wilkins equation. Not at all!

"I hope you do not mind that I made reservations at Costa Mare?" he asked with a boyish grin.

Costa Mare was renowned for its Italian food and even more renowned for the fact that it took months to get a reservation. "You were able to make a reservation there?" I asked in awe, my mouth gaping in response.

Sinjin shrugged. "As a rule, I never take no for an answer." Then he chuckled as if he was making a joke. But you know what people say about jokes—there's always an underlying element of truth to them. It would not at all have come as a surprise to me to learn that Sinjin Sinclair was accustomed to getting his way.

For the next fifteen minutes, we made small talk—discussing things like the weather, his flat tire, and the history of my friendship with Christa. Before I knew it, we'd pulled in front of Costa Mare and Sinjin was handing his keys to the valet. Sinjin shook his head at the doorman who attempted to open my door, insisting that he would do it himself. I couldn't remember the last time a man had opened a car door for me. The guys in LA weren't exactly gentlemen.

I took Sinjin's proffered arm and allowed him to escort me into the restaurant, where the staff seemed to fuss over him like he was some great messiah. They led us through a weaving path of tables, sparkling marble flooring, and dim candlelight, finally designating us to an isolated table in a corner of the room. Potted bamboos acted as a screen from the rest of the restaurant.

"Where would you prefer to sit?" Sinjin asked me with a polished smile.

"It doesn't matter," I answered as I waited for him to pull out my chair. He chose the seat with the best view of the restaurant, but I hadn't been lying—I really didn't care.

The host, a rotund, short man, who was probably in his late forties, offered us our menus, placed our napkins on our laps, and left us to our own devices.

"A man should always choose his seat wisely," Sinjin commented, glancing at me with a smirk.

"Why is that?" I asked, wondering what he was getting at.

He nodded as if he was about to divulge a long and interesting story. "In times long past, it could mean death if a man's back was to his enemies."

"And you're still practicing that, I see?" I asked with a smile, suddenly feeling comfortable with him. It was strange because I wasn't a person who was, in general, comfortable around anyone I didn't know.

"It is my duty to ensure your safety, poppet."

I wasn't sure why, but the word *poppet* seemed so familiar to me, even though I was pretty sure I'd never heard it before. It was a sudden moment of déjà vu, of that feeling that somewhere, sometime, I'd experienced this exact moment. It made no sense, but I couldn't help but feel haunted by it all the same.

"Well, I'm sure things are safer in this day and age," I said, trying to shake off the weird feeling. It wouldn't budge. There was just something so . . . familiar about all this. I took a deep breath and started perusing the menu, hoping to banish my wayward thoughts. Feeling as if Sinjin was staring at me, I glanced up and found his eyes fastened on me. He didn't even try to hide the fact, and when I caught him, he smiled.

This one was smooth.

"Have you selected your supper?" he asked, his mouth spreading into a wide smile as if he was in on some inside joke that I wasn't privy to.

I swallowed hard, suddenly more than aware that this whole date might just be the setup for a one-night stand. That was when it struck me—that's *exactly* what it was. Sinjin was traveling from Britain, and he probably wanted to taste everything the United States had to offer, including its women. Well, unluckily for him, I wasn't on the menu. I felt my lips tightening into a line, and I tried to keep my cool. But inside I was fuming—mainly at my own idiocy. Had I really been out of the game so long that this hadn't dawned on me from the get-go?

"I think so," I muttered and concealed myself with my menu.

"What is on your mind?" Sinjin asked as he pushed my menu down with his index finger, forcing me to look at him. I could feel my cheeks coloring. He had nerve . . .

"Nothing," I answered and dropped my eyes.

"Please, Jolie, do not insult my intelligence."

I took a deep breath. If he wanted to know what was on my mind, he was about to get an earful. "I'm not into one-night stands," I said stiffly.

Sinjin narrowed his eyes, but the smile on his lips revealed the fact that he was amused. "A wise policy."

So he was still playing this game, was he? "Well, I think you should . . . be aware of that . . . in case you . . . in case you . . ."

"In case I what?"

I could feel sweat breaking out along the small of my back. He was forcing me into a corner, and that damn smile was still in full effect. "In case you . . . were, uh, looking for that . . . that sort of thing."

He didn't drop his attention from my face. If anything, his eyes were even more focused, challenging. "Is that what you imagined I was in search of?"

So he was going to make this tough on me, was he? He was going to make me spell it out for him and embarrass myself? Well, I might not be in his league, but I wouldn't be made a fool of. I was way too smart for that. "Without a doubt."

"And what, pray tell, gave you that impression, if I may be so bold as to inquire?"

"I . . . um." I cleared my throat and forced myself to look him straight in the eyes. "I couldn't figure out why else you'd be here with . . . with me tonight."

Sinjin took a deep breath, and it seemed to take him forever to exhale it. "I see."

"So, if you are . . . expecting that, you might as well take me home now . . . no harm done," I finished and held his gaze for another three seconds before I picked up my ice water and began chugging it.

"Very well," he answered, and his voice was tender.

I dropped the menu and reached for my purse, feeling something icy forming in my gut as I readied myself to leave. I wasn't angry, no, but I was humiliated. Strangely enough, though, relief was beginning to suffuse me . . . relief at the fact that I could end this farce and lick my wounds in the comfort and serenity of my house. After collecting my things, I stood up and noticed that Sinjin hadn't moved an inch.

"What are you doing?" I demanded.

"Perhaps I should ask the same of you?"

I swallowed hard. "I thought we were leaving?"

"Why would we be leaving? We have not even ordered yet."

"But I thought," I started before my voice was swallowed up by the fact that I was at a complete loss.

Sinjin smiled up at me and shook his head, pulling out my chair. "Please have a seat, love," he said. "You misunderstood my intentions."

"But you said 'very well,'" I started, even as I sat down and pulled myself to the table again.

"I was simply agreeing with your assessment of the fact that you are quite opposed to 'one-night stands,' as you so fittingly termed them." He smiled again, cocking his brow. "And while I find you to be quite a delectable package, poppet, I am afraid I quite agree with you regarding the more intimate side of our association . . . for the time being, at least."

So he wasn't looking for a one-night stand? Or maybe he was so smooth, he was just faking it and he'd put his plan of attack into action once I was no longer suspicious. I took a deep breath and lifted my menu again, wishing I'd never agreed to this date in the first place. "Oh."

"Would you be averse to the notion of . . . starting over?" he asked and leaned back into his chair as he studied me.

I felt an embarrassed smile pulling at my lips even though I still wasn't sure what his intentions were. Well, either way, it took two to tango and my tango shoes were in a box in my closet, covered with dust. "No, that sounds good."